REDSHIFT
RENDEZVOUS

Ace Books by John E. Stith

SCAPESCOPE
MEMORY BLANK
DEATH TOLLS
DEEP QUARRY
REDSHIFT RENDEZVOUS

REDSHIFT RENDEZVOUS

JOHN E. STITH

ACE BOOKS, NEW YORK

Quality Printing and Binding by:
Berryville Graphics
P. O. Box 272
Berryville, VA 22611 U.S.A.

For Jean Archibald,
Margie and Pete Cotton,
Rita and Northwood Kenway,
and Julie and James Peace.

And for Annette.

CONTENTS

Passenger Guide   viii

1   Prelude to Hyperspace   1

2   A Fish Dinner in Hyperspace   15

3   To Die in Hyperspace   30

4   Hunters of the *Redshift*   42

5   The Door into Hyperspace   56

6   Hyperspace Swimmers   72

7   Captives of the *Redshift*   87

8   Hyperspace Voyage   100

9   Destination Xanahalla   113

10 A Hyperspace Odyssey   124

11 Expedition to Xanahalla   138

12 Jason's Run   151

13 Downbelow Xanahalla   164

14 All the Traps of Xanahalla   175

15 Something Wicked This Way Jumps   190

16 Ring Around the *Redshift*   201

Phenomena Aboard the *Redshift*   212

Inventing the *Redshift*   215

PASSENGER GUIDE

The environment aboard a hyperspace craft is quite safe as long as you are careful. The management reminds you that *the speed of light on board this craft is ten meters per second,* or about 30 million times slower than what you are used to. This means you will frequently encounter relativistic effects and optical illusions.

NEVER TAMPER WITH YOUR LIFEBELT OR ATTEMPT TO UNFASTEN IT. THE FIELD IT GENERATES ALLOWS YOUR NEURAL TRANSMISSIONS TO OPERATE AT NORMAL SPEEDS AND IT IS ABSOLUTELY ESSENTIAL TO YOUR HEALTH.

1. Use only the ship's master clock displays. Do not rely on your personal timepiece; it will accurately record your personal subjective time, but it will never agree with any other timepieces until you reset it when you leave the ship.
2. Remember that everything you see and hear is at least slightly in the past, due to the time it takes sound and light to travel. The closest things to you are the most current.
3. Trust what your hands tell you rather than believing your eyes. Bending light can make you think a convex floor is concave. Colors may shift and shapes may distort.
4. Go slow. Limit your speed to a fast walk until you are familiar with the environment. Please heed the traffic rules. By running fast, it is possible to exceed the speed of sound, which is only 6.7 meters per second.
5. Never assume anything.
6. Have a nice trip.

"Phenomena Aboard the *Redshift*" (page 213) gives
further details, as well as the required liability disclaimer.

REDSHIFT RENDEZVOUS

1

Prelude to Hyperspace

Either she wanted to be found, or I simply had a stroke of luck in coming upon her at just the right moment. Since luck and I had never been on very good terms, I naturally assumed Jenni Sonders had been waiting for someone to show up.

I was down on level two of the *Redshift,* on my rounds, making sure my eyes told me the same story I got from the ship's status panels and the rest of the crew. Not that I distrusted either the indicators or the people—I just didn't like to rely entirely on reported observations, even if the optical illusions on the *Redshift* were enough to make my own eyes less trustworthy than sensors.

In the high-gee field of level two, my feet scuffed the floor as I walked along the equatorial corridor. Closely spaced ceiling lights lit the gray corridor walls and the charcoal deck floor. The cargo bays I'd surveyed so far had been packed with expensive machinery, containers of rare metals, exotic foods, unique fabrics . . . the staples of a typical hyperspace run: items not universally available, and expensive enough to justify passage. Nothing so far had been out of the ordinary, but ahead and on my right a cargo bay door was not entirely closed.

The door was open the width of a hand. I glanced through the gap and then slid the door all the way open. The bay was full of labeled crates, mostly rectangular, in a multitude of sizes. Near the center of the bay, a passenger sat atop a tall stack of crates, hugging her knees, looking forlorn and tired, like a lost child. The woman's hair nearly touched the deck overhead. She must have crawled up a staircase of crates to reach her resting place near the center aisle.

The woman was Jenni Sonders. I remembered seeing her boarding, and I had talked to her once briefly at dinner. She looked to be in her late twenties, about my age. She was a redhead, narrow-hipped, perpetually sad—at least I hadn't seen her smile since she boarded the *Redshift* at Megorath. Her red curls hung slightly lower than normal in the strong gravity down here. She wore off-white pants and a matching long-sleeved blouse. The cuffs of both the pants and blouse were circled with violet bands in a chic paramilitary style that looked good on her.

Jenni was far enough from me that I stood by the door and waited for indications of my arrival to reach her.

After a delay long enough for light to reach her and return, I saw her head turn toward me. Suddenly she was in motion, scrambling off her perch and behind a crate that nearly touched the overhead.

I frowned, trying to imagine what she might have been doing down here, wondering what was going on in her head right now. She wouldn't be trying to steal; every cargo crate was securely locked. And she was obviously ill at ease in the hyperspace environment; otherwise she would have remembered that I'd had ample time to see her before she hid.

I waited a moment, saying nothing, partly because I didn't know what to say, partly because I was curious about what she would do next. She stayed hidden.

Finally, I called out, "I know you're there, Ms. Sonders. Why don't you come on out?"

There was a long delay, even longer than simple sound-transmission time, so she must have taken time to think about her response. Finally her head showed to one side of the crate. She said nothing.

"What are you doing down here?" I asked, and began walking toward her.

A panicked expression came over her face and her lips moved before I heard her words. "Don't come any closer." Her voice was scratchy, as though on the edge of tears.

I stopped where I was. This wasn't going at all the way I had expected. "I'm Jason Kraft, the first officer, Ms. Sonders. What's the problem?"

"Go away," was all she said. I got the feeling it took quite an effort for her to say even that much. She got back up on a high crate and scooted closer to the edge. She looked down at the floor from there, and turned back to me. "Go *away.*"

"Look, I can't just go away. I'm responsible for—"

"Go away or I'll jump."

There was such pain in her voice that for an instant I considered honoring her request, but I couldn't. I finally realized what this was all about. For whatever reason, she was apparently near suicide. I hadn't a clue what to do about it. I could call the ship's doctor, but by then she might have jumped off a pile of crates.

Maybe someone trained in how to deal with people like this would have done things differently. I did the only thing that came into my mind; I decided to try to distract her from whatever it was that was eating at her.

"I would have thought the beds in the passenger cabins were more comfortable than a stack of shipping crates." Impatient with the long delays of large rooms, I waited for her reply.

She remained silent, perched on the lip of the crate.

Calmly, softly, I said, "This delay between sentences makes it tough to talk. Would you mind if I come closer?"

"Stay away," she said through clenched teeth.

I backed up to the wall and made a point of not moving at all for a good part of a minute. At last I said, "You come here often? You don't look like one of the regulars."

Jenni sobbed once and was silent. Her lips opened and closed several times without speech, and finally she said, so softly that I could barely hear, "Not funny."

"Ms. Sonders, I know how to fire a crew member who's not making the required effort. I know how to tell the skipper when she's made a rare bad decision. I don't have the smallest notion of how to deal with someone who wants to commit suicide."

She tacitly confirmed her intentions by not correcting my statement, but she glared at me as though I *should* know exactly what to do with a suicider, as though this kind of problem had a solution as straightforward as artificial respiration. I felt suddenly inadequate, and at the same time a little like an intruder. Maybe someone else would have decided the fairest thing to do was to go away and quit meddling, but I couldn't do that.

As she sat there fidgeting, looking over the edge, I shifted my weight slightly so I'd be able to move quickly if I needed to. I tried again to think of a way to get her thoughts away from whatever pain had caused all this. "You know," I said finally, "a fall from that height might not be fatal. You might just put yourself in a lot of pain."

Some of her words were too soft to hear, or she wasn't able to speak clearly. ". . . be condescending . . ." "I wasn't being condescending," I said truthfully. "You probably read the brochure that says the gravity is two and a half gees on this level, but that's only at the floor. The

4 John E. Stith

gravity tapers off. Up where you are, it's probably only one point five to one point seven. That means the average from you to the floor is about two. And your terminal velocity will be greater than a fall in one gee by only a factor of the square root of that increase. Do you think hitting the floor at one point four times faster than normal will guarantee results?"

I hoped the overly clinical techtalk might jog her out of the rut she was in. Another way of looking at the numbers was that she would hit the floor from her current perch as though she had fallen from a point twice as high in one gee, but there was no point in giving her that encouragement.

While she appeared to think about what I'd said, I considered running toward her. With light traveling so slowly in this layer of hyperspace, I could run almost as fast as the speed of light. I could certainly run faster than the speed of sound. If I were to run as fast as possible, I probably could reach her before she had time to react. I hesitated, thinking a better plan would be to talk her out of it, or to keep her talking long enough for the mood to pass.

"Have you felt this way long?" I asked, changing the subject.

After a long silence she said, "What way?"

"I don't know what way you feel. I've never contemplated suicide. I've felt the urge to kill someone else, but I imagine that's not quite the same thing. Why are you up there?"

"I don't want to live."

I wasn't sure it was progress for her to say that out loud or not. *"Why* don't you want to live?"

". . . none of your business."

Feeling less sure I was approaching this correctly, I went ahead anyway and said, "None of my business? How can you say that? Have you any idea how many forms I'll have to fill out if you do this on our ship? And with me as a witness?"

She sobbed again. She was still awhile and then drew a deep breath. She said clearly, "I understand what you're doing. But I have to do this."

"Ms. Sonders, when I came down the corridor this door was open. I don't know if you consciously wanted to talk with someone, or whether the thought was just at the back of your mind. But somewhere in that brain of yours there's a voice saying you want to talk. I'm here. This may be your last opportunity. How about if you tell me about it?"

She was silent for a disturbing length of time, but finally she said, "It's everything. One thing after another. This was supposed to be my honeymoon trip." Her voice caught. Then she swallowed hard and went on. "Two days before we were supposed to leave, he told me he thought this was all a mistake. He had changed his mind. He's always changing his mind. He's still on Megorath." She drew a deep breath. "At first I thought going away and deliberately having a good time without him would help, but it was a mistake."

Being spurned had caused all her pain? I felt a guilty sting of comfort that I would never be hurt that way.

"So you're in such pain that you don't want to live?" I asked at last, trying hard to understand. "Or you want to get back at him?"

Her head jerked around when my words reached her. "How can you say that I'd be doing this to—" She broke off, staring at me for a long moment before she looked down. She clenched her fists and said, "This isn't just because of him. It isn't. *It isn't.*" Her words were muffled since she didn't face me as she spoke.

"Say, I've got an idea," I said, deciding that moving to this topic had been one of my bad ideas. "I'm starved. Let's go up to the galley and get a late-night snack. Layne Koffer fixes a terrific sweet-java."

She shook her head just as I finished speaking. She edged closer to the drop to the deck.

"Wait just a minute," I said quickly. "I almost forgot. A message came in for you over the network. It was—" I never finished the lie I had started. Instead I ran.

I pushed against the wall behind me, and I accelerated as rapidly as I could move my body in the high gravity. If I could have reached the speed of light instantly, Jenni would have had no warning that I was on my way until I was already with her. As it was, I outdistanced a couple of my words but still gave her a little warning.

I ran straight along the row between crates, my view of Jenni shifting into blue and then violet as I ran fast enough for Doppler shift to tint the world ahead. The view of stacked crates to either side of me contracted.

Jenni must have seen my violet blur as I approached, because she pushed herself off the stack of crates, tilting backward so she would land on her head. I was nearly too late.

As I ran, I held my arms outstretched. Catching her was awkward, even though I tried to compensate for her extra weight on this level. Her body hit my arms at about the same instant that the sonic boom I had generated sounded loudly in my ears. I thought at first I had her, but a second later I dropped her after all. At least I had been able to slow her down and reorient her so her heels and buttocks hit the deck simultaneously. I fell heavily to one side.

She had been yelling from the moment I first touched her. "Get away from me. What are you—ouch!" Hitting the deck stopped the flow of words for only an instant; then the impact laced her words with pain. "You've got no right. Get away!"

Her remaining restraint broke and she began to pummel my chest with her fists. I grabbed for her wrists to force her to stop.

Even up close the speed-of-light delay made it hard to anticipate Jenni's moves. My first attempts to restrain her missed, but she knew what I was trying to do because she changed her tactics. She slapped my face and a moment later I felt the wet result of four fingernails scratching deeply into my cheek.

Finally I got good grips on both of her wrists, which left only the possibility of being kicked or kneed. She didn't waste any time. Fortunately she landed only two kicks before I was able to force her down against the deck, straddle her, and pin her fists to the deck.

She lay on her back, breathing heavily, looking up at me because she had no choice. As my adrenaline level began its descent to normal, I looked back at her. What had appeared from a distance to be a tan was instead closely spaced freckles. *"Damn* you," she said slowly, vehemently.

Jenni was unmoving for a long moment as anger put creases between her eyebrows and anger burned in her eyes. Suddenly she put on a burst of energy, moving her hips, twisting her body, trying to jerk her arms away from my grasp. I felt terribly like a rapist and I didn't know what to do next.

Jenni couldn't get free. It took her a while, but I could see her coming to the realization that she was trapped until I decided to let her up. She lay still, looking up at me, while tears formed in her eyes. She averted her gaze, clenched her jaw, and drew several deep breaths, staring blindly past my ear.

Her face plainly showed the effort it was costing her not to cry. The next minute she seemed to draw back from the brink and just when I thought maybe she wouldn't cry after all, her body abruptly relaxed, her eyelids closed, and tears began streaming out of the corners of her eyes.

I felt angry at myself because I'd thought I had an answer for every possible question, and here I was possibly causing more pain than I was preventing.

I loosened my grip on her wrists, and Jenni began to sob. I let go entirely of one wrist, and her arm stayed limp as her sobbing deepened and every muscle in her face seemed to tighten. I leaned back, letting both of her arms lie unrestrained over her head.

I retreated a little more, and after a short time she moved her hands to cover her eyes. As if she didn't want me to watch her cry, she raised her head and chest and put her arms around me, burying her face against my chest. Her sobbing was convulsive.

I put my arms around her and let her cry.

She cried for what seemed to be a long time, only occasionally stopping for a series of deep breaths, finally exhausting herself with dry sobs that gradually came farther and farther apart.

When she had been calm long enough that I didn't think she would start crying again, I said softly, "This deck is probably no better than those crates. I'd better get you back to your cabin so you can sleep."

She nodded her head against my chest.

I let Jenni dry her eyes on my shirt sleeve.

As I helped her stand up, my knees felt weak. I blamed it on the high gravity.

"What's your stateroom number?" I asked.

She didn't give any indication that she'd heard me.

I asked again and still got no response. Her thoughts seemed to be far away.

I walked her slowly from the center of the cargo bay to the door. In the corridor, I used a comm panel to call the skipper, Bella Fendell. The rate-of-time difference between the level-two cargo bay and the bridge up on level four pushed Bella's voice pitch high enough to make her sound almost girlish and excitable. Bella was neither.

"Is Doc available?" I said.

"What's the problem?" Bella asked.

"Minor incident. It's under control. I'll explain when I get back to the bridge, but would you please have him meet me at Jenni Sonders' cabin? I'm on my way there now."

"Will do. Anything else?"

"Yes. Which cabin is hers?"

There was a short delay as Bella looked it up. She did an outstanding job of keeping her curiosity in check.

In the elevator, I pushed the button for *five*, the main passenger cabin level, farther out from the center of the onion-skinned *Redshift*. Jenni sagged against one wall. She looked away when I glanced at her. I didn't know whether I had made an enemy for life—however short her life might turn out to be—or if she was feeling a mixture of gratitude and embarrassment.

I looked instead at the elevator ceiling. The four corners had appeared to curve upward when we boarded on level two. As we rose out of the high-gee field, and light started traveling in a straighter path, the corners began to droop until the ceiling looked almost level. The less than one-half gee on level five made it seem the elevator was still slowing down when the doors opened onto a wide, gray corridor edged with black handrails.

The corridor dipped out of sight in the distance in both directions. The *Redshift* was a spherical ship with the gravitational warp at the center. Here we were far enough from the warp to be in a comfortable gravity. Jenni walked by my side, staring straight ahead, a reasonably attractive zombie with bloodshot eyes.

The heads and shoulders of a couple of passengers were visible in the distance, but we reached Jenni's cabin without getting close enough to have to greet anyone. She hesitated at the combination pad long enough that I was about to use the master, but then she opened her door. I took that to be a good sign.

Light from the hallway spilled into the cabin and bounced around the interior until it reached equilibrium. The phenomenon repeated itself when I switched on the overhead lamps. A glance around Jenni's cabin gave no obvious indication that she had settled in; all of her possessions must have been behind closed doors and in concealed compartments.

"Jenni, I want you to lie down on the bed," I told her with my best command voice. I went to the closest bedside table and opened the drawer. Besides a *Wayfarer Word,* there was nothing inside.

She moved listlessly to the large bed and fell slowly backward onto it. Her limp body bounced once before coming to rest. Her arms were flung over her head, and the violet rings on her sleeves looked for an instant like handcuffs.

I continued my search, my shadow on the wall lagging behind my motions. The second bedside table and the wall-mounted drawers were similarly devoid of drugs and weapons. I was about to check the bathroom when the visitor chime sounded.

I opened the door to Rory Willett. He stood there with his case in his hand. His long sideburns together with his growing bald spot gave the first impression that his hair was migrating. Prominent laugh lines showed at the corners of his eyes. His white jacket seemed a little too small on his beefy frame. He looked more like a seasoned gambler than a competent doctor.

"Come on in, Doc," I said.

"What happened to you?" he asked. He blinked a couple of times; probably he'd been asleep when he was called.

For an instant I didn't know what he was talking about, but his gaze at my cheek reminded me how sharp Jenni's fingernails were. "I'm fine," I said. "The resident here is the one who needs help."

I explained briefly what had happened in the cargo bay. Rory nodded a couple of times, glancing past me once to look at Jenni Sonders lying on the bed.

Rory was either a good acquaintance or what some people might call a casual friend. When no tension was present, his good humor was always ready; when rapid action and the right decision were required, he was cool without being distant.

When I finished explaining, I said, "I'm not sure what you can do for her, but I thought your bedside manner would be better than mine."

"I certainly don't doubt that." Rory nudged me from time to time about what he and others considered my standoffishness, but he knew I liked him. He moved past me toward Jenni, and I went to the bathroom to complete my search.

In front of the mirror, I realized the scratches on my cheek looked nastier than they felt. I used Jenni's sink to clean off the dried blood.

As I had expected, nothing in her cabin seemed to be usable as a weapon, unless she chose to strangle herself with her clothes. If she wanted that badly to die, I wouldn't stand in her way.

Rory was sitting on the bed next to her, talking softly, when I joined them. Jenni's gaze moved from Rory's face, over his shoulder, and into my eyes. Her eyes didn't seem to be focusing very well, and she looked puzzled.

"Whatever he's saying is bound to be right," I told her. "The doc knows all about this kind of thing."

Rory reached into his case and retrieved a puffer of what I guessed to be a tranquilizer. He said something to Jenni that I couldn't hear, and she looked back at him. She moved her arm closer to him, and he puffed the medication into the skin near the crook of her elbow.

She still looked puzzled as she gazed back up at me. She didn't look away until the drug destroyed her ability to keep her eyes open. After another moment, the faint lines on her face vanished.

Rory removed the cover from a small vial. He brushed Jenni's hair aside and swabbed medication near her ear. Once finished, he looked up at me. "Some night, huh, Jason?"

"Women will just die to get near me."

Rory nodded as though that was the type of comment he expected. He rummaged in his case for a moment and handed me a small tube. "Put some of this on your cheek twice a day. Three times a day if you spend a lot of time on level seven. It will heal faster."

"What have you got for her?"

"I'll talk to her when she's had a chance to rest. I don't know if she's a chronic or if this is her first time. I'll keep a close check on her." His eyebrows rose and he looked at me questioningly. "Unless you'd rather do that. She might hate you for interfering, or she might actually be grateful if this was more to get attention than to finish her life."

"Don't try to get me involved. I don't know anything about medicine."

"You know that's not the issue. It would probably do you as much good as her if you did get involved. Getting close to someone wouldn't hurt you."

I didn't want to talk about it, so I forced the thoughts away. I grinned at him and deepened my voice. "A man's gotta do what a man's gotta do."

"You're wrong, Jason. A man does what he chooses to do."

I took my time on the way to the bridge. I hadn't been officially on duty anyway.

I found Bella Fendell leaning back in a comfortable chair she had long ago moved from her cabin to the bridge. Her feet were propped up on the console, and before her were multiple circular status panels showing the current condition of systems all over the *Redshift*. We were cruising in hyperspace layer ten at nine meters per second, nine-tenths of the speed of light in this layer. Measured by the corresponding locations in layer zero, we were effectively traveling at about 1000 times the normal speed of light. And the wind didn't even ruffle my hair.

"You're looking really nice tonight," she said, noting my fresh scratches. "I assume your opponent came out second best." She didn't ask me outright what had happened, pretending that she wasn't intensely curious. I refrained from volunteering information so she'd *have* to ask me. It was one of our rituals.

Bella Fendell was a large woman, described by some as maternal. Since I had never known my mother, the expression was hard to evaluate, but Bella was rarely afraid to ask personal questions, whether they were intrusive and prying or not. Not only was she obviously curious about my scratches, she was probably even more interested in my having been down on level two in a cargo bay with a woman.

She waited a moment longer for my reply and then shook her head, amused. She grinned, her round cheeks puffing out farther, and said, "So tell me. What was the minor incident?"

"One of the passengers, Jenni Sonders, wanted to kill herself." I gave her the whole story.

When I finished, Bella asked, "Do you think she'll keep trying?"

"Ask Rory. I'm no judge. How far is she traveling with us?"

"She's paid through Far Star." Bella knew that without having to look it up. When I had called for Jenni's cabin number, Bella would have found out all there was to know about Jenni.

I glanced at the schedule on a wall screen. "Ten more days. I suppose Rory would get in trouble if he kept her sedated that long."

Bella gave me a wry grin. "She is a paying passenger. We can't treat her like a sick pet."

"But she is sick, right? I mean she did try to kill herself."

"Who's to say what's sick and what's not? Even you might do the same thing if you ever let someone get that close to you and then dump you. Of course with you that's one awful big 'if.' "

"That's Rory and you both, tonight. And I'm not even on duty."

Bella looked up at me speculatively. "That's your trouble, Jason. You're always on duty."

The next day the *Redshift* was scheduled to dock near Vestry. I was on the bridge to supervise the maneuver. The layer-ten velocity readout had switched from percent of c down to micrometers per second now that we were closing in on the dock. The corresponding layer-zero readout showing the normal-space equivalent, was down in the kilometers-per-second range.

Razzi Luxon, the second officer, was there, too, her blonde hair held by a clasp at the back of her neck. At least *she* wasn't giving me a difficult time about my lifestyle. Aside from the immediate preoccupation of being engaged in docking, she rarely seemed inclined to offer me advice.

Razzi sat in her chair, leaning forward in anticipation, even though her command goggles eliminated speed-of-light delays. I shouldn't have been, but I was occasionally surprised that Razzi was so thorough and competent, not that she looked unprofessional, but because she viewed her duties on ship as simply a means to an end: travel. She loved to visit star systems wherever our route took us, and whenever we had a long enough layover to get off the ship.

The central display showed Vestry's orbital dock as we approached.

A scanner constantly translated back and forth between the *Redshift* in layer ten and normal space, layer zero. Beacons on the dock guided our craft slowly into position.

Vestry's dock consisted of a long, narrow hallway in an orbital station.

Hatches and doors were seldom used on the *Redshift.* When you could translate a passenger or piece of freight directly from a layer-zero loading platform into the correct corridor aboard the ship, all you really needed to do is make absolutely certain that the source and destination were perfectly lined up. Having an unprotected passenger step from a comfortable loading dock into the hard vacuum of layer ten was bad for repeat business.

Actually, passengers did have some protection, as did the crew. We all wore lifebelts that generated a field allowing our bodies to function at regular speed. Put a human body in layer ten with synapse speeds limited by our speed of light, and you had just a dead body. The master clock lines and selected equipment aboard were aided by the same fields, but protecting the entire *Redshift* would have cost more than the ship was worth.

Razzi pressed a switch, leaned back in her chair, pushed her goggles onto her forehead, and turned toward me. "Everything looks smooth."

The *Redshift* glided slowly into position, matching the dock's motion with propulsion since the ship in layer ten couldn't take advantage of Vestry's layer-zero planetary mass to force the ship into a natural orbit.

"We're in sync," Razzi said, once the status panel showed a perfect overlap. The ship's control system would keep maneuvering the *Redshift* to keep us superimposed with the dock as it orbited Vestry.

"Thanks," I said. "I'll be watching the loading if you need me."

Razzi nodded, her attention again on the status panel showing the portal, currently lined up with level seven of the *Redshift,* opening for outbound traffic.

I left the bridge, wondering how one person could be driven to consider killing herself, while another person was apparently content with temporary liaisons on whatever worlds she found herself.

I considered skipping the level-seven activity since most of the cargo up there was staying aboard, but I went anyway. The unloading progressed smoothly, so it was soon time to go down to level six. Level six's ceiling was more than fifty percent higher than the ceilings on any other level, and this far from the center of the ship the gravity was only about a third of a gee, so most of the cargo here normally was contained in large, bulky crates.

Shipping crates vanished one after another through the portal leading to the dock in layer zero. Once offloading on every level was complete, the portal would be reversed to accommodate loading cargo originating on Vestry. We could have activated a portal for each direction simultaneously, but we had only so many of the crew available for loading, and completing the process one step at a time was less confusing.

With activity on level six doing fine, I went down to level five, the main passenger cabin level.

Bensode, the third officer, was in charge. I was sure he enjoyed his job, but he never looked very happy. His large, dark eyes made him appear perpetually apologetic. He reminded me of a night person who'd had to get up early in the morning after too little sleep. His salt-and-pepper hair made him look years older than me, but he wasn't.

"Only two passengers got off," he said when he saw me. "We're just about to reverse the portal."

"Carry on." My timing was good. I always felt more comfortable when I was able to see the new passengers as they arrived.

The first passenger on Bensode's list was a Marj Lendelson. I looked toward the portal just in time to see a pointed toe enter layer ten. The portal surface, as always, turned shiny when it was penetrated. Iridescent ripples spread rapidly out from the toe as the passenger moved forward. More ripples moved outward from the outline of Marj's body as she completed her transition and then stumbled.

Conrad Delingo, one of the newest of our crew members, caught her arm, gave her a broad smile, and said, "Welcome to the *Redshift*, Ms. Lendelson. I can give you directions to your cabin." Conrad wasn't normally assigned to this duty, but he was so energetic and interested in everything that happened on board I was sure Bensode had let him volunteer. Bensode and Conrad together gave the impression of an invalid with a new puppy on a leash. Conrad must have spent a fair amount of the shift on level seven, because his cheeks were already showing dark stubble.

Marj Lendelson said nothing for a moment, no doubt coping with the brief disorientation that sometimes came with using the portal. She looked to be about forty-five years old—forty-five good years if her appearance was an accurate indicator. She wore a dress cut in simple lines but obviously made of expensive material. Her eyes were alert and watchful. She held her chin high in an almost regal posture.

Absently, she scratched at her waist. Almost everyone did that at first, unaccustomed as they were to wearing lifebelts next to their skin. Finally she nodded to Conrad and he led her away from the portal, the puppy escorting the queen to her chambers.

Next through was a short, dark man named Daniel Haffalt. He came through the portal smoothly, showing no signs of disorientation. His closely cropped black hair lay flat, spreading over the top of his head like short, trampled grass. His piercing dark eyes gave me the feeling he could see a coin at a hundred meters. When a crew member offered directions to his cabin, he said, "I'm fine," and began walking along the corridor toward the downward-dipping horizon. He was easy to peg as a frequent traveler.

The boarding list showed a married couple following Haffalt. The man, Wade Pesek Midsel, came through first. A broad-shouldered fellow, he blinked his heavy-lidded eyes a couple of times and then he turned to face the portal he had just come through. He moved with an easy grace, as though he, too, might be a frequent traveler, but the expression on his face was more open, more inquisitive than Haffalt's. He wasn't actually smiling, but a submerged smile seemed to be ready to surface, as though he was thinking pleasant thoughts.

Midsel's wife, Tara Pesek Cline, followed. Her hand showed first, as rippling shimmers spread across the portal. She came through grinning unabashedly, and pushing strands of her long, black hair away from her blue eyes. Tara took her husband's outstretched hand even though she obviously didn't need support. She wore a short-sleeved pullover and pants. She was the only passenger so far to look at anything except the nearest crew member and the corridor ahead. As her gaze swung past me, she nodded, still smiling. Her smile was somehow mischievous, making her look younger than she probably was.

Almost against my volition, I smiled back, but she moved the focus of her inspection fast enough that the speed-of-light delay meant my gesture was lost on her.

"Come on, darling," Wade Midsel said to her, waving away an offer of assistance from the crew. He put his arm around Tara's waist. As they walked away, Wade's head swung tightly from side to side, and Tara's head bobbed as she looked first in one direction and then another. She seemed to have even more enthusiasm than Conrad Delingo had on his very first day.

I watched them disappear down the corridor, my complete attention absorbed. Even later I couldn't say whether I was simply captivated by the energy Tara Cline exuded or that something about her made me think my routine was to be unsettled.

= 2 =

A Fish Dinner in Hyperspace

I saw Jenni Sonders again sooner than I had expected. After losing my ritual argument with Bella, the skipper insisting that I dine with the passengers, I found my way to the dining hall on level four. The room held about two dozen tables for ten. The ship was fairly full, so most of the chairs were occupied. There was one empty chair at my table: mine.

The standard procedure was for the rest of the table to be occupied by the newest passengers, but some serious scheming had obviously been going on tonight. Not only was Jenni Sonders at the table, but Amanda Queverra was as well. And Amanda was seated next to my chair.

To one side of the room, a young blonde girl, probably impatient for dinner, was playing in front of one of the mirrors. She was pivoting at just the right speed to see the reflection of her back when she looked at the mirror.

I walked toward the table, trying hard not to show my discomfort with the seating arrangements. I wasn't bothered so much by Jenni being seated there; probably Rory had arranged that. Amanda, however, was a person I'd already spent more time with than I cared to.

Amanda was nice enough to look at, and pleasant enough for the first ten minutes, but she seemed to be a compulsive flirt, to whom the word "no" appeared to mean the opposite. Or maybe she viewed me as a challenge. If so, she was right. Either she was not exceptionally bright, or she was extremely skilled at making men feel superior so they wouldn't be intimidated. I didn't care whether it was an act or the real thing. If someone dropped a heavy piece of equipment on your fingers, your first concern wasn't necessarily whether the act was deliberate or an accident.

Naturally, Amanda was the first to notice me as I approached the table. "Hello, Jason," she said warmly. She had on a simple but very low cut blouse with a matching skirt. The moderate gravity on this level definitely assisted her figure.

I forced a weak grin on my lips and strode boldly forward.

"We thought you weren't going to make it," she said, pushing her long blonde hair back over her shoulder. Her eyelids were tinted a deep blue-violet. "You're almost late."

"Sorry. Duties," I said, sitting down and looking around the table. Actually I always arrived as late as I could, and left as early as possible.

Directly opposite me, down the length of the table, was Jenni Sonders. She looked pale tonight, but she acknowledged my nod. Her red hair was prettier in the better light here on level four. Her curls lifted slightly higher in the lighter gravity. Her expression was neutral, so I couldn't tell if she was ashamed, grateful, embarrassed, angry, numb, or something else entirely.

Amanda played the hostess and introduced me to each of the people seated at the table. Some of them I recognized already. Next to Amanda was Emil Frankton, an aging, portly businessman, and his aide, Juan Absome, who seemed too young to look so prune-faced. Between them and Jenni sat a smiling, handsome man in his mid-twenties, named Karl Welmot. Maybe I could get him interested in Amanda so she'd leave me alone.

On Jenni's other side were Tara Pesek Cline and her husband, Wade Pesek Midsel. Tara still managed to appear slightly mischievous and Wade was still a bit smug. I wondered what conversation I had interrupted. They both nodded in my direction slightly after they were introduced, and with an effort I pulled my gaze away from Tara.

Next to Wade was a sandy-haired young man named Merle Trentlin who seemed barely old enough to travel alone. He was the only one at the table who fidgeted. Between Merle and me, sat Daniel Haffalt, looking totally at ease, if not bored. He did smile wryly, though, when his gaze reached the scratches on my cheek.

Introductions complete, I raised a toast to new friends and new ports of call—the standard list that Bella would have toasted if she were here. But she never was. I envied her job for that reason as much as any other; with her rank, no one could tell her she had to mingle with the passengers.

Raised non-spill mugs rippled down the table. Images of the nearest people drinking reached me before the sounds of each container clinking against the next arrived in a series of tiny clicks. One pair of mugs came together almost hard enough to knock a mug from a hand; probably one person or both had underestimated the speed-of-light delay. Jenni was apparently the last to drink since she was the farthest away.

Trying to adjust to the perceptible time delays aboard the *Redshift* gave newcomers some of the symptoms of a hangover. A precision marching team would have turned in their retirement requests before they had to work in this environment.

Jenni seemed more at ease tonight. I watched her for a moment, wondering if she was truly feeling better, or if she was just putting on a show for the sake of the others. Off to one side of my vision sat Tara Cline. An instant later Jenni caught my eye and gave me a brief puzzled glance. I averted my gaze, knowing that she would see me watching her for a large part of a second anyway.

Fortunately, dinner arrived right on time, so the food temporarily occupied people's attention. Aboard the *Redshift* most meals looked terrible and tasted great. It took people a while to adjust to eating a meal in which everything on the menu came in motley shades of gray and charcoal, but soon they realized the color loss was just an artifact of this bizarre environment, and the taste was unaffected. Food, just like anything aboard the *Redshift* that wasn't protected by a field, or specially treated, reflected most of the light that struck it.

Layne's new assistant chef must have been responsible for this evening's meal. Layne preferred the standard three-course approach. His assistant favored four courses, and she showed a tendency to prepare more exotic variations than did Layne. I imagined it wouldn't be long before Layne felt the competition and began trying for more variety himself. Tonight we had deep-water fish from a water-planet called Misty. They were stuffed with a filling made from tubular plants from Archon. Layne needed to start watching out.

As we ate, I occasionally looked at the passengers. I glanced in Jenni's direction more often than Amanda's, but I found myself watching Tara out of the corner of my eye, noticing her dimples and her slight, playful smile. And realizing that she was also glancing at me occasionally, her dark blue eyes looking almost black from this distance.

Tara raised a small morsel of fish on her fork. The biteful passed between her lips, and it turned indigo as it entered the field surrounding her body.

"Where have you been keeping yourself, Jason?" Amanda asked, her knee "accidentally" brushing my leg.

I was staying away from the passenger cabin deck. I moved my leg back. "I stay fairly busy."

"I don't doubt that," said Daniel Haffalt. Opposite Amanda, he was grinning, his gaze focused on my scratches.

"Just an accident," I said softly, not looking toward Jenni.

Daniel Haffalt was apparently ready to let the subject die, but then Amanda spoke up. "Whatever are you two talking about?"

Trying not to look toward Jenni, I got a glimpse of Tara's mischievous expression turning sober.

Daniel said, "Nothing much. The first officer just has a few scratches on his cheek. Made, no doubt, by running into a door."

I tried to make light of it, to indicate it was no big problem. "Actually," I said, "I cut myself with my depilatory cream."

Daniel smiled knowingly and nodded. Wade chuckled smugly. Amanda put her hand to my chin and turned my head until she could see the scratches.

"Jason," she said, something between amusement and surprise in her voice, "that looks like war paint. I guess you're not as shy as you let on." She smiled at me. It was a predator's smile.

"It was simply an accident," I said calmly. "Why don't we talk about something else?"

"But, Jason, I—"

"Don't you have any more questions about the ship, Amanda? It seems that everyone new to traveling in hyperspace has more questions than the brochure answers." I didn't add that if they read the *entire* brochure that they wouldn't have so many questions. I tried not to even think about Jenni.

Amanda was obviously more curious about my scratches than about hyperspace phenomena, but for the moment she quit pressing. "All right. I didn't feel the ship slow down before we docked at Vestry, and I didn't feel us start to move again afterward. Are we moving at all?"

I was about to answer when our youngest passenger, Merle Trentlin, spoke up rapidly. "I know the answer to that. Would you let—would it be all right if I answered that, Mr. Kraft?"

Merle was obviously far more interested in this than he had been in my scratches. He looked at me and then at Amanda and then back at me, his eyes unblinking. His dark hair was combed forward over his forehead and cut in an arc so perfect that it suggested the careful use of a compass. His ears stuck out wide.

Happy to be out of the focus of attention, I said, "Sure. Go ahead."

"It's because they warp space. I know—it sounds almost like getting something for nothing, but it isn't. You see, they focus a warp outside of the ship. It's like gravity—or like a pond. You know, if you scoop out some water next to a piece of wood floating on a pond, the wood floats toward the depression. They warp space outside the ship to create a depression, and the ship falls in that direction. If they just created a warp at a fixed distance, the ship wouldn't fall toward it, because that's just like holding a magnet near your belt buckle to pull yourself forward. They create a warp and let it go, and it takes a small amount of time before it dies away. While it's dying away, it attracts the ship. And once the ship is started, inertia keeps it moving."

He paused and looked at me for confirmation.

"Close enough," I said.

"But you can't scoop vacuum like you scoop water," Amanda said. "I mean, there's nothing there to scoop."

"It's just an analogy," I said. "The ship uses energy to create a gravity well that's outside the ship—the same kind of gravity well that would be generated by a close, massive object. We create the well, and fall partway down into it before it collapses. We use that same general technique to generate gravity aboard the ship. There's a warped space, a gravity well, inside level zero that creates the same effect that would be generated by having a small, very dense planet at the core of the ship."

"Okay," Amanda said. "But when the ship is starting or stopping, why don't we feel like we're falling then?"

Merle was ready for that one. "Because we're all falling together— the ship and us—we're all moving with each other, just like we were in free fall. And the ship's internal gravity isn't affected."

I was impressed. Most passengers didn't even read enough of the brochure to understand why you could generate sonic booms by running, and they still got confused when their wristcomp time never agreed with ship time.

Amanda must have read my mind. Her next question was, "How come my wristcomp time never agrees with the clocks on the ship?"

I was suddenly very pleased that Merle was sitting at our table. I nodded at him the instant I saw him look toward me.

Merle leaned forward. "It's because time runs at different rates all over the ship. It's just like general relativity—time goes slower the closer you are to the gravity at the center of the ship. Because gravity slows down time."

"But the time doesn't seem consistent even when I stay on one level."

"It isn't like that. I mean time doesn't go at the same rate even on one level. It runs slower at your feet than at your head. Because the lower you are the stronger the gravity is. Hold your wristcomp over your head and it will speed up. That's true in normal space, too, but since the speed of light is so much faster there, the effects aren't so easy to measure."

"This is all really true, Jason?" Amanda said, disbelief showing plainly in the cocking of her head and the pursing of her lips.

"He's exactly right. That's why you don't have to clip your toenails as often as your fingernails."

She looked closely at me.

"I'm not joking. Or at least I'm not saying anything untrue. But there are other reasons for your wristcomp time being wrong."

"That's right," Merle said, taking over again. "If you run—or if you just move quickly, time slows down for you. It's all because the speed of light is so slow. Relativity—relativistic effects happen at low speeds."

I could tell from expressions on other faces around the table that some of this was news to more people than Amanda. "He's right," I said. "The faster you run, the slower time goes for you, so in a sense, jogging really is good for your life span."

A few of the passengers gave slight serious nods of comprehension. Only Daniel Haffalt smiled.

Amanda seemed to have run out of questions, and no one else was asking any. The conversation picked up sporadically as the passengers began to talk about their jobs, their destinations, the food.

I was thinking that I had been successful in diverting the topic, when Amanda said, "I know!"

I looked everywhere but at Amanda and at Jenni.

Amanda put her hand on my arm. "This morning a steward told me there was an incident with one of the passengers last night. I'll bet that's where you got your scratches."

If that had been the entire message Amanda received, I could probably have squelched the conversation again, but not a second later Jenni set her mug down on top of Tara's mug, and it tipped over with a loud crash. Jenni's face paled.

Amanda either knew more than she had said, or she simply read Jenni's expression accurately. "It was you, wasn't it?" she asked, leaning forward and looking directly at Jenni.

I said, "That's enough. Stop it, will you?" but Jenni nodded before my words reached her, as though she had no other choice, a guilty child caught by a persecuting parent carrying inescapable evidence.

Every head at the table seemed to swivel toward Jenni in unison. Those at the far end of the table had seen her response first, but their images were delayed the most to my eyes. No one spoke for a long moment.

"Well," Amanda said, stretching out the word, and she looked back at me. She blinked her midnight-blue eyelids.

"Amanda," I said, "that's enough. It was just a simple accident. It didn't involve anyone here."

"Oh, stop it!" Jenni said suddenly, more animation in her eyes than I had seen since we were on level two. "Quit badgering the man. He's too much of a gentleman to admit that I did it."

Jenni looked down at her lap and then back up at me and eight expectant faces. Tara lifted her eyebrows. Jenni went on. "It isn't what you're thinking. Mr. Kraft—Jason—was helping me."

Perhaps she would have left it there, but Wade Midsel said, "Helping you, or helping himself?" He grinned broadly at Tara, but since shedding her mischievous grin, she had stayed solemn. I wouldn't have wanted that stony look directed toward me.

From the pained expression on Jenni's face, she clearly didn't want to explain her personal problems to nine strangers. She said, "I was in need of—that is, I was—oh, damn it all! I got myself in trouble and I panicked. Jason helped me." This last sentence she directed my way, accompanied by a smile meek enough to make it difficult to recall the ferocity in her eyes last night.

Layne Koffer's new assistant would be unhappy; no one was eating.

Now everyone was looking at me, as though this were some bizarre sporting match and it was my turn to hit the ball toward Jenni so the eight heads could swivel back and the game would continue. Jenni didn't seem to need the concentrated attention, however, so I said, "It's all in a day's work. I think we've delved deeply enough into Jenni's personal concerns. The lounge is open in case anyone wants to relax after dinner."

Wade Midsel snorted loudly enough for me to hear. Clearly, he couldn't have been more displeased if I had thrown down my racket and stormed off the court, but he didn't say anything to divert the conversation back to Jenni.

No one moved from the table. Silence prevailed a moment longer until Amanda blurted out, "You were committing suicide?" Whoever had talked to her must have given her a clue.

Jenni shot Amanda a cold stare that I could easily read: *What business is it of yours?*

Emil Frankton, the businessman, finally took the cue I had planted earlier. He rose, gesturing for his aide, Juan Absome, to join him. "I think we will retire to the lounge after all. Will anyone join us?" Emil looked a little uneasy, but I couldn't tell if that was the result of tensions at the table, trouble adjusting to the ship's day-night cycle, or perhaps a common malady that sometimes hit newcomers to the environment: c-sickness.

No one accepted Emil's invitation. At least Emil was doing his part to defuse the situation. "Perhaps later," he said, and then he left with his aide.

"Surely you've got more questions about the ship," I said to the remaining passengers.

Wade Midsel must have decided to be no more cooperative than Amanda had been. He had to have realized that with her silence Jenni had tacitly admitted her intentions. He turned away from me. "You've piqued our curiosity, Jenni. Is what Amanda said true?"

I was momentarily stunned at his callousness, but realized that he had asked his question the way I had probably asked mine last night, and this time I heard the submerged message that I had presumably sent also: *You want to take your own life? Why are you such a freak that you want to do something so alien to what I think is normal?*

I was about to renew my request to change the topic and insist on it, but Jenni replied calmly. Maybe she needed to talk, even if the only alternative meant doing so in a group. Perhaps the fact that the group had recently dwindled made it easier for her.

"Don't you get brief flashes—once in a while?" she said. "Angry times when you just don't want to go on any longer? Sometimes life is just too complicated." Jenni faced me, as though I were the only one at the table. "Those moods come and go, but they've been with me a long time now, long enough that they seem normal." She looked back at Wade when she finished, as though to indicate the answer had been for him even though she had faced me.

I didn't know if she wanted to talk about all the pain that must have been required to bring her to where she was, or if she wanted to talk about where she would go from here. In her position, I imagined I would want to look ahead, so I said, "Why is death a solution?"

She gave me a puzzled look for an instant and then said, "It isn't that death is a solution; it's that life doesn't seem to be the answer. It's not that I want death; it's that sometimes I don't want life."

It must have been a compulsion with me to talk her out of wanting to die. I knew enough about the situation to realize the issue was an emotional one, but that didn't stop me from trying to intellectualize it. "But suppose death is even worse?" I said. "Were you brought up in a religion that talks about a rewarding afterlife?"

She nodded yes.

"Haven't you ever wondered if all that talk wasn't simply a way of making people less afraid of dying? And maybe more afraid of causing pain, because they get punished for that? What if the truth is that the afterlife is even worse than life? For all we know, it might be the equivalent of waiting in some doctor's office for eternity, with only some old disease-prevention videos to watch."

Jenni's eyes clouded. "You just don't understand."

"That's true. I don't. But I'm trying to. If you just don't like life, if you want to quit living, quit contributing, quit feeling, why don't you just go to Xanahalla?"

In the slow-speed environment aboard the *Redshift,* communications delays were usually disconcerting. This time, however, the delay was useful. I had already stopped talking and was watching Jenni when I saw two people suddenly turn their heads in my direction, check the motion, and then turn casually back to Jenni. The two were Wade and Tara.

"What's Xanahalla?" Jenni asked.

Tara's lips opened slowly, as though she was going to answer, but Karl Welmot spoke up first. "I thought everybody had heard of it." He glanced at the rest of us before he looked back at Jenni and continued. "Xanahalla is a religious retreat. I don't know where it is, but I hear about it once in a while. You apparently have to buy your way in—by contributing heavily to charity or doing a huge amount of community service.

"It's supposed to be a paradise of some sort, a reward for people who have made their contribution. Everyone lives in comfort, spending whatever time they choose contemplating the mysteries of the universe and communing with God." Karl waved his hands in the air, indicating someone gesturing to God.

Jenni looked at me. "I don't understand. Why do you compare that to suicide?"

I said, "I just meant there's a whole group of people who have checked out of the universe. They've done all they intend to do to influence the quality of life and all those other trite popular causes. They've made the same decision you're considering, but they have the advantage of being able to change their minds later. They're just suiciders without the fortitude to make it permanent."

"You must be quite an expert on Xanahalla, Mr. First Officer," Tara

Cline said, quietly. Her voice was a pleasant contralto, but her words and tone told me instantly I had hit a sensitive area. "You damn so many people in a few short sentences, that surely you must know an enormous amount about the people who go there."

I looked into her eyes for a long moment. "I apologize if I've offended you, Ms. Cline. Sometimes I say things to see what will happen, precisely because I *don't* know all the answers. But it does occur to me that perhaps *you're* an authority on this subject."

Wade made a motion to keep his wife from replying, but that didn't stop Tara. "I suppose I am. You see, I've *been* to Xanahalla."

At the same time Tara spoke, I felt a hand on my leg. I took the opportunity to move my chair back and make myself more comfortable, farther from Amanda. When I looked up, all heads had swiveled to face Tara.

"I've never met anyone who has been to Xanahalla," I said. "Did you fall from grace or get a weekend pass or what?"

Wade scowled at me. "She chose to leave. That's her business."

Tara frowned in my direction. Whether the frown was for me or due to her husband answering questions directed at her, I couldn't tell. Whatever the cause, I found that it bothered me.

Karl Welmot leaned forward. "We don't need to know why you left. But tell us about Xanahalla, would you?"

Tara hesitated, but she had already gone too far, and she proceeded to answer the question. "It's an idyllic world, absolutely peaceful. The makers built every single structure on Xanahalla to be in harmony with the beauty of plant life from dozens of worlds," she said, the frown leaving her face. As her words arrived, I could see she was warming to her description. She struck me as someone who wouldn't stay angry for long.

"If you stand near the peak of the Tower of Worship, you can see rich greens and blues all the way to the horizon; thousands of people live there without trampling the natural beauty. Stone walkways join some of the buildings, and each building is custom-designed for the exact location it occupies. If the makers wanted a building in the path of a stream, they built it on stilts so the stream could pass beneath, or they built it so the stream could pass right through a large atrium. I've never seen so many atriums and skylights. A network of tunnels connects the Tower of Worship to every building."

Tara's eyes had acquired a faraway look that could have been wistfulness. I wondered if she wished she was back there. Maybe on Xanahalla no one asked questions people didn't want to answer. Maybe they asked only questions that had no answers. Or perhaps they already had all the answers.

"What's the Tower of Worship?" asked Karl.

"It's the largest temple I've seen in my life. It's magnificent. It's pyramid-shaped, with elevators and corner stairways that go almost all the way to the peak. The peak is so high the weather at the top is different from the weather on the ground. It must be 500 meters tall." Wade glanced at Tara and she concluded her description. "It's simply a beautiful and serene place."

The following silence was awkward. When it was obvious that Tara wasn't going to add anything more without another question being asked, Amanda went back to the hints I had dropped when I didn't want to talk about the scratches on my cheek.

"You know," Amanda said, "I *did* have several questions about this fine ship of yours, Jason. Do you think you might have some time tonight to answer one or two of them for me?"

The tables next to ours were starting to empty. If I didn't move now, I risked being stuck with Amanda or having to be even more rude to her. I rose abruptly. "I'm sorry, Amanda. I'm afraid I need to excuse myself, ladies and gentlemen. If you've got any more questions about the *Redshift*, I'm sure that Merle should be able to answer them. Or ask any of the crew. Good evening and I hope you have a pleasant voyage."

Amanda's eyes narrowed almost imperceptibly as she grasped the message underneath, but she smiled brightly in Merle's direction. I noticed Wade start to look more relaxed than he had for the last few minutes.

Merle ducked his head and smiled in embarrassment at the compliment before he looked around the table to see if people were going to ask more questions. I retreated.

The exiting crowd was large enough to make it impossible to move quickly without running into people, so I cautiously edged my way between a couple of standing passengers and headed for the door. I was almost there when someone called my name.

I turned and found Jenni Sonders right behind me.

"I wanted to—to say I was sorry about last night," she said. "And for making you the focus of curiosity tonight. Whatever Doctor Willett gave me has got me thinking more clearly." She touched the skin behind her ear. Jenni looked somber, but I couldn't see the pain in her eyes that I had seen last night. She was prettier when she wasn't hurting so badly.

"Let's go out in the corridor," I said.

In the hallway, we took a right on the equator and walked a few meters in silence. I wasn't sure what to say, so I started with, "You really don't need to apologize to me, Ms. Sonders. For all I know, I should be apologizing to you. No law says a person can't commit suicide if she wants to. Even now I don't know if I did the right thing."

"It's Jenni. And you'd do it all over again if you found yourself in that position."

"Yes," I admitted. "I probably would at that."

We continued walking. We passed the service entrance to the galley and took a right at the next north-south corridor. From the middle of the intersection, the floors arcing down and out of sight in all four directions gave the feeling that we stood on top of the world. Or at least on top of a small world.

I looked more closely at Jenni than I had last night. Her eyes were green flecked with blue. "Do you feel better tonight?" I asked, hoping that she did, and thinking it would help her to admit it.

"Yes. And no. I'm still confused about everything. Maybe I feel a little better. I guess I do."

"And this is all because of recent events?"

She shook her head. "I thought so for a while. But I guess it's bigger than that. I haven't been happy for a long time."

"How far back? Parents?"

"You, too?" she asked, facing me suddenly.

"Lucky guess," I said, and swallowed.

We lapsed into silence as we passed a passenger.

"Why did you originally go down to level two last night?" I asked, to change the subject.

"If you mean did I go down there explicitly to commit suicide, the answer is no. I like to explore. I was feeling really depressed and I thought that exploring might cheer me up. It wasn't enough." She grinned ruefully.

"Tell me about your parents."

Jenni clasped her hands behind her back and swung her shoulders to and fro as she walked. I interpreted the gesture to mean she was trying to be casual, but her voice was strained, breathy. "On a scale of ten for rigidity, they were, oh, maybe an eleven. Maybe a twelve. I was the first of three children, so I got to be the test case for everything. My brother and sister got treated a little more like human beings with minds of their own, but only after I fought—and fought and fought. Enough to destroy whatever bonds had existed between me and my parents.

"One time my father locked me in an empty room for punishment. I had returned late from some school function. Do you have any idea how long twenty-four hours can seem when there's absolutely nothing to do but feel the hate building inside you?"

Jenni almost choked on the last few words, so I said nothing for a time. Soft, long-delayed echoes of our footsteps were almost the only sounds.

"You know," I said at last, "the message transmitted isn't always the message received."

"I've understood most everything you've said until now."

"I don't know that I should even speculate. But I mean if you kill yourself, part of the reason could be that you want to send a message to your parents. Something like, 'Look what happened to me because you two messed me up so badly.' "

Jenni stopped right there in the hall. She looked at me, a tiny frown creasing the skin at the center of her forehead, her curiosity entirely transparent. "Go on."

"Think about it for a minute. How do you think they'd actually react if they heard about your suicide? Do you think they'd say, 'Gosh, we were terrible parents to have forced our daughter into doing such a thing.' Or do you think they'd say, 'So after all our sacrifices, Jenni went and killed herself. So this is the thanks we get.' "

Jenni looked at me for what seemed like a long time, staring blindly for part of the time, and then shifting her gaze from one of my eyes to the other. She said softly, "It sounds like we had the same parents."

"Not if you knew yours," I began and then stopped before I said anything else.

"What—"

"Nothing. Look, I guess what I'm trying to say is that you obviously can go ahead and commit suicide if that's what you feel you have to do; no one can stop you. But maybe it won't accomplish your goals."

Jenni drew a deep breath and let it out slowly. "You give people a lot to think about."

"If that's good, thank me by doing me a favor."

"And what's that?" Her voice hardened just enough to convince me that she hadn't necessarily received very good treatment from men.

"Call me immediately if you feel you have to go ahead with suicide. You can get me through the bridge at any comm panel. Any time."

Her intense look vanished and she lost some of her stiffness. "I don't honestly know if I can do that. I don't think very clearly when I'm feeling that bad. But I promise to try."

I nodded.

"Where are we anyway?" she asked, looking down the corridor toward the next intersection.

"We've walked almost entirely around the ship. That corridor ahead is the equator, where we started."

She looked back the way we had come and then ahead to the intersection. She nodded as though she had her bearings again.

I walked her to the junction and started to take a left to go to the bridge. "You *will* call?" I said.

"Yes. I'll try." Jenni was turning right, toward the dining hall and the lounge, when she stopped in the middle of the intersection. No one else was nearby at the moment. "Jason, I—" Her voice caught and she grinned too brightly, inhaling through her nose as though to clear her head. "I don't know what all of your duties are aboard this ship, but I'm quite sure they don't pay you enough."

I was tired when I finally went back to my cabin for the night. Dealing with Jenni Sonders and dinner had drained me of more than mere physical strength.

Weary as I was, I took the time to look at the single picture that occupied my wall.

Black-and-white images were the only ones that could exist on the *Redshift* without a protective field, and even then they had to be specially produced so the appropriate sections absorbed light. The long focal length required for this particular photo had flattened the image to begin with. The processing to make the image usable in this crazy environment had robbed it of what little depth of field remained.

I stared at that picture of my father long enough that when I looked away I saw a vivid negative afterimage.

Sometimes I wondered why I kept the picture. By now, I couldn't have erased the image if I tried.

And I wondered if he was still there.

The next morning, I was walking from my cabin to breakfast when the nearest comm panel chimed with the coded tone that meant a summons. Faint echoes from comm panels farther away followed in succession.

I punched the button and said, "Jason here."

Razzi was on the bridge. She sounded unsettled. "You're needed up on level six." She supplied a bay number.

"Can you give me the rest? I'm alone."

"We've had a fatality. A passenger. The name is—" The speaker was silent for a moment while she probably decided she couldn't get out of being the one to tell me. "Jenni Sonders."

= 3 =

To Die in Hyperspace

"Hell of a way to kill yourself," Bella said. She and Bensode, the third officer, stood near Jenni Sonders' body as Rory continued his examination.

I had been the last to arrive. Conrad Delingo had discovered the body. He was now stationed at the level-six cargo bay door to keep out any wandering passengers. This was the first time I could remember seeing his enthusiasm dampened.

Bensode and I made no reply to Bella's comment; Bensode could probably tell as well as I which of her remarks were rhetorical. Bensode's normal doleful expression had magnified so much that I didn't think he could look any sadder if someone had killed half the people at one of his family reunions.

Rory knelt on the far side of Jenni's body, so my view was nearly unobstructed. She wore the same clothes she had at dinner last night: a light blouse and loose, royal-blue pants. She lay on her back, her feet splayed. A tie-down cord was wrapped in a single loop around her neck and knotted in front. The loop was almost hidden by the puffy flesh it bit into, except for the knot, which covered a small bruise. Jenni's face was calm, but the bluish tinge on her lips and ears remained as a testimony to the pain caused by oxygen deprivation. One of her hands still gripped an outstretched end of the line. The other end of the line snaked away like a severed umbilical cord. Her eyes were closed.

On my way here, I had felt anger—burning anger, the kind I had for a time been able to fool myself into thinking I'd grown immune to. I was angry at Jenni for breaking her promise to call me. I was angry at her for doing this to herself. And I was angry at myself for letting her get close to me.

According to Jason's first law of motion, everybody continues in a consistent direction unless acted on by an outside force. Jenni had jogged me out of my comfortable path.

If this were the first time I'd seen Jenni, I could have maintained my immunity. She would have been just another stranger who faltered in her journey from one place to another. Just another carcass along the road to kingdom come.

But she wasn't. I looked back at her face, and I saw the sadness that had been there before, and I hurt.

I guess I must have been staring at Jenni's face when I felt a hand tug at my elbow.

"Jason, are you all right?" Bensode stood next to me, looking concerned.

"What? Oh, yeah. I'm fine."

Bensode hesitated, as though he wasn't sure whether to believe me, and then he said, "I've sent someone after a stretcher. Is there anything else you want?" His eyes seemed darker than usual. In a slightly altered scene, he could have been a creditor, waiting for the right moment to be able to intrude on the bereaved family's grief.

I looked at Bella. She had heard Bensode's question and shook her head at me. I said, "No. Thanks."

I forced myself not to look at Jenni's body. Instead I occupied myself by taking a quick scan of the cargo bay. Large individually locked crates came close to the high ceiling in several places. A straight path led from the door to the opposite wall, and four paths cut sideways across the central lane. Jenni's body lay on the floor at the intersection of two walkways.

Rory appeared to be finishing his preliminary examination. He had pushed Jenni's blouse up to expose the lifebelt around her midriff. He looked up at Bensode. "What's her code?"

After a brief call to the bridge, Bensode gave him a five-number sequence which Rory proceeded to enter on the front keypad. Once he finished, the lifebelt beeped loudly several times. Rory keyed in the number a second time and the lifebelt turned itself off and unlocked. The field took a moment to die; as it did, the red in Jenni's hair and what little color was still in her face disappeared. The royal-blue in her clothes, no longer exposed to the fringes of the field, faded to shades of gray.

Rory used a sharp blade from his case to cut the cord around Jenni's neck. He removed the cord carefully. The depression it left behind seemed just as deep as it had been with the cord biting into it. Rory unwrapped the end of the cord from Jenni's right hand and deposited the cord in a transparent container from his case. Finally, he took a protected-field, subjective-time counter and strapped it onto Jenni's wrist. He rose slowly. Since the gravity here was only one-third gee, his sluggishness obviously wasn't due to lack of strength.

The dual display in the rectangular strip indicated the moment it had begun counting, and a running total of elapsed subjective time since then. Except for the time before Jenni's body had been discovered, the counter could have been labeled "Time AJ."

Rory faced Bella, Bensode, and me and said, "This is preliminary only." He scratched his bald pate and sighed.

Bella nodded.

"She died by strangulation, apparently self-inflicted." Rory squinted at the master clock next to the door. "Given that time progresses almost twenty percent faster here than on level four, I'd say she died near midnight. She has three bruises on the back of her head, one probably caused a day earlier than death, the other two occurring shortly before she died or as she was dying. She's got several minor cuts and bumps and scrapes on her arms and legs, none of which are more severe than one would expect to be caused by crawling onto shipping crates and exploring.

"What we have is what it looks like: a completed suicide. I'll do some checks for drugs and a few other things, but I don't expect to change my opinion."

Bella nodded.

I said, "There's no chance one of those blows on the back of her head was responsible for her death?"

Rory shook his head instantly. "If you're suggesting that someone killed her with a heavy blow, and then tied the cord around her neck, that couldn't be. She was still alive when the cord was tied around her neck, and the cord tightening was the cause of death. I'm sure of that much. If she hadn't tied the knot, she would still be alive, because she couldn't have maintained pressure on the cord after she passed out."

"Why are you so sure she asphyxiated?" I asked.

"Petechial hemorrhages—the increased blood pressure ruptures small capillaries in the eyes. Those little dots are unmistakable indicators of oxygen deprivation."

Bella's eyes narrowed and she said, "What's behind your questions, Jason? You think anyone had a reason to murder her?"

"Not one reason in the world," I said. At least not one good reason. Jenni had promised to call me before she did anything like this and she hadn't called. But that might simply mean she lied, or she couldn't bring herself to make the call, or she didn't think clearly when she was feeling at her worst, just as she had said. "I'm just trying to rule out possibilities."

"Those bruises are probably the result of spasms caused by the pain of death," Rory said. "A cord tightened around the neck can kill you at least two ways. If it's tight enough, it can do extensive nerve damage, and you die quickly. If it's a little looser, it merely cuts off either blood flow to the brain or air flow through the throat, or both. That's the way Jenni died. It's a lot more painful since it lasts longer."

I knelt beside Jenni's body, wondering what it felt like to be unable to untie the knot even if she changed her mind. I wondered if she had tried to struggle with the knot once she felt short of breath. Would that burning pain make a person wonder if there were another choice, or would it just cause another unpleasant minute or two on the way to a long-sought goal? "Why the scratches on her neck?"

"Probably her reaction to the pain—trying to get the rope loose. I've read reports of people who *almost* died that way. As I said, it's a painful way to go."

"So she really did it, huh, Doc?" I said.

Rory looked at me quizzically. "Yes, I already said it looks that way."

He had at that. I stood up. I told myself to settle back and start thinking with my brain instead of my gut. "Thanks, Doc. I guess I'm not thinking too clearly. I'll be back to normal in a few minutes."

To the side of my vision, I saw Bella and Bensode exchange glances.

Despite the grim setting, Rory looked at me with what seemed to be a weak smile on his lips, and he shook his head lightly. "Don't worry about it. That's actually just a very normal human reaction."

"Are you surprised that Jenni Sonders killed herself?" I asked Rory in his office on level four. The room contained a desk and four chairs. The walls were gray, lined with closed compartments everywhere except for the two doors.

He offered me a drink, which I declined. He warmed his hands on his mug for a long moment. "I don't know if I have enough data to be surprised or not surprised. I talked to her for a few minutes before I sedated her, then for about an hour yesterday, and maybe another fifteen minutes last night. Even now I don't know enough to say for sure

whether she was a long-term or a spontaneous. She had some characteristics of both. The medication should have helped—I thought it was
helping. If I had to guess, I would have said she was recovering, coming
out of the worst of it. But it's hard to know what's really going on inside
other people's heads. You seemed to make quite an impression on her,
though."

"Don't you have that backward?" I said, rubbing my cheek.

Rory took one of the visitor's chairs and sat down beside me. "Joke
about it, but at least half the time I spent with her she was asking
questions about you. What you did before you got onto a hyperspace
crew, what relationships you were in now or in the past. I felt a little
silly saying, 'I don't know' to most of her questions."

Rory looked at me expectantly, but I felt even less like talking about
myself now than I usually did. Jenni's body lay in suspension in the
next room, a reminder of the cost of letting other people get too close.

"Yes, I talked with Jenni Sonders last night—in the lounge, after
dinner," Wade Midsel told me. "Both Tara and I did."

Wade and I sat in facing chairs in the business office just down the
hall from the bridge. On the wall behind Wade was an enormous cross-
sectioned illustration of the *Redshift*. Cut open like an orange with
several slices missing, it showed a portion of each level. Next to it were
seven pairs of circular maps showing for each spherical level the equatorial corridors, the other latitudinal corridors, the meridian corridors,
and every room with its labeled function. On level four was a small
arrow with a sign saying "You Are Here."

I already knew what Wade had told me was true; I had received the
same information from three different people on duty in the lounge last
night. "How did she seem to you?" I asked.

Wade dropped his eyelids a fraction lower as he formulated his reply.
The reaction made him look sleepy, but nothing in his manner indicated
fatigue. He appeared calm, in control of himself, and unaccustomed to
nervous gestures that spent unnecessary energy. "Depressed, I suppose.
She didn't talk about suicide while I was there, but it isn't too hard to
recognize the signs of a woman who's clearly unhappy. She had to stop
once in a while in mid-sentence to keep control. She never looked relaxed even when she smiled. She fidgeted."

I didn't see that the things Wade pointed out applied only to women,
but he was answering my question so I said nothing.

He went on. "I'm a little surprised that she went ahead and did it, but that's probably because suicide isn't something I hear about every day. There's no telling what some women will do."

"I guess it's hard to predict anyone. I've lost count of the stories I've heard about someone going out of control and killing a bunch of innocent people and then every friend interviewed says, 'But he or she was such a normal person. Who would have guessed?' "

"That's true; the unexpected happens. But I'm afraid I can't tell you much more about Jenni Sonders."

"Thank you, Mr. Midsel. Perhaps your wife will be able to tell me more. I understand she stayed in the lounge with Jenni after you left."

"You're wasting your time. Tara doesn't know anything that will help you."

"Thanks, but I'll be the judge of that." Even as I said it, I was aware that once again lately my feelings were interfering with my judgment. I wanted to find out more about Jenni's mood last night, but I was also curious about Tara.

"Yes, I am surprised that she went ahead and did it," Tara Cline said. "Very surprised. I thought Jenni was feeling much better."

Tara sat in the same chair Wade had occupied. She didn't look nearly so happy as she had when she'd boarded the *Redshift*. And today, she didn't have Wade's composure. Jenni's death seemed to have touched her in a way it hadn't touched Wade. Tara's dark-blue eyes looked sad, and they lacked yesterday's easy inquisitiveness. At the moment she didn't look mischievous at all. She looked vulnerable.

I was actually glad to know that Wade and Tara disagreed on something. That indicated they hadn't compared notes and arranged a standard story. But I was still curious about the discrepancy. "Your husband told me he thought Jenni was still very depressed last night. I'm getting the feeling from you that she didn't seem that bad."

"Mr. Kraft—"

"Jason."

"Jason." She nodded. "Wade didn't stay talking with us for all that long. Jenni and I talked at least another hour after he left. I don't know that he had as much opportunity to see how she felt." Tara crossed her legs.

"You and Jenni left the lounge at the same time—about two hours before midnight?"

"Right. She was on her way to her cabin and I went to mine. Wade's and mine."

"Did Jenni mention any plans she had last night?"

"No. I thought she was going to bed. She thanked me for talking with her—I told her I didn't need any thanks for doing something I wanted to do—and she said something like, 'A little sleep couldn't hurt anything.' "

"What did you two talk about after Wade left?"

Tara clasped her hands together in her lap and looked at them for a moment. "We talked about several things. Mostly, I guess, suicide and Xanahalla—and you." She looked directly at me then, as though measuring my reactions. Maybe it was my imagination, but Tara's eyes seemed to have regained some of their inquisitiveness.

"Tell me what she said about suicide," I said quickly, feeling uncomfortable that the conversation might switch its focus to me.

The barest smile touched Tara's lips and then it was gone. Or maybe I imagined it, too. I wondered if I was imagining way too much lately.

"She told me about her conversations with you—about some of the things she said in anger which you might not even have heard for all the reaction they got."

I opened my mouth to protest this change in direction of the conversation, but Tara went right on.

"She told me about the questions you asked her—questions that slowed her down and made her think. Questions that gave her some time to wonder if she was really doing the right thing. I didn't really talk to Jenni before those conversations you had with her, but I'd be surprised if the change wasn't significant. I think part of what she wanted was simply a friend. She was beginning to feel that she owed you something."

I swallowed and then hesitated, amazed that I could be touched by thinking that Jenni had felt I made some difference. "Really, Ms. Cline, I—"

"Tara."

"Tara. I think we're getting off the subject."

"Are we?" Again on Tara's somber face there seemed to come that briefest hint of the mischievous smile I had seen yesterday. She dropped her gaze to the floor.

"Why did Xanahalla come up in your conversation last night?" I asked, to get to a more comfortable topic.

"Because of you."

"Oh, come on. Let's start over and—"

"I'm serious. It was because of your comments at dinner. Surely you remember comparing going to Xanahalla to committing suicide."

"Look, I've already apologized for that."

"I don't know that you need to. Jenni and I talked about ourselves, about why we had done the things we had so far. We had more in common than I thought. Perhaps I *was* dropping out. I had never thought of it that way, but going back has some of the same appeal that Jenni felt suicide offered."

"Going back?"

"Did I say that? I meant going there. I was rude last night not to answer your question about why I left. I can tell you now if you're still curious." Actually Wade was the one who had been rude; Tara's loyalty was refreshing.

I said, "Please go on." I was still curious about Xanahalla, and Tara was the final person I planned to question about Jenni so there was no rush. And actually, I was still a little curious about Tara, too.

"I left Xanahalla because eventually I came to feel I was just killing time. Maybe it was some of what you talked about last night. I didn't feel like I was contributing any longer; I was bored. As far as I could tell, a lot of the wealth I donated ended up in the Tower of Worship, either for beautification, or for the emergency fund—to be used if some enormous disaster should ever happen anywhere. But it seemed to me that more should be spent now; there are people in need on a hundred worlds right now. I thought we should have been looking to the nearer future. I guess maybe being there is a little like dropping out."

"Why is beautification so expensive?"

"The Tower of Worship isn't just any temple. I mean, you always want to make a place of worship as beautiful as you can, to honor God, but this temple is special. I think I said it's probably the largest in existence. They don't just have massive textured windows and all the rest of the typical trappings; at the center of the Tower of Worship there are supplication benches with inset panels made of pure gold. There are prayer benches lined with gemstones. The whole effect is stunning."

"Don't they worry about theft?" I asked.

"By whom? The residents don't have any use for extra wealth. And no one else could get there."

I must have looked dubious, because she continued. "It's not like you just look up Xanahalla in a tour guide and go there. You have to be taken there. And those few who leave, like me, go via a ship that deposits them quietly near a standard dock far enough away that they don't know how to get back."

"How did you get there in the first place?"

"I ran into another recruiter, and I agreed to go there. Eventually I received directions to take a trip. At one of the brief layovers, I was approached by a Xanahalla representative and I left directly from the layover point."

"Why do you say 'another recruiter'? Are you one now, too?"

"Yes. To me recruiting seems more constructive than staying there." Tara had appeared to relax as she talked about a topic that didn't involve Jenni. She rested her arms on the sides of her chair.

"What does a recruiter do? And are you on a recruiting trip now?"

"No, not actively; this is mainly a pleasure trip. Mostly I keep watch on the news wherever I am. If I see a story about someone who's made a significant effort to help others in need, or if I hear of someone wealthy who might be persuaded to make a large donation to the cause, I notify him or her and, if there's interest, give directions for making contact."

"And what did you donate?"

What was apparently a moderately large sum to her was an inordinately large amount to me. She named a figure that was more than I would earn in twenty standard years—even if I charged extra every time someone asked me to explain why wristcomp time didn't agree with the ship's clock.

"That probably seems a lot," she said, "but I took over a business that my mother had started, and I was lucky enough to get it to grow rapidly. I decided my good fortune should be shared."

"So you met Wade after you left Xanahalla?" Somehow the idea of Wade letting go of that much wealth seemed improbable. Maybe I wasn't feeling very charitable myself.

"Yes. He's been very good for me. He's even interested in history, too." Tara pushed a few stray strands of black hair away from her eyes. Somehow she had undergone a subtle transformation since I had first seen her. Earlier she had been a moderately attractive stranger. Now that I knew a little more about her, or I had simply seen more of her, she seemed unaccountably more beautiful. I was sure that when she was happy again, once the ugliness of Jenni's death had faded further into history, the word "radiant" would be apt. For the moment, the radiance was submerged, waiting for a better time.

"History?" I said, for the moment forgetting the original topic.

"Yes. History's my hobby. Old folk tales and children's stories especially. I'm fascinated by the past."

"Somehow you seem more a live-for-the-present person."

"I don't mean I dwell in the past. I just think we're all strongly influenced by the past. We're reacting to the past as often as to the present."

I agreed with her, but said, "Then you should feel right at home on the *Redshift.*"

"I don't follow you."

"I mean *everything* you see here is in the past. Makes you feel old, huh?"

Tara smiled, and my thoughts finally returned to the reason we had started talking. I said, "I didn't mean to stay off the subject for so long. Can you think of anything else that might explain why Jenni seemed to have a change of heart?"

"No I can't. She seemed appreciative that she had you as a friend."

"I really didn't do that much. I'm flattered that Jenni told you I seemed to make a difference, but I think—"

"You know, I think you see out better than you see in."

"—we should—I beg your pardon?"

"You hide behind your barriers, but you see out. Jenni talked about it and I can see what she meant. You shy away from anything that would get someone started talking about you—as though you had no feelings. I don't think that barrier means you don't have feelings—you have just as many feelings as anyone, but you're afraid of them."

"Really, I—"

"You know, you said that people who go to Xanahalla are just committing suicide in a socially acceptable manner. I think maybe you're doing the same thing by shutting out the rest of the world."

I was speechless. I opened my mouth to say something and realized I had absolutely no idea of what I had intended to say.

Tara drew her head down abruptly and focused her eyes on her hands before she looked up at me. "I'm sorry. I have no idea what possessed me to say all that to someone I hardly know."

She rose. "Just forget everything I said, Jason. I've no right to talk about how you run your life. I—I'd better leave. Unless you have any other questions?"

Still mute, I shook my head no.

Tara left and slid the door gently closed behind her. Only later did I wonder if her comments had been meant to deliberately unsettle me, to keep me distracted while I asked questions about Jenni's death.

The bridge was quiet, the atmosphere still somber. Losing a passenger was a relatively rare occurrence, and the effects seemed to have reached every member of the crew. People were subdued, pensive.

I leaned back in my chair and watched the stars drift by—not that obvious motion was easy to detect; the most noticeable changes happened when a nearby star occluded a more distant star. The fact that the screen was flat rather than three-dimensional robbed the star-field image of some of its majesty. For all that, the view was still spectacular. We were near enough the center of the galaxy for the stars to be more closely spaced than snowflakes in a dense storm.

The display wasn't truly representative of the view from *Redshift,* however, even if we had been in normal space, because it was impossible to travel this fast in normal space. The view was continually being constructed from positional information delivered by the network.

The network was a regular grid of transponders residing in hyper-space layer fifteen. That layer was more hazardous to human life than was layer ten, but not so harsh that hardened, redundant electronic and photonic systems couldn't survive quite a while. Since the effective transmission rate was thirty-two times the rate here in layer ten, we could communicate fairly rapidly with Confederation planets and other ships. Each transponder employed one sensor that rapidly shifted back and forth between normal space and layer fifteen; on board the *Redshift* was one that translated between layer fifteen and our layer ten.

The sound of a chime broke my reverie. I glanced over and saw Razzi making a quick check.

"It's for you," she said. Razzi usually wasn't much more talkative than I was; today she was especially quiet. She looked tired, but that was probably just an illusion. She kept fit by running, partly because a side benefit of running was that ship time speeded up. She could have used the treadmill in the gymnasium to get her exercise, but then her off-time would go slowly. She wanted her off-time to go slowly only when she was away from the ship.

I overlaid the star field with the incoming message. It was a reply to the query I had sent with Jenni's death notice shortly after the discovery. No, as far as the family knew, no friends of Jenni's were traveling on the *Redshift.* The ex-fiancé's name was Todd Armentio. The last line of the message gave permission for an autopsy.

A cross-check of the passenger log showed no Todds and no Armentios. Only two passengers had the initials T. A. and they were both female.

I forwarded the reply to Rory Willett and then returned the star field to the central viewer. I leaned back and lost myself in the mesmerizing scene. Wherever Jenni was, I hoped she was at peace.

And Tara. I had been comfortable for a long while, able to cultivate my isolation and find fulfillment in my job. And now it seemed that Jason's third law of emotions was resurfacing: for every emotion, there's an equal but opposite emotion. I was unexpectedly attracted to Tara, and at the same time I felt guilty about the attraction. She had made a commitment to Wade, and she seemed happy with that.

My thoughts drifted back to Jenni. My first reaction had been normal to me: why had I gotten involved? It was only now that I was asking myself the question, what might have happened had I gotten *more* involved?

Even when you're at rest, time is relative. Only moments later, it seemed, my reflections were interrupted by Bensode's arrival at the bridge.

"I'm afraid we have some more trouble, Jason," he said. He sat down next to me and loosened his uniform collar. His shadowed eyes gave me the impression that whatever he was about to tell me was his fault, even though he was surely only the messenger.

"Tell me about it," I said.

"Fenn Melgard is assigned to the swing crew on level six. He didn't report for duty today, and he doesn't answer any calls to his cabin."

Bensode had cause to be concerned. Crew members who didn't take their responsibilities seriously didn't last long on the *Redshift*. The explanation for Fenn Melgard's absence was quite unlikely to be as simple as oversleeping or forgetfulness.

= 4 =

Hunters of the *Redshift*

"Do you make any sense out of this, Jason?" Bella asked. She leaned back in her comfortable chair on the bridge and shook her head.

"Not yet. We've got too many possibilities. Melgard's going missing about the time Jenni Sonders died seems suspicious, but I think we need to stay open to any possibility." Fenn Melgard had not responded to a ship-wide summons.

A chime sounded on the comm panel. Razzi leaned over to answer the call. A moment later, Rory Willett's voice came through. "Would you tell Jason that Melgard's not in his cabin? His bed is made. Everything's tidy. Apparently all his personal effects are still here. No sign of a struggle."

"He got the message," Razzi said. "Thanks."

Oblivious to the surrounding status panels, we sat in a circle of chairs on the bridge: Bensode, Razzi, Bella, and me. Bella had joined us just a few minutes after I called her with Bensode's bad news. The somber mood following Jenni's death had transmuted into a tense uneasiness.

Bella drummed her fingernails on the chair arms. "I think a thorough search of the ship is in order. Any disagreement?"

"It's underway already," I said. "I figured we could always stop if you didn't want to alarm the passengers, and the odds of Melgard just having overslept were too tiny to accept. A crew started on level six."

Bella nodded, obviously unsurprised by my anticipating her order. "All right then. You're in charge of the search, Jason. Let me know if you find him or if you cross a level off your list. How long do you think it will take?"

"It could be finished at any moment if we find him right away. Several hours if he's staying in one place where he doesn't want to be found. Even longer if he's actively evading us. I don't know what to expect yet."

Motion at the corner of my eye told me the door to the corridor had opened. Conrad Delingo strode quickly toward us, and an instant later there came the muffled "pop" of the sonic boom he had generated on his way here.

"You sent for me, sir?" he said, looking at me and standing erect.

"Right. Relax and have a chair."

Conrad moved an empty chair closer to our circle and we made way for him. He sat stiffly in the chair and looked straight at me. His white uniform was immaculate, and every one of his tiny pocket flaps was neatly closed.

I said, "We just need some information from you. There's no need for formality. I understand you're a good friend of Fenn Melgard." After Conrad nodded, I added, "You've probably heard that he's missing. Tell us what you know about him, anything you can think of that might help us locate him or figure out why he's disappeared."

Conrad swallowed hard and looked around the circle of serious expressions. "I'm not sure I've got anything useful to say, sir, but I'll tell you what I know. Fenn—Melgard is—this isn't like him. He's a reliable guy. Friendly. He's spent a fair amount of his off-time helping me learn about the areas I haven't worked in yet. I can't imagine what could be the problem."

"Is there anyone special on the crew that he spends lots of time with —male or female?"

"No, sir. Fenn likes company as much as any of the guys do, but, as far as I know, no one special woman. He always says he likes variety."

"What about passengers?"

"You mean does he socialize with passengers? No, not much at all. He knows that's discouraged, and he thinks the crew is large enough for, ah, entertainment between shore leaves." Conrad was studiously avoiding looking at Bella and Razzi, as though this were somehow exclusively "man talk."

"So he didn't mention having met Jenni Sonders?"

"No, sir."

"When's the last time you saw him?"

"Last night. About halfway through swing shift, around eight. When we dock at Tangent today, we have to unload some cargo that was behind a bunch of crates that don't come out until Far Star, so Fenn and I and Thompsil and Hendern reshuffled the load."

I scratched my forehead. "Did Melgard seem all right? Was there anything bothering him?"

"He seemed fine. Maybe a little quieter than normal, but not enough to make me think anything was wrong." Conrad had apparently overcome his initial nervousness.

"Did he have any financial troubles?"

"Not that I heard about. He managed all right."

I leaned back and spread my hands. "Anyone else?"

No one had any additional questions for Conrad, so I let him return to duty.

I turned to Bella. "We can't let passengers off at Tangent if Melgard's still missing."

"But we can't *not* let them off. If we try to keep them here, we have to wait until the search is complete, or we keep them with us and drop them off later for a return trip. Either way, we're going to have a passenger revolt. Search fast, Jason."

I sat in the growing silence a moment longer before I said, "I suppose I'd better go up and see how the search is progressing."

"Keep me posted."

Bensode and I rose to leave. I reached the door to the corridor first. I was sliding the door open when there came the loud *pop* of a sonic boom, and a kid half my height flashed past the doorway. Deep-pitched footfalls sounded in the wake of the short, red-shifted figure vanishing down the hallway. The runner's shadow followed behind, as if it were a separate entity, a slithering dark disciple holding back a respectful distance.

I had better things to do at the moment, but I immediately followed. As I picked up speed, the sounds of the kid's footsteps came up closer to normal pitch and his back shifted first to orange and then into the normal spectrum. His feet, flashing back and forth between red and blue with each stride, seemed to speed up as my rate of time dropped.

I ran faster, feeling an increase in wind resistance, and suddenly the sound of my own footfalls dropped out of hearing and I passed the sound barrier. The sounds of the kid ahead and of air rushing against my ears were all I could hear. Calling ahead to him would do no good because the sound would never reach him. Now all I had to do was gain on him.

On level four the orbital velocity was about eighty percent of the speed of light, so you didn't push for every speck of speed—unless you wanted to put yourself in orbit. Getting into orbit wasn't hard; unless you were lucky, though, the unpleasant part was stopping. What was most likely to happen was that you'd start to tumble slowly, and, when air friction slowed you down enough to hit the floor, your feet were unlikely to be conveniently positioned. Jason's law of orbits says the part of the body to hit first is almost always the back of the head.

Fortunately, the kid wasn't pushing to the limit. He might not even be able to run that fast anyway. I kept low to the ground, running as fast as I dared, and I started to gain. Unless he looked behind, he'd have no clue I was approaching.

The corridor had contracted perceptibly as I gained speed. The walls ahead acquired a distinct blue tinge. I slowly closed the gap between us until I was just a step behind, breathing smoothly, hearing my breath only in my head. I reached forward and managed to grab the back of the kid's collar and I lifted.

The kid squawked. We were so close to orbital velocity that he was easy to hoist. With him dangling by the shirt collar, his legs still pedaling, I slowed down abruptly. The corridor grew to its normal length and the kid's weight increased. I let him down but kept a solid grip on the collar.

The sonic boom hit us then, a deep, several-second rumbling that finally faded like distant thunder. If we had been going a little slower, say just above the speed of sound, the boom would have been sharper, shorter, louder. As it was, it seemed to startle the kid even more than my sudden grab.

I twisted him around to face me and realized I had been chasing a girl rather than a boy. She was the same girl I had seen twirling in front of a mirror in the dining hall. There was a gap between her two front teeth. Her freckles reminded me vaguely and disconcertingly of Jenni, but her hair was blonde rather than red. Although her wide eyes were suddenly filled with apprehension, I was sure that in five minutes this girl would be as carefree as she was five minutes ago. No burden of pain showed in her face, just a sudden pursing of the lips that said, "Oh no. I got caught."

I knelt next to her to put our heads level. "Young lady, we have regulations about running that fast aboard the ship. Do you know what they are?"

Her eyes widened still farther as she saw the rank insignia at my collar, but her voice was completely unruffled. "No, sir. What are they?"

"One, if you have to run in a busy corridor, always stay on the right side. Two, if you don't have to—if you're just running for the fun of it—you're supposed to confine yourself to the corridors that are specially marked for running. They have footprints painted on the walls. Now, is there an emergency I should know about?"

She shook her head very solemnly. "No, sir. There isn't."

I had to smile at her seriousness. For all I knew, she'd be back at it the moment I was gone, but she put up a good front. "What's your name?"

"Becky."

"Well, Becky, the closest corridor where you can run is upstairs one level, two intersections from here in that direction. It runs north and south. How about if you try it instead of this one?"

"Yes, sir. Does that mean I'm free to go? You're not going to lock me up?"

"Yes, you're free. We don't lock up first offenders."

I still couldn't tell if she was merely humoring me, ready to run and tell her playmates how she had the first officer completely fooled, or whether she was scared and doing her best to conceal it. I decided to play safe and add, "We don't really lock up children we catch running. We just don't want anyone hurt. When you run that fast, people in your path don't have much time to see you coming, and they're just as likely to walk into your path as out of it. Your internal time goes slower when you're running; that's why other people look speeded up. Since your time is slow, you can't react as easily to avoid them. Does that all make sense?"

"Yes, sir. I'm sorry, sir. I won't do it again—except in the right place, that is."

"No harm done this time." I rose to my feet and turned to leave.

"Are you really the first officer?" she asked suddenly, looking up at me.

"Yes. Is there anything I can do for you?"

Becky shook her head no and gave me a sudden shy smile, dimples on her cheeks. She backed away three paces and turned to leave. Her pace picked up before she caught herself, and then she slowed down to the fastest possible walk. She gave me a last backward glance, as if to say she *was* going to take me seriously.

I found myself watching her disappear down the corridor, her arms swinging briskly forward and back, tinged alternately red and blue, and I felt an unexpected twinge. Whether the pang was envy of someone who was privileged to enjoy a happy childhood, or some unbidden urge to provide a happy childhood for someone like her, or some feeling even more foreign, I couldn't tell.

Maybe Tara had been right about my being unable to see inside very clearly.

The search on level six had turned up no sign of Fenn Melgard so far. That wasn't so startling; lately it was taking more and more to surprise me.

Level six constituted about a quarter of the ship's useful floor space. If it were divided into moderate-sized office cubicles of about ten square meters each, it would have held more than 400 offices. Lots of room for a person to get lost in if he wanted to be lost. Or if someone else wanted him lost.

The cargo bay where Jenni had been found was empty of searchers; the search crew had already moved well out in an expanding circle from the epicenter. I walked the length of the main path through the rows of shipping crates, wondering what had happened to precipitate Melgard's disappearance.

Maybe he had found Jenni just after it was too late to do anything and he had worried that suicide might look like murder. Maybe Jenni had seen him engaged in some activity he shouldn't have been engaged in and he killed her. If that were the case, he would be waiting, hiding, until he could get off the ship the next time we docked.

I moved to the comm panel and called the bridge. Razzi answered.

"I want three crew members stationed at the portal when we dock at Tangent today," I said. "No one gets off who's not supposed to."

Razzi acknowledged and switched off.

I slowly toured the cargo hold, letting my mind run unchecked as it spun through various possibilities. Jenni's death being an isolated event. Melgard independently disappearing. Jenni and Melgard linked somehow. The silent crates gave me no help at all. None stood unlocked and opened as though Jenni had caught Melgard as he was checking the contents of something he was smuggling. None showed bloodstains. None were marked CLASSIFIED SHIPMENT. DO NOT LEAVE UNATTENDED. They were all just simple rectangular crates ranging in size from a few barely large enough to contain a well-cushioned egg to one large enough to house a generator even taller than me, each with a secure lock, each unimaginatively marked on every side with the owner, origination point, and destination.

I moved back to the comm panel and made another call to the bridge. "Razzi, I want a complete list of every shipping container in the bay where we found Jenni Sonders. Not just what we've already got in our docket. I want a list of planets of manufacture, destination, names of company officers, the type of business they're engaged in, the companies they own, the companies who own them, the board of directors and company officers. And get that information for everything in the six bays nearest to this one. Run every name against the crew—and the passenger list."

"That may take a little while. Over and above transmission time delays."

"Whatever it takes, it'll take. But let me know if you get some preliminaries."

I flipped off the light at the door. Darkness sped into the cargo bay, swirling into every corner, leaving an afterimage of coffins in a variety of sizes and shapes—as though the inhabitants of an entire zoo had all died and were being sent home to rest in peace.

Before the search party completed their examination of level six, we docked at Tangent. Tangent was an active trade center, kept in business by high volume more than by any intrinsic value of the planet itself. On level five, feeling frustrated, I watched passengers disembark.

Emil Frankton and his aide, Juan Absome, left us at Tangent. Emil still seemed a little shaky. Marj Lendelson left also, wearing a deep-blue blouse and a matching skirt, looking as graceful and regal as when she had come aboard. A dozen other passengers I remembered seeing board at earlier stops left, too, but no one who got off could possibly have been a disguised Fenn Melgard.

Bensode and two helpers courteously stood nearby in case a passenger needed assistance.

The search continued on level seven, to delay alarming the passengers on level five. Since level seven was the farthest out from the center, it was the largest level, fifty percent bigger than level six.

I personally searched the primary computer and communications room. Only officers were allowed the access code, and I was nearby, so I made myself useful. The room was no larger than the doc's waiting room, but instead of closed, gray cabinets, half-meter-wide racks were stacked with thin, horizontal equipment cabinets, each with its own lettering and indicators on the front panel, each secured tightly in its own space.

Every critical component in the room was backed up by redundant equipment, and the entire room itself was backed up by its counterpart on the opposite side of the ship, also on level seven. Having the computers on level seven instead of near the bridge on level four allowed them to be slower and therefore smaller. Time ran about twenty-five percent faster here than on the bridge.

Searching this room took only one action: looking behind the desk. Fenn Melgard wasn't there, either hiding or dead.

I was growing more and more pessimistic that we would ever see him again.

We searched level three next, again postponing having to tell the passengers something was amiss. Level three was the strangest level aboard the *Redshift*.

Level three also consisted almost entirely of large cargo bays. There was more apparent activity here, primarily because the entire length of the corridor was visible, the result of a unique optical illusion that made the corridor look straight. In fact, if I wanted to wait about seven seconds, I could see myself in the distance. In fourteen seconds, I would be able to see yet another image, twice as far away.

On level three, near eye level, the speed of light matched the orbital velocity. That meant a photon launched horizontally would travel the circumference of the corridor. Since it came straight on at the eye, the brain said it originated far out in front, instead of starting out from right behind the observer's head. That phenomenon was responsible for the illusion that level three was straight and flat, even though the floor and ceiling were both spheres, just like every other level of the ship.

If I'd had a pair of binoculars, I could have used them to see if Melgard had been here recently. For centuries, astronomers have re-signed themselves to seeing only the past through their eyepieces and on their screens. It took a while to adjust to the situation, but on a limited scale the same was true aboard *Redshift*. The corridor faded into infin-ity in much the same way as a view between face-to-face mirrors, the dark handrails disappearing into the distance like levitational transit tracks.

The search of level three turned up no sign of Melgard, so I gave orders to start on level two. I reached the nearest stairwell and started down. The stair-lights formed a quantized rainbow ranging from blue near my feet, green and yellow farther down, reaching a dim red near the next landing. The stairs below that were low enough to be red-shifted into black invisibility.

While I descended, the hues from the stair-lights kept pace as the component colors in the spectrum shifted up from red toward violet. They generated the illusion that I was fixed in space, walking down a rising escalator. Violet remained near eye level, blue near my feet, and red farther down. The visibility decreased as I neared the level-two landing, and the gravity grew stronger.

I closed the stairwell door behind me, turned, and started walking east along the equator. Level two was enough smaller than level three that it held only two corridors—one circle around the equator, and one meridian joining the north and south poles.

I walked rapidly along the corridor, my feet scuffing the floor, my lowered center of gravity making my body lean slightly forward. The gravity differential down here gave the feeling of wading through water. The corridor curved upward and out of sight, as though I were standing at the bottom of an enormous bowl, instead of on one of the seven onion-skin levels of the *Redshift*. Bending light could make anything appear different from reality. Distorted arcade mirrors had nothing on the view on level two.

Overhead, the ceiling lights were more closely spaced than on the higher levels. The off-white corridor walls showed V-shaped shadows near the ceiling, between lights.

The search party crew members were retrieving hand-lamps from a hallway equipment panel when I reached them. Conrad Delingo was last in line and he handed me a lamp.

He tilted his hand-lamp up at the wall, holding the lamp the way he would hold a water hose because light fell quickly this close to the center of the spherical ship. With a yellow lamp pointed straight up from the floor down here, light turned red by the time it reached eye level, and was fading into infrared as it reached the ceiling. Shine a lamp horizontally at a wall five meters away and the light would drop almost half that distance on the way there.

The search went faster than on level three since level two had only about half the area, but the fact that time ran slower here eliminated some of the differential.

Melgard wasn't here either, so I sent all of the crew except Conrad up to level four to search all the non-public areas.

At the nearest elevator, I called the bridge. Bella was on duty this time.

"Conrad Delingo and I are going down to level one," I said. "Can you check on us if we're not back in a few minutes?"

"Will do. So that means level two was empty also?"

" 'Fraid so. And I'm not optimistic about finding him down there either, but we've got to look."

Bella signed off, and Conrad and I stepped into the elevator and pushed the "one" indicator followed by a crew access code. The gravity on the floor of level one was almost four and a half gees. Even at eye level it was still over two and a half. A person could manage to walk, but it wasn't an easy task, and it was always safer to use the buddy system.

My ears popped as the elevator pulled to a halt on level one; the higher gravity made me feel that the elevator had pulled to a panic stop after having fallen fifty stories. The elevator door opened.

I still had my hand-lamp, but it wasn't of much use here since even with the lamp pointing forty-five degrees upward the beam still couldn't reach very far. Besides that, the ceiling was entirely covered with lights. We shuffled out of the elevator into the single corridor on level one.

The corridor seemed to rise so steeply that we would need stairs to climb, but I shuffled forward, my feet telling me that the corridor floor actually fell away as it circled the center of the *Redshift*. Everything down here seemed to tilt toward you. The floor was lined with edges of access panels used to get to the guts of the warp generator. I didn't worry about opening them; anyone whose body entered that compartment when the warp was on would instantly disintegrate first into molecules, then into atoms, and then into subatomic particles. If someone merely opened an access panel, a pressure suit would be mandatory, because the air on level one would immediately get sucked down into the singularity.

"I've never been down here before," Conrad said. "It's a little spooky." He looked jowly because the gravity tugged so hard on his cheeks.

"It isn't all that different," I said. "Same rules as everywhere else; it's just that the gravity makes everything more obvious."

We walked forward, as though we were inside a large, well-lit tire. I kept a fair amount of attention on balancing. I supposed walking around in a high-gee field was a little like being enormously overweight, but not quite that simple. You had some of the same problems: the extra weight loads placed on your feet, legs, and spine. But the big differences were how fast you lost your balance if you leaned a little too far, and how fast you fell if you lost your balance. Walking on level one made me feel old and tired.

Conrad reached toward the low ceiling at the axis and pulled his hand back quickly. "The ceiling feels warm."

I looked sideways at him, and the perspective changed the way it would when a fisheye lens turned. "Nothing's wrong. The lights are just strong on the infrared end of the spectrum because as the light falls it shifts up into the visible spectrum."

"Of course," he said, abashed.

Level one held only two bays. I took the south hemisphere, and Conrad took the north. The walls were as wide as I could spread my fingers, and the bays were segmented into several areas separated by more thick support walls. The crates down here were similar to ones on higher levels, but each had its own wheeled carrier.

Walking among the crates gave me the feeling of wearing a visor that heavily distorted my vision. A crate I knew to be rectangular, when looked at from the front had a level top, but the side edges curved upward. When I walked to the side of the crate, the side edges appeared level and the front and rear edges curved upward.

"Nothing here," I said moments later, back in the hall.

"Or here," Conrad replied.

We walked the remaining distance down the corridor and arrived back at the elevator. From level two I called Bella.

"We're clear of level one," I said. "Negative."

"The crew here on four hasn't found anything either. We're going to have to tell the passengers soon. You think we're going to find him? Oh, before I forget, I've got a message for you from Razzi.

"She says the bay directly south of the one we found Jenni Sonders in contains cargo being shipped by a company owned by Daniel Haffalt, a passenger. And four bays away is a shipment in the name of Sunrise Limited, of which a passenger named Harold Summertree is an employee."

"I'll check on them later," I said. "And no, I don't think we're going to find Melgard." I glanced at Conrad, but he was expressionless.

"There's got to be an explanation."

"Either there's a missing jumpsuit or he smuggled himself out in a crate that went to Tangent. My bet is the jumpsuit. No one has seen any crate contents strewn about." A jumpsuit was a pressurized lifesuit equipped with a hyperspace translator, for use in emergencies.

"Sounds risky to me."

"If he's somehow involved with Jenni Sonders' death, maybe he thought it was worth the risk."

"If he did, then he could have got off at Tangent on his own," Bella said.

"Or he could be riding on the skin of the ship. Or, if he made a tiny miscalculation, he could be adrift in space, whatever layer he stayed in, waiting for his air to run out."

"I'll have someone check the suits while you're finishing the search.

And I suppose we'd better alert the passengers that we're going to be searching their rooms."

I looked at the clock on the comm panel. Less than two hours to midnight. "I'd rather you didn't issue a bulletin. If everyone gets the word like that, they'll be out milling in the halls. How about if we just tell them door-to-door and ask them to stay inside for the next few hours? That will make it harder for Melgard to change locations if he's still on board."

"Asking paying passengers to confine themselves to their cabins— even when they'd probably be sleeping anyway—may lose us a few repeat passengers. What do you suggest we tell them?"

"Tell them there's an escaped krugerbear loose on the ship. Tell them it's in heat and masses eight times what you and I do. Tell them when it's in heat, it's so frantic it can't tell a human from another krugerbear, let alone distinguish human males and females."

The speaker was silent a moment. A grin touched Conrad's face before he turned away from me and studiously faced down the corridor.

Finally Bella said, "Have any suggestions on how to explain why such a creature is on the ship?"

"Sure. Tell them it's in the officer-training program. Wait! I've got an even better idea. We could tell them the truth."

"Let's go with the truth just this once, Jason."

Today's luck continued to be unremittingly bad. The next passenger cabin on my list to search was Amanda Queverra's. Too bad we weren't searching level five using the buddy system.

This wasn't a firstshift, but it felt like one. You don't have to work on a hyperspace craft to know there are more hours in a firstshift than in a lastshift.

The time was close to midnight when I rang Amanda's visitor chime. I hoped she was out so I could use the master combination, search quickly, and be gone before she returned.

No such luck. A fissure formed between the door and the frame, and then the door slid open wide to expose Amanda in a filmy blue night-dress so revealing that for an instant I couldn't find my voice.

"Why, Jason, this is a surprise," Amanda said. "Come on in."

"I'm afraid this isn't a social call. I'm on duty and we're searching all the cabins for a missing person."

"Oh, are you going to search me?" Amanda said. She raised her arms and twisted slowly to the right and then back. Light from the bedside table shone through her dress as she pivoted. Fenn Melgard definitely wasn't hiding behind this lady's skirt. Aside from the thin outline of her lifebelt, Amanda couldn't have been hiding a pimple.

For just a second I thought perhaps a little frisking never hurt anyone, and then for a curious instant I was thinking of Tara Cline instead of seeing Amanda Queverra. The moment passed and I said, "I'm sorry. This really is business. I'm sure you wouldn't be harboring a fugitive, but I have to check anyway."

Amanda pursed her lips disappointedly and stood aside so I could enter. Her cabin showed many more signs of habitation than Jenni's had. Amanda had twice as much luggage as I would have thought necessary. The bathroom countertop was crowded with cosmetics, and three dresses lay draped over the shower door.

Only a few places are large enough for an adult to hide in a passenger cabin, so my search took only a matter of seconds. When I turned to leave, I realized Amanda had closed the door.

"Really, Jason, all you had to do was let me know you wanted to see me. There wasn't any need for you to go through this charade." Her voice was breathy, as though her words were somehow formed solely by her mouth, rather than originating with vocal cords. Before I reacted, she had her arms around me.

Suddenly flustered, I pulled back, pulling her with me, moving her inadvertently toward the bed. Probably that was why she came so willingly, and why her smile intensified. "I'm sorry," I managed to say. "I was serious. A search really is going on. I've got to get back to work."

With that, I pulled loose from her embrace and moved quickly to the door.

"But, Jason—"

I opened the door, stepped outside, and slid the door closed quickly enough to cut off whatever she had to say. I stood there a moment, leaning on the door and breathing more heavily than I had when I chased Becky.

"Is something the matter, sir?" One of the junior members, a dark-haired young woman whose parents had both been in the merchant marine, had halted nearby and was looking at me, concerned.

I straightened immediately. "No, just a krugerbear," I said without forethought.

"Sir?"

"Ahh, nothing. No problem."

I searched four more cabins, receiving reactions that included amused tolerance, a sense of adventure, puzzled incomprehension, and litigious annoyance. I was moving on to search the next cabin on my list, the one belonging to Tara Pesek Cline and Wade Pesek Midsel, when I heard a summons. I went to the nearest comm panel.

Rory was at the bridge. I told him I was alone so he could talk freely, and he said, "I've just completed a preliminary on Jenni Sonders. I'm afraid she didn't commit suicide. She was murdered."

=== 5 ===

The Door into Hyperspace

I met Rory and Bella in the privacy of the bridge. A public comm panel wasn't the right place to discuss Rory's statement that Jenni Sonders had been murdered.

The status panels all indicated normal conditions, as though stubbornly insisting that the recent death and disappearance were events beneath concern, unimportant to the destiny of a craft as large as the *Redshift*. The master clock's digits changed silently every second. A nearby row of clocks, all running slightly faster, showed local times for the planetary docks on our route, including ones for Tangent and our next stop, Leviathan.

Even before I had reached the bridge, I found myself wanting to believe Rory. For some reason, I felt a strong need to believe that Jenni had been telling me the truth when she said she'd call. If she had indeed been murdered, the implication that the *Redshift* might have had a killer as a member of the crew seemed for the moment less important. Maybe I didn't want to picture her as a quitter; or maybe I just didn't like the thought that I had been lied to.

As I tried to understand my feelings, I once again recalled Tara's words about my not seeing inside very well. I could make out some of the overall conditions of my feelings—the result of perhaps several different desires mingling—but I couldn't see below the surface to resolve the individual issues. It would have been just as easy to figure out the recipe for some exotic concoction by knowing only how it tasted. Maybe I was an emotional black hole; I could see everything outside my horizon, but nothing inside.

I looked at Rory and said, "You're absolutely sure Jenni Sonders was murdered?" I said.

Rory sighed and slowly nodded to me and Bella. He looked tired. Probably my fruitless search for Melgard was a lot less demanding than performing an autopsy on someone you had known. "There's no doubt about it. Rigor mortis set in faster than normal, even assuming she died no more than fifteen minutes after she started for her cabin. That speed implies her metabolism was racing when she died—probably from a struggle, not just the strangulation panic itself.

"Plus, her hyoid bone was broken. It's a bone in the throat, just above the Adam's apple. The cord couldn't have damaged it, but manual strangulation would. Someone must have started to strangle her, breaking the bone, and finished the job with the cord when she was too weak to resist."

The air temperature on the bridge seemed to drop as Rory spoke. I felt chilly for a moment until the heat of anger started warming me. I said nothing. Fenn Melgard would not want me to be the person who found him.

"All right," Bella said. "We'd better warn the search party."

"Right," I said. At the console, I summoned Bensode. When he responded from a hallway comm panel and indicated he was alone, I said, "Doc has got evidence that Jenni Sonders was murdered. Warn the rest of the crew and have each of them issued disablers. If anyone sees Melgard, the orders are to sound the alarm; I don't want anyone going after him alone." As I talked, I looked at Bella to see if she objected to anything I was saying. She didn't.

When I switched off, Rory raised his eyebrows. He said, "I thought you figured he wasn't on the ship anymore—that the search was more a formality than anything else."

"I did. But I'd prefer to have the passengers a little upset than to take a chance of losing anyone else."

"I agree," Bella said. "It's enough to make me want to retire." Bella probably wasn't any nearer to wanting retirement than I was; she just said things like that whenever things got unpleasant for too long.

"Nothing else has gone wrong?" I asked, more out of politeness than from any suspicion.

"No. At least nothing like Sonders or Melgard. One of the passengers got off at Tangent just to look around while we were docked. She never got back on. So now we'll get a reprimand for leaving early or some other nonsense."

"Who was it?" I asked.

Bella leaned back farther in her chair. "Marj Lendelson. She boarded at Vestry."

I remembered her. Middle-aged, formal, a wintry smile. Coincidences are always worth examining, but there was no obvious link between Lendelson and either Fenn Melgard or Jenni Sonders.

I also remembered my instructions to Bensode. I rose from my chair and moved to the weapon locker. I found a disabler and clipped it onto my belt. "I'll be rejoining the search party unless you've got anything else," I said to Bella.

Bella shook her head dispiritedly. Maybe she actually *was* considering retirement this time.

"Cheer up," I said, and foolishly added, "What else can go wrong?"

"You want to *what?*" Wade Pesek Midsel squinted at me through the gap in the doorway to his and Tara's cabin. He looked even sleepier than normal.

"I said I need to search your cabin." I tried to give the appearance of patience, but my irritation had been gradually growing during the long day. "Jenni Sonders didn't commit suicide."

"You mean she was murdered? So there's a murderer on the ship?"

"We don't know. Someone familiar with jumpsuits could have left the ship at Tangent. But we're making a thorough search to be sure."

Wade looked at his wristcomp, apparently realized his mistake, and glanced back at the master clock display near his door. "Do you have any idea what time it is?"

"Don't tell me; let me guess. I know it's late. We usually schedule ship-wide emergencies just after lunch so no one has to be bothered too much, but our scheduler is on leave and her substitute just doesn't understand the rules. I can't wait until Marlys gets back."

For a moment Wade did nothing more constructive than blink at me. Finally the sarcasm must have penetrated, because he said, "All right. Just a minute," and shut the door. From Wade's vantage point just inside the door, he should have been easily able to read the poster explaining, among other things, that what I was doing right now was in fact legal.

I stood in the hall less than a minute before the door slid open again.

Wade, barefooted, was dressed in a turquoise robe. The hem of the robe was far enough from his lifebelt field that it looked soiled. He curtly gestured me inside. The Peseks' cabin was larger than the last few I had searched. A small entrance L opened onto a brightly lit bedroom. On one side of the bed the wrinkled bottom sheet showed where Wade had been before he answered the door.

On the other side of the bed sat Tara, also dressed in a turquoise robe. She averted her gaze, as though she was embarrassed, but her robe exposed far less skin than Amanda's dinner dress had. The bed was the same size as the one in my cabin, but somehow this one looked smaller because there was someone else on it.

"I apologize for the intrusion," I said. I entered the bathroom and found an empty shower and nothing except a neat array of perfume, soap, and tooth spray near a haphazard pile of underwear, depilatory cream, a bank stick, and a comb. I moved fast enough that a glance at the reflected image of my face in the mirror showed my head just beginning to turn that direction.

Back in the bedroom, I cautiously opened the closet and found nothing more suspicious and threatening than a row of clothes on hangers.

I said nothing more and I was moving toward the front door when Tara spoke. "You said that Jenni was murdered?"

I almost didn't make out her words, because at the same moment she had spoken, Wade had said, "I intend to file a complaint, you know."

I ignored Wade and looked at Tara. "Yes, she was. The ship's doctor is convinced. Besides the fact that I'd believe him anyway, I'm satisfied by what he says. The crew member we're searching for may be the killer."

"You want him because he killed a passenger or because he killed Jenni Sonders?"

Without knowing why, I found myself irritated by what seemed to be a strange question. "I'm just doing my job. I'd do the same for you or your husband." Well, I'd certainly do it for her anyway.

I held my hand palm-out to indicate I hadn't meant to sound as harsh as I must have, and I turned toward the door to the hallway. "Please stay in your cabin until six."

Wade came closer and said, "I mean it. I'm going to file a complaint."

I paused to face him. "You'd better file it fast. If there's a killer on board, you could be next."

He was beginning to show more signs of irritation as I spun away from him and left. I slid the cabin door shut behind me with a great deal more force than I had intended.

Maybe I get cranky when I'm up late.

• • •

Less than an hour later, I was again on the bridge. Seated next to Bella were Razzi and Bensode, all three looking unhappy. The search had uncovered no trace of Fenn Melgard. Picture me unsurprised.

"So," I said to Bella, "that must mean the check on jumpsuits showed one missing."

"True enough," Bella said. "The bay on level seven nearest the north pole is one short."

"So, to complete the search someone should check out the hull."

"Whom do you have in mind?" Bella asked.

After a day this long, I couldn't bring myself to ask anyone else to do another job that was almost certain to be a waste of time. "Me."

Bella nodded, knowing me, and undoubtedly aware that the job had to be done even if it was of dubious value. "Right, Jason. We'll try to keep course corrections to a minimum while you're out there." Her gentle humor was probably intended to cheer me up.

"I'd appreciate that."

"Oh, I've sent word to Tangent. I'll call you if I hear they've found Melgard there."

"Thanks. But don't call me for any other reason. If he *is* out there in a suit, he'll hear, too, and I'll have a bigger problem on my hands."

I dropped the jumpsuit on the floor just outside the level-seven north-pole airlock and then knelt beside it. I fastened the front of the empty suit, secured the helmet, and punched the diagnostic button on the neckline of the suit.

The jumpsuit promptly began to enlarge, unfolding its arms and legs, the wrinkles snapping into smoothness with soft creaks and pops. The read-out on the chest said the internal pressure was five atmospheres and holding. The two-minute diagnostic proceeded to check out the rest of the functions and pronounced the suit healthy. I punched the ready button and the wrinkles appeared again and the suit sagged.

I donned the jumpsuit and stepped into the airlock. With me I carried a flash and a 180-meter lifebelt which I promptly secured to a ring on the side of the wall. The other end of the lifebelt I fastened to the ring on the belt of my suit.

Accompanied by the quiet rush of circulating air, the sound of my breathing came louder now inside the closed helmet. My check of the jumpsuit internals indicated all was well; I could clearly see the status displays reflected off the inside of the visor, and as I focused my eyes first on a command symbol and then on the execute symbol, the suit responded properly. The rush of air increased. Temporarily I turned off the helmet display.

I slid the airlock door closed behind me as quietly as I could and secured it. A few commands on the lighted airlock panel started the airlock cycling down to vacuum, dumping air into the ship slowly enough to avoid transmitting much noise through the hull. I still doubted that Fenn Melgard was out there on the hull, and I doubted even more strongly that he would be waiting directly over the airlock that could have brought him out, but skipping simple precautions had cost a fair number of lives aboard hyperspace crafts. And probably in more than a few bathtubs.

When the indicator showed hard vacuum, I cut the lights. Within a few seconds the falling light level outpaced my adjusting eyes. I took a few more seconds for the chamber to get totally dark, and then I manually turned the control for the overhead exit door, slowly enough again to avoid sending vibrations through the hull. If Melgard were out here, the search would be a lot easier if he was stationary than if he was trying to evade me. At least there was no light outside to make me visible to him. Running lights on a hyperspace craft were as necessary as windshield cleaners and roll bars.

Finally the door was open wide and the darkness was so complete that the only image before me was triggered by retinal flashes that would keep diminishing. Overhead the endless blackness of the starless empty space in layer ten stretched away to infinity. I knew that intellectually; actually I could have been inside a closed shipping container and not have known any difference. All I really knew was that I couldn't see a damned thing.

I climbed up the wall ladder far enough to confirm with my hands that the door had indeed opened, and then I stepped back down and stood in the center of the floor. I took a deep breath and jumped straight up as hard as I could.

Weightlessness overtook me.

When I guessed my jump had carried me as high as it was going to, I turned on my jets. Still in total darkness, with no way of knowing if my body had started a slow spin, I relied on the programmed jets to push me directly away from the largest mass my suit could detect. The burst of acceleration twisted me to one side briefly before it stabilized.

The jets cut off after the programmed interval. I turned on my visor display and watched my range increase. When the proper distance was behind me, I commanded my jets to flip my body ninety degrees forward and I triggered the flash for a brief second.

At first I saw nothing more than light speeding down my umbilical cord, as though the cord were an enormously long fuse burning rapidly down toward the *Redshift,* leaving darkness behind it. As the light sped away, I gave my jets another command to push me farther away from the ship and draw the line taut. Moments later, I bounced on the end of my line, and told the jets to maintain just enough thrust to keep me suspended over the ship.

More than a half-minute later, the light from the flash finally had reached the ship and reflected all the way back to me. I saw the open airlock illuminated first, and then the light sped out in an expanding ring. A couple of seconds later, the circle of light reached the outer edge of the *Redshift*'s hull, having lit the whole hemisphere I faced. The whole *empty* hemisphere.

From here the *Redshift* was smaller than a basketball held in my outstretched hand. Fenn Melgard would have been merely an insect crawling on its surface, but I would have seen him if he had been there. So either he was on the other side, or he was no longer with us. The dull black surface of the sphere gave no clues.

I gave my jets another command, this time at an angle chosen to keep my umbilical cord tight, but also to start me in an orbit around the ship, a decaying orbit limited by my lifeline winding around the ship.

I watched the time. Fortunately, the gravity fell off gradually enough that I could ignore rate-of-time problems caused by gravity differentials. When I was in position for the next glimpse, I set the flash to start going off at ten-second intervals.

The first image of the ship was visible more quickly this time. It was much larger than before, but the surface was still barren.

I watched carefully each time I saw a new image of the hull of the *Redshift.* Each image was closer and larger, but still vacant. When I had traveled most of the way around the *Redshift*'s hull, I turned on my shoulder lamps and left them on.

The open airlock door showed itself directly under me and I turned on one final blast from the jets to ease my impact. A speed-of-light miscalculation drove me to fall forward as I landed. I bounced off the hull and then fell gently back in one-sixth gee.

I untangled my lifeline and regained my footing. I walked back a few steps to the airlock cavity, flicking the extra few meters of lifeline out of my way. A switch next to the open door turned the airlock lights back on. I jumped lightly down into the opening.

In the airlock, I linked a shorter line from my suit to a hook on the wall, disconnected my long tether and started reeling it in. It was only after my gaze wandered while I was pulling in the lifeline that I noticed the blood.

I *assumed* it was blood, anyway. There wasn't much else it could have been. Since this environment leached the color from anything not protected by a field or specially treated, the drops on the floor were almost the same shade of gray as the floor itself, but they definitely looked like blood spatters—several circular drops of different sizes, each with rippled edges. I suddenly changed my mind about where Fenn Melgard must be. If I was right, he had died a long way from home.

I had let my preoccupation with Tara Cline and Jenni Sonders inhibit the flow of possibilities. One theory I hadn't explored was that Jenni and Fenn Melgard were both murdered by a third party. Or could Fenn have found a second victim? I discarded that possibility for now since no one else had been reported missing.

If Fenn had been dripping blood when he was in the airlock, he certainly hadn't been wearing a jumpsuit. He must have taken his trip outside at someone else's insistence, assuming he was even alive at that point. And that someone else had either jettisoned a jumpsuit with Fenn, or hidden it somewhere, or pushed the right buttons to send it into another layer of space. No matter which way it was done, that third party certainly had known a missing body with no missing suit would instantly tell us we should be looking for someone else.

So not only did we have a killer on board, we had no clues whatsoever to the killer's identity.

I finished reeling in the lifeline as I considered the options. My first instinct, to call Bella on the bridge and warn her, felt unwise even before I reached to close the overhead airlock door. If the killer were a crew member, the communications lines could be monitored. The one slim advantage we had at the moment was that the killer should believe no one yet suspected the truth.

With the ceiling door closed against the endless night, I started admitting air to the airlock. The digital display of pressure as a percentage of normal began to rise rapidly from 00, climbed steadily to the low 90s, and gradually slowed down until it stopped at 100.

Even after such a brief outing, I was eager to get out of my jumpsuit. Having to turn my torso to see the view at the edge of my vision made me slightly claustrophobic, so I unfastened my helmet before I reached to open the inner airlock door.

I didn't complete my attempt to open the airlock door. I didn't even get my helmet entirely off. I had unlocked the neck seal and was starting to lift the helmet off my head when I became aware of a sweet smell in the air—a smell that shouldn't have been there.

I tried to refasten my helmet but my fingers refused to cooperate. A black fog at the edge of my vision grew thicker and expanded toward the center until it obscured everything before my eyes.

I'm sure I felt nothing as I crumpled to the floor.

A sharp pain at the side of my neck was my first sensation as I revived.

For a long disoriented moment, I thought I was back on Redwall, recovering from a beating at the hands of several of the older kids. I bitterly swore at my parents, whoever they were, for delivering me here.

But something wasn't right. I wasn't lying on a filthy cot in what everyone sarcastically called "the dormitory." The light filtering through my partly open eyelids was not coming from high, barred windows.

Finally I realized that the pain was caused by the lip of a jumpsuit helmet biting into my neck. I was lying on the floor of a closed airlock, an airlock aboard the *Redshift*.

I forced myself to a sitting position and took off the helmet, remembering the odor I had smelled just before I passed out. I twisted my head around to see the master clock display. The airlock whirled. I felt hung over. My eyes refocused on the display.

I had been out for several hours.

Too many things didn't make sense. Why would someone gas me in the airlock and then just leave me here without killing me or doing something further? And if I had been lying here the whole time, why had no one come to investigate?

Maybe it wasn't just me, I realized finally, as my head began to clear still more. Gassing a person in an airlock and then doing nothing to him made no sense. Maybe the whole ship had been gassed and maybe no one awake knew I was here in a closed, seldom-used airlock.

I stood up and leaned on the wall. In a moment the trembling in my legs subsided. I shook my head and fortunately it felt as though it was still firmly attached.

A cloying odor hung in the air, but the remnants of whatever knock-out gas had been used seemed impotent. I started to reach for the comm panel but caution stopped me.

Still working with the theory that there was no obvious reason to gas only me and then do nothing else, and that the rest of the ship *must* have been gassed also, I followed the chain of conclusions. When I filled the airlock with air from the ship, I had gassed myself. Assuming the effects wore off after a predictable length of time, whoever else was on level seven was also reviving now. People below, where time was moving more slowly, would be coming out of it in stages: level six, then level five, on down to level one. It would probably take people on the bridge another hour to recover.

So by calling the bridge right now, not only wouldn't I get any questions answered, but I'd probably alert whoever was responsible.

Staying in the airlock suddenly seemed the wrong thing to do. The jumpsuit would be too noisy for covert investigation, so I unfastened it and shrugged out of it. I could always get another if I needed one.

I unlocked the inner airlock door and slid it open a few millimeters. I listened for several seconds. Nothing. I slid the door open far enough to be able to get a glimpse of the corridor in both directions. Empty. I slid the door all the way open and cautiously peered first in one direction and then the other. No one.

I closed the airlock behind me and moved quietly toward the nearby intersection. I hunched down to limit my visibility. No one was up and about in the cross corridor either.

I unlocked a nearby emergency panel and retrieved my disabler.

The nearest stairwell was back the way I had come. I listened at the door for several seconds before opening it. After entering the stairwell, I closed the door gently behind me and went down one flight as softly as I could. A small gap in the doorway on level six revealed no signs of activity. I went down another level.

On level five I was even more cautious. Movement in the hall sent gentle vibrations into the door frame. So someone else was up after bedtime. I opened a slit between the door and the frame and peered through. At first nothing was visible, but then two figures in black ran quickly by my field of view. The men's features were subtly contracted and distorted by their speed, but not enough to keep me from being sure I hadn't seen them before. Both men wore scabbards with knives. And they weren't dinner knives.

I squeezed the door closed and hesitated, wondering if I should hide temporarily in a cargo bay so they'd have time to decide I was no longer alive, and therefore, have time to forget about me. The trouble with the plan was that it gave whoever "they" were more time to do whatever they were doing. It seemed to me that my best chance to disrupt activities was before they were totally organized and settled into a routine.

Hoping activities weren't in fact totally organized already, I reached for my disabler.

For another moment, I waited at the stairwell door to level five, wondering what the takeover was all about. Theft from passengers? Theft of cargo? Killing one or more of the passengers or crew? At least the fact that they had gassed the ship was probably in my favor. That meant they could handle the operation with a smaller crew than they would have to use if they were counting on being able to muscle their way into control. A smaller crew meant fewer people I'd have to deal with.

And I definitely planned to deal with them. An armed contingent taking over the ship deserved no second chances. Whatever lay behind all this, it was not a misunderstanding or an accident. And it must certainly tie in with Jenni's murder and the assumed murder of Fenn Melgard.

I opened the doorway just a crack and peered through. No one was there, no sound. I opened the crack wider and could see farther down the hall to an open cabin doorway. I figured I might be able to tell from the shape that cabin was in whether someone was looting the cabins. Almost ready to investigate, I paused as a sound reached my ears.

The slow speed of sound destroyed the normal positional delay cues the ears rely on, so the source of the sound was a little difficult to determine, but it certainly came from the corridor and not the stairwell. An instant later, there was motion in the cabin doorway. A black-suited figure was dragging an unconscious or dead passenger from the room. Evidently the team knew enough about the ship to get the master combination from the bridge computer.

I waited. He would either go past me or start down the corridor in the opposite direction.

He started my way. I got a firm grip on the door, and tightened my fingers around my disabler. Whatever was happening, I was unlikely to get a better opportunity to deal with individuals. If the team knew I was up and about, I would have much tougher obstacles.

The man in the black suit faced backward as he dragged the limp passenger down the corridor toward my hiding place. As he approached, his head was turned away from me. I slid the door quietly open and moved toward him. Either he heard my foot scuff the floor, or the nature of his job had finely tuned his protective instincts. Just before I reached him, he released his grip on the passenger and started to turn rapidly toward me. I feinted high toward his head and neck.

Newcomers already had reaction-time problems with the environment, so feints were especially hard for them to deal with. People took a while to get used to the fact that everything they saw was in the past. Feints aggravated the problem by adding reaction times to the delay. He started to check my thrust, obviously realizing far too late what was really happening. I slid my disabler around his side, so it was directly in front of his lifebelt. His arm bounced off the side of my head too late to deter me.

I clicked the disabler just as he turned suddenly and powerfully in my arms, but surprise had given me too much of a head start. A moment later, he sagged in my arms as the disabler turned off his lifebelt field.

Color bleached out of his cheeks and uniform. Inside his body, the chain of command from neuron to neuron through the intervening synapses had slowed down too much for his brain to retain control. I had started the downward drift into death, reversible only by the converse function of my disabler, or a jump to a shallower layer of space.

Despite my having been able to overcome the guy in black without getting hurt, I judged him to be a professional. He hadn't tried to speak or waste energy in any way; he'd just done what little he could to preserve his life.

I glanced around. As far as I could tell, no one had witnessed the scuffle. Moving quickly, I dragged his body and the shallowly breathing passenger's body back into the cabin. Black-suit's face was completely unfamiliar to me. I ripped a sheet from the bed and bound the black-suit's arms behind him. Sitting astride him, I reactivated his lifebelt.

Color immediately flooded back into the man's pasty-white features, and his uniform turned from gray to black. His eyes began to move under his eyelids as though he was dreaming, but it took a moment longer for his brain to resync and for his breathing to resume.

He coughed a few times before his eyes opened. They were brown, and full of questions. A second or two later, hostility supplanted the questions and he struggled, obviously realizing how helpless he was.

"I'm going to give you one chance," I said evenly and clearly. "Make absolutely no mistake here when you answer me. I am not bluffing. I will do exactly as I say I will."

What looked to me to be belief showed in his eyes as his facial muscles relaxed from his attempt to rise. The stakes were so high, I forced myself to speak slowly. "I'm the first officer and I want to know exactly what is going on aboard my ship. Until I know more, I have no option but to assume you are a hostile, endangering the lives of everyone aboard this ship. That gives me the legal right to turn your lifebelt back off and let you die. If you can provide me proof that the situation is something else, for instance some bizarre exercise initiated by the home office, I'll take the time to bind you securely enough that you won't get free on your own. If you *are* a hostile, but you tell me enough about your operation and where your boss is—same thing. If you refuse, I turn you off. And you die."

The man was silent, staring up at me.

"Do you understand what I said?"

He nodded.

"Do you believe that I'm bluffing?"

He hesitated, then shook his head.

"Are you going to talk?"

Another hesitation, then a swallow. He shook his head.

I sighed. "All right. If that's the way it has to be. I can't afford the time to secure you. On the count of three, I turn your switch."

Those implacable brown eyes stared up at me, unblinking.

"One."

"Two."

"Three."

I pressed the switch.

Color faded from his face and eyes for a final time as he began his journey into death. My own breathing had stopped at the same moment his had. With an effort, I pushed aside the pain of killing, forced myself to resume breathing, and thought desperate thoughts about my job and duty. Damn him for refusing to talk. Damn him.

I slowly rose from the body and for a fleeting instant, I marveled at how quickly I could slip back into the kill-or-be-killed frame of mind. Finally, I began to move faster.

I stripped off the man's suit, and pulled the suit on over my own clothes. The suit turned black again as it entered my lifebelt field. Protective coloring was precious little defense, but I needed every edge I could get. A quick check of his pockets turned up nothing at all in the way of identification, just a map of the *Redshift* and a couple of coins. They were about as useful as a set of stereo speakers on this ship.

Only as I hid the body behind the bed did I realize that besides being mystified and tense, I was also powerfully angry. I almost wished that guy were still alive, so he could resist again and I could get rid of some of my frustration and tension by fighting with him. That's not the way I am most of the time; I suppose the *Redshift* herself was my only real friend, and someone was methodically violating her.

I checked my appearance in the bathroom mirror, not wanting an exposed part of my uniform to flag me immediately as an imposter. My expression was grim, much more troubled than one would expect of a man who had first killed at age fourteen.

I put the man's knife in a scabbard hanging from my new belt. I dragged the passenger back out in the empty hallway. He was an elderly man, dressed in long, thin bedclothes. I hoped he didn't have to go through much more of this.

I was dragging him in the direction my predecessor had been traveling, wondering what to do next, when another black-suiter came out of a nearby cabin, dragging yet another passenger. This passenger was a middle-aged woman, her torso partially covered by a blanket. Providing her with modest covering for when she woke up was a touching gesture, but I wasn't impressed. The two ends of the blanket wound under the victim's arms and back up her neck where they made a convenient carrying grip.

I kept my head down until I was almost next to the black-suiter and he was probably starting to wonder why I was quiet. Making a silent apology to my charge, I dropped his head and shoulders onto the deck, making an exclamation calculated to make the black-suit think it was accidental, and to divert his attention to the passenger I dropped almost at his feet. While he was reacting to this display of bad manners, I wasted no time grabbing my disabler. I shouldered him against the wall, keeping him off balance, and moved the disabler into position and clicked it.

This intruder was a professional, too, but not so quiet about being caught. Only when I heard the voice painfully cursing me did I realize I was dealing with a woman. She wore her hair closely cropped, and my furtive glances toward her hadn't been attentive enough to note her small breasts.

I felt guilty this time, too, but anyone doing what these two people were doing knew the chances and had already made a choice. I wasn't about to die by trying to hit someone only hard enough to disable him. Knives and delayed reactions made for an instantly deadly result with just the smallest miscalculation. I filed away the grief. Later I'd have to deal with how I felt about the killings, but letting them occupy me now would be fatal.

I pulled the two slumbering passengers and my victim into the cabin the black-suit had just left. I didn't recognize this black-suit either. I left the female passenger lying on the floor, hid the dead black-suit behind the bed, and hid her knife under a pillow. I felt the bile rise in my throat as I took a last look at the black-suit, but I couldn't afford the time to secure her adequately and let her live.

The sleeping elderly gentleman made no complaints as I resumed my journey with him in tow. I hoped he was having a good dream, but he was probably dreaming about flying and falling.

No one else was in the corridor. I pulled my charge slowly, hoping for some clue to what was going on. Evidently the takeover was not planned to be ending in an hour or two. Otherwise, there would be no reason to round everyone up and, presumably, keep them under guard.

I wondered, too, about the size of the takeover crew. In the last few minutes I might have been lucky enough to eliminate two out of six, but the numbers were probably more like two out of ten or twenty, assuming they had enough people to fetch all the passengers and crew before anyone woke up. Unless they were planning to release another batch of knockout gas soon.

I nearly stopped right then and picked a place to hide in case more gas was on the way, but, at the same moment, one of my backward glances picked out another black-suit in the corridor. Without a break in stride, I kept moving closer, keeping my face averted.

This guy evidently didn't realize I wasn't a friend, but he did seem sure I wasn't the one he was looking for. "Where the hell is Murphy? He should have been back here by now."

I said nothing for fear my voice would tell him I wasn't on his side. Instead, improvising, I released one hand and made a rude gesture indicating that maybe Murphy was taking liberties with a female passenger who was still unconscious.

"You're kidding," came the enraged reply. "I'll have him sucking vacuum. Where is he?"

I motioned toward an open cabin door and kept pulling my passenger along the floor.

Black-suit came briskly along the corridor. When he was almost even with me, I rammed him against the wall, and, before he could recover, I used the disabler on his lifebelt. I felt more and more angry at being forced into a position of having to do what was now required of me.

As I concealed the third body, some corner of my brain reviewed possibilities such as these black-suiters were just employees hired by the home office management to see how we responded to an emergency. Or they were Confederation agents resorting to unusual measures to capture a very difficult most-wanted fugitive. Or maybe these people really were performing a criminal action, but their motivation was simply to stage a takeover to demonstrate the effortlessness to the media. Or they were working under Bella's orders to test the crew.

But I didn't honestly believe any of those possibilities for one second.

Gassing the entire crew and passengers and then towing them along the halls to some unknown destination was in itself a process that stood a significant risk of killing any passengers with health problems. The black-suiters were prepared to take that risk, so they had to be prepared for far more. Getting myself killed by merely trying to lock up a black-suiter who got free would eliminate the only advantage I could see we had. And the more time I reflected on what was required of me, however distasteful, the more time the opposition had to realize a few of their party were missing, and to do something about the problem.

I started back along the corridor with my passenger companion. No one else was in sight. I hoped that I'd get an indication of where people were being collected before I got to the next intersection.

I reached the intersection without finding out, but a peek around the corner gave me my answer. There, down the hall, at the door into the ship's swimming pool, were two guards stationed at the door. Two more black-suiters were dragging limp passengers toward the doorway. I figured the collection process should be almost complete; by my reckoning the victims on this level should be recovering from the gas sometime soon. If I managed to free a few critical members of the crew from captivity, we could really get serious about regaining control.

I nestled my disabler against my palm. Then I carefully took hold of my charge's limp wrist so the disabler would be instantly ready. When the two collectors had departed alone, I moved around the corner and proceeded toward the two guards.

I had never been less interested in going to the swimming pool. This situation definitely called for more than a life preserver and a squeaky duck.

6

Hyperspace Swimmers

Long before I reached the two black-suited guards at the door to the swimming pool, I had second thoughts about whether this was the right course of action.

Maybe I should have stayed where I was and waited for more opportunities to attack individual black-suits as they moved about the ship. Maybe I should have gone back to the cabin I had just been in and feigned sleep. Then I could have attacked whoever came to empty the cabin. But it was too late now to change my mind. I forced the other possibilities out of my head and continued pulling my unconscious passenger closer to the two guards.

I drew nearer, feeling highly exposed with my back to them. I stole occasional glances out of the corner of my eye, watchful for a sudden reaction from either guard or the return of another collector.

My right hand still concealed my disabler held next to the passenger's arm. My left hand gripped the man's other wrist and a sleeve fastener under my fingers gave me an idea. Holding both of his arms gripped in one hand for a moment, I pulled a coin from my pocket. I held the coin against the man's wrist and continued on my way.

From my third victim's reaction, I knew that the back of my head had at least a superficial resemblance to one of the collectors, probably my first victim, who had dark hair also. That advantage, coupled with surprise, wasn't enough to make me cocky. I drew closer.

I was almost even with the closer guard before either of them responded. One said, "What took you? We should be done by now."

I passed the closer guard, gaining the position I had to have—directly between the two. In answer to his comment, I jerked my head in the direction I had come from, as though to indicate the explanation was in that direction. A fraction of a second later, when I hoped he was looking down the corridor and not at me, I jerked my hand quickly and tossed the coin in the direction I had indicated.

I kept moving casually for another part of a second, and then I went into action. While the guard I had just passed was reacting—I hoped— to the image of me gesturing down the hall, and hearing the delayed sounds of the coin as it skittered across the floor, I whipped my disabler toward the other guard's midriff. My passenger dropped to the floor again.

Even before the guard began to slump, I was pulling away and pivoting toward the first guard. He had still been reacting to the past, but was beginning to turn toward me. I moved in with the disabler, but the second guard had been moving faster than I realized from his delayed image. His hand swung in a sweeping arc. He knocked the disabler from my grip even as he began to back up.

A meter apart, we faced each other. He drew his knife, and for just an instant his glance flickered toward where my fallen disabler was skittering across the floor. He bent slightly forward, holding his knife horizontally. He grinned, a grin filled with more malice than I had seen recently. He actually seemed glad about this disruption in his activities.

I moved away from the wall, toward my disabler, and he moved carefully to block my path. What vestiges of doubt I'd had about this group of unusually dressed people dissipated into nothingness.

He lunged and I backed away just in time. My qualms about recent actions vanished. I began to maneuver. From that point I was constantly in motion, never in the place where the black-suit's eyes told him I was. My one advantage was my familiarity with the environment, and I had to use it to the fullest.

The black-suit made a couple of lunges toward me, slicing his knife through the air in strong, horizontal sweeps. He came nowhere near me either time, and his malevolent grin faded into compressed lips that said he was taking the situation more seriously than before.

To maximize his confusion, I said, "Get him, Harry!" and, as I closed my mouth, approached him fast, feinting to my right, and then moving around him to the left. No doubt confused by the apparently simultaneous cry and feint, he defended himself against my image's attack, leaving himself exposed. From behind him, I snapped my arm around his neck and put pressure on his Adam's apple. My other hand grabbed his knife hand and swung it into the wall.

The knife hit the wall point-first, and his hand slipped over the haft, onto the blade. The knife dropped to the floor. He couldn't cry out, though, because I was cutting off all his air.

With the knife no longer an immediate threat, I kicked against the nearer wall and managed to twist his body so his head smashed heavily against the opposite wall. The man went limp instantly.

I retrieved his knife and my disabler as quickly as I could. He was still unconscious when I turned off his lifebelt and the color faded from his skin and uniform. I took a couple of deep breaths and then dragged both bodies into a service closet across the hall and dumped them inside.

I hurried back to the doorway leading into the swimming pool. I would have gone inside right then, but, if I had been observed just now, the action would do nothing except ensure my capture. I assumed a guard position next to the door and looked carefully first one direction then the other. I saw no one. But, if someone had entered this section of the hallway a few seconds ago, the speed-of-light delay meant his image would just now be reaching me, and he would be seeing whatever I had been doing a few seconds ago.

Seconds went by with no activity visible, so I opened the door to the swimming pool and pulled my much-abused passenger inside. The back of his head would be sore when he woke up, but in the under-one-half gee on this level, he shouldn't have a concussion. I resumed my position outside the door for long enough to make sure no one had been watching me, then I went back inside.

The swimming pool foyer was deserted. Side halls led to men's and women's changing rooms. I towed my passenger straight through the foyer to the arched walkway directly opposite the hallway entrance, and around the corner.

The creamy-white surface of the pool water was placid, narrowing as it stretched toward the rear wall. Around the pool were far more people than I could ever remember seeing here before, but there was no activity in the water. The entire room was still. Bodies had been distributed in a giant ring around the pool, a few draped across one another. Many were in nightclothes; the rest were wrapped in blankets or sheets that looked like togas. I could see the ones closest to me shallowly breathing, rib cages gently heaving in and then out. The scene could almost have been a pleasure-planet orgy in the pass-out-when-it's-over stage.

This was just a guess, but these folks were probably going to be really perturbed when they woke up.

I deposited my passenger, happy to be free of the load, relieved that I wouldn't have to bang him around any more. Then even as I straightened back upright, I realized what was bothering me.

In this massive collection of slumbering men, women, and children, there was no sign of a crew uniform.

At the very least, anyone on duty should have still been in uniform. Therefore, the crew members were being treated differently, or being held elsewhere. I took a quick look around to verify that only passengers were here. I saw Wade Pesek Midsel and Tara Pesek Cline. I saw Merle Trentlin, his nightclothes making him look even younger than he had at dinner ages ago. I saw a few passengers whose heads were shaking slightly, as though they were coming out of it. I saw not one crew member.

So my plan of freeing a few key crew members was on hold. I moved back to the main door and listened. Nothing.

I casually opened the door, prepared to act quickly, but the corridor was still empty. I assumed the guard position outside and I started to think furiously.

Where would they be keeping the crew? I was narrowing down the likely possibilities when I caught sight of motion in the corner of my eye. Another black-suit was approaching.

If I ran, I instantly gave my advantage away. The approaching figure was far enough away to make it difficult to recognize someone, so I gestured quickly at him, indicating for him to follow me, and I went inside the foyer.

All he had to do, if he was really suspicious, was to summon backup. He must have been only faintly suspicious, because he followed me inside with his knife drawn.

Keeping my face averted, I gestured for him to follow me into the room beyond the foyer. Obediently, he came along. As he turned the corner behind me, I swung at him, hard.

In what must have been his last conscious effort, he slashed at me. His knife bit through my black sleeve and I could feel the tingling that told me the blade had sliced into my arm. Then the edge of my hand caught him quite hard in the throat. He made a noise somewhere between a gasp and a choke. I grabbed his arm, moved in and under him, and twisted him over my shoulder, hurling him past the steps into the pool.

His body arced through the air and he landed head-first in the white water. Water splashed high in the weak gravity. Reflected patterns of light rippled across the ceiling. Black-suit's knife had fallen into the water, but it was on a step near enough the surface for me to retrieve it without getting more than my hand wet. I would have left it there otherwise. I couldn't afford to be sneaking around the ship going *squish squish squish*. Spray from my opponent's fall showered onto several of the nearby passengers. They were going to wake up *really* irritated.

I stood at the edge of the pool, armed with two knives and a disabler, wondering how to handle this guy. A moment later, it was obvious that I didn't have to do anything else. He was floating face down. The black suit in the white water stood out like a pregnant woman in a house of pleasure, but I couldn't afford the time to retrieve and hide the body. I kept an eye on him just in case he was faking.

I turned toward the door, and as my gaze flashed past the array of passengers, I saw Tara's eyes open. Instantly I moved toward her.

"What?" she said when I knelt beside her. She shakily swept strands of hair away from her cheek and looked at me with obvious puzzlement in her eyes. She wore the turquoise robe I had seen her in when I had searched her cabin.

"Don't say anything," I said. "Just listen to me. And listen carefully. This is important."

"Where am—" She began to look around her and her frown deepened.

We had no time. I put my hand on her chin and moved her head to face me again. "*Listen* to me, and listen closely. The ship is being taken over. Everyone was gassed and the passengers were brought here. I'm going to try to find the crew so I can get help. Take this and hide it." I handed her one of the knives.

She widened her eyes in comprehension. I thought at first I was going too fast for her, but then she reached out and grabbed the knife. She tucked it under her, and she frowned again as she apparently realized how she was dressed. She pressed her lips together in a gesture that seemed to say *All right, some things I'm just going to have to worry about later.* I admired her reactions.

"I'm going to look at the emergency exit from the outside after I leave here." I pointed to the sign at the far side of the pool. "I assume they've jammed it closed."

Next to Tara, Wade rubbed his eyes.

I went on quickly. "As soon as enough people are awake, you've got to get people out of here. We can't fight back from in here. Have one or two of them fish that guy out of the pool in case anyone investigates."

She nodded. I rose and ran back to the foyer. I hesitated just inside the door. If a black-suit had arrived and found the door unguarded, he'd be suspicious. But he'd probably also open the door and investigate. No one was here investigating, so probably no one was just outside.

To play safe, just in case this dazzling display of deduction had led me to the wrong conclusion, I opened the door and backed out, trying to indicate I was talking to someone who was following me. "Uh-huh. Right." I nodded.

The effort was wasted. The corridor was empty. Any other collectors must have finished and headed elsewhere to join their compatriots.

I moved down the hall as quickly as I could while still appearing to be a legitimate black-suit. I turned the corner onto another empty corridor arcing downward in the distance. Even if I didn't find the crew, a group of over 200 passengers was bound to include several strong, resourceful people. And now they should have a chance even if I got caught.

I opened the door to the hallway leading to the rear door to the pool. In the empty, doorless hallway I ran. As I got close to the emergency exit door, I saw how prepared the hijackers had been.

The door to the pool was set into the side of the corridor, almost at the end of the hall. Between the door, which opened onto this hallway, and the opposite wall, was a rectangular grid of rods fastened together in a cube-like structure. If the door had been the standard sliding variety, the blockage wouldn't have worked, but emergency exit doors were swinging doors wherever possible. Undoubtedly the hijackers had known ahead of time what to expect.

When I reached the grid, I could see it was fastened together with twist-lock rings. It had probably been carried here unassembled, just a container full of rods. I started disconnecting key junctions. The twist-rings were stubborn, as though they had been tightened by someone jumping on a two-meter torque wrench, but finally I was able to pull some of the key assembly parts out of the way.

To see how many of the passengers were starting to recover, I pulled the door open just a crack. In the instant I realized what I was seeing, I tried to shoulder the door closed again, but this time I reacted too slowly. On the other side of the door was still another black-suiter, his boot raised to kick open the door.

The kick connected with the door. The door connected with my shoulder and then my chest. My head connected with the wall behind me.

My brain disconnected.

• • •

My head hurt. My arm hurt. My throat felt constricted. I was turning into a real complainer.

This time, though, when I came to, I wasn't lying on the floor. I was in a chair. But no chair had been in the hallway behind the pool. And there had been no voices.

I opened my eyes. I was on the bridge. Probably the least important detail was the one I noticed first; I was no longer wearing the borrowed black suit over my uniform. My disabler was gone, too. A section of my white uniform sleeve was blackened by dried blood, but the modest pain gave me hope that no severe damage had been done. I vaguely wondered why no one had attended to my arm.

"So you're finally awake," someone said.

I looked up and saw that the speaker was Daniel Haffalt, my short dinner companion from a couple of nights ago. And he *was* wearing a black suit. He seemed taller than he had before because of my vantage point. Small circles under his eyes told me he hadn't had much more sleep than I'd had tonight. He said, "Before you get any creative ideas about resistance, feel around your neck."

I followed his advice and found that I was wearing a very heavy necklace.

"That collar," Daniel said, "contains a small receiver and a spool of monomolecular filament. If you don't follow instructions, the filament cuts all the way to your spinal cord. You comprehend?"

"I gotcha. No more headaches."

"At least two people have controls. Two of them have orders to stay on opposite sides of the room."

My mind was clearing fast. His point was that even if I could get away with a speed-of-light attack on one of the two, the other would activate my collar. "I understand."

I realized finally that, besides Daniel Haffalt and the two guards, other people were in the room. Wade Midsel stood nearby, also wearing a black suit. Now I really felt left out of the gang.

Beyond him in a chair sat Tara, looking as unhappy as I felt. She also wore a collar. It really didn't go very well with her bathrobe. Her hair was a little mussed from having been slept on, but she was a welcome sight. She nodded at me a moment after I looked in her direction.

Sitting near Tara were Bella and Razzi. The pattern would have been obvious even to a child. One either wore a black suit or one wore a collar. Bella and Razzi wore collars and grim expressions. Bella was also still in uniform. Razzi wore a jogging suit with green stripes along the outside of the arms and legs.

Wade moved closer to Daniel. Daniel's head came up to Wade's shoulder. I wondered which one was the boss.

"You caused us a lot of trouble, Mr. Kraft," Daniel said. "The man you threw in the pool drowned, and you came uncomfortably close to letting all the passengers loose. It's lucky for us that Wade was able to get help quickly."

Wade shifted his weight on his feet, as though he was uncomfortable with praise. If I went around doing things like he did, I hoped I wouldn't get much praise either. Daniel hadn't explained why Wade happened to be in with the rest of the passengers. Perhaps that had been deliberate, just in case someone in the recovering group knew something the team hadn't anticipated. I filed away the question.

Daniel continued. "But we need all our resources right now. I want to know where to find the rest of our assistants."

"How many are here?"

"Nice try," Wade interjected, stepping closer, "but you don't need to know that. Obviously you're someone who should get as little information as possible." Wade's voice had changed subtly since I talked to him last. More natural, but more angry. As though he had shed an uncomfortable persona. Before he had seemed to be a possessive husband. Now his eyes were filled with the intensity of a performer on an adrenaline high.

As he talked, I looked around the bridge at the status screens. We were not on our original course.

"Where can we find them, Mr. Kraft?" Wade asked again. His voice was still casual, but it felt to me that he was on the edge, ready to resort to calm, quiet threats.

"Well, two are—"

"Jason," Bella said sharply, "you can't give these men any assistance."

"It's all right. I don't mind. Two are in the service closet across the hall from the pool. The other three are in individual staterooms." I gave him the approximate room numbers.

"Thank you," Wade said. "See, this isn't so difficult after all, is it?" He gave instructions to someone behind me to release the missing black-suits.

As the door slid closed behind whoever was on the way to search, Bella said with surprise, "Jason, that was a direct order."

I looked over at her. "Don't be too quick to discard what you already know about me, Bella. That information won't do him any good."

Daniel moved toward me menacingly. "What exactly do you mean by that? They're not where you said?"

"I mean that by now they're all dead."

Responses arrived in haphazard fashion because of varying reaction times and speed-of-light delays.

Daniel clenched his fists and said, "They're *what?* Half of our—"

"Shut up, Daniel," Wade said quickly. This time I could hear more of the submerged anger.

Tara gasped, just loudly enough for me to hear in the short lull.

I glanced at Bella in time to see her nodding her head slowly in understanding. Razzi looked like a passenger with c-sickness. The guard on their side of the room merely clenched his jaw.

Wade calmly carried a chair over close to me, locked it into the floor grid, and then sat in it. He carefully straightened the seam of his trousers before he said, "I'm to understand that you killed six of my men, Mr. Kraft?"

"Nothing personal, but yes. Five men and a woman, actually. You don't seem too amazed."

"I guess I'm more surprised by the number than by their fate," he said. "So somehow you awoke earlier than the others, saw my men roaming the ship, and simply killed them."

I stared at him for a moment. "Let's not pretend the situation is something other than what it is. A passenger and one of our crew members were murdered in the last two days. I can't for a minute believe that wasn't your fault, or the fault of one of your team.

"I don't recognize any of your help, but I normally see everyone who comes aboard. Therefore, they must have been smuggled aboard inside a cargo crate. Jenni Sonders was probably exploring and had the misfortune to see something she shouldn't have—maybe a hinged crate wall moving. Therefore, she couldn't be allowed to live. Fenn Melgard, one of our crew assigned to level six, probably arrived just in time to be another witness who couldn't be allowed to talk.

"Besides that, you're taking chances with all of our lives, first by gassing the ship, and then by illegally altering the ship's course. These collars aren't entirely risk-free, and I imagine you are quite prepared to use them if you feel it necessary." I was saying more than necessary. Maybe I was trying to eliminate some of the guilt I felt.

I went on. "And even if I didn't have two almost certain murders to go on, specific rules established required actions when illegal acts are committed aboard ship. One of those rules is that anyone suspected of wrongdoing is guilty until proven innocent. The skipper could probably court-martial me if I had merely tied up those folks and then they got loose and killed more of the crew or passengers."

"You aren't saying you killed my assistants because you were afraid of court-martial, are you, Mr. Kraft?"

"No," I said evenly, "I'm not saying that at all."

"No," he echoed. "I really didn't think so." He looked up at Daniel and said, "I think we'd better be quite careful with this man, and with the entire crew, if he's representative."

Daniel said, too quietly, "How about if I just take him someplace where I can be real careful with him for about an hour?"

Wade shook his head emphatically. "If he's telling us the truth, and I'm sure he is, we're going to have to re-evaluate our plans. Hibbard and Babcalut were both—" He glanced at me and paused, obviously not wanting to say anything more.

"Where are we going?" I asked.

"You mean there's something you don't know?" Wade said. He gave me a mild wry grin.

"I know we're no longer bound for Leviathan."

The conversation was interrupted by the sound of the door opening and closing. "They're dead," said a feminine voice I didn't recognize. "Every damn one of them." Her voice contained more anger than Wade's, showing no effort to submerge it. I wouldn't want her in charge of fixing up my arm right then.

All too often it seems that the people who are willing to break the rules for their own personal gain are the same ones who are quick to take offense when someone else defends what he owns or what he is charged with protecting.

"Yes," Wade said. "We've just now learned about that. Put the bodies out one of the airlocks, and go back to your station." He looked past my shoulder long enough to make me think this assistant was taking things fairly personally. "Nothing can be done about it now," Wade added quietly as he leaned back in his chair. Finally, with no more words being spoken, I heard the door open and close again.

They'd have to throw the bodies out fairly fast if they didn't want them to fall back to the hull, but I said nothing. A moment later I began to think more clearly and I realized they must already know that, since Fenn Melgard's body hadn't been on the hull.

A beep from the console drew Daniel Haffalt to one of the large screens. He stood there hesitating before the control panel that handled course corrections. A status indicator said the beep had indicated a transmission receipt.

A flash of intuition suddenly gave me one more possible answer. I waited until Daniel had turned back toward me, lowered my gaze to my feet, and said, "I hear Xanahalla is lovely this time of year." I hesitated long enough that when they heard my words they would see me looking away, and then I looked back toward Daniel and Wade.

Wade gave no reaction to my words, but Daniel's eyes immediately narrowed and he said, "I thought you said—" He stopped abruptly without having to be cut off by Wade, but the admission had already been made.

Wade gave Daniel a slow, withering glance and then looked back at me. "You seem to know a lot more than you let on. How is it that you're so knowledgeable?"

"Just a lucky guess."

"Based on what?"

At first I considered saying nothing, but the more I could confirm, and the more I could pass on to Razzi and Bella, the better off I assumed we all would be. "Several things. If you wanted to go to a regularly scheduled destination, you wouldn't have had to go through all these contortions. So you're going someplace private. The person in charge of the takeover team is married to one of the few people around who knows how to start someone on the way to Xanahalla, a very private place. A private place with an enormous hoard of wealth, if that same person can be believed.

"You're taking readings as though you're following someone who must have a fairly sophisticated layer-fifteen transmitter making periodic position transmissions. The one passenger you have on the bridge is a woman whom one would think you don't care for very much after all, and whose true value may therefore be the fact that she knows her way around Xanahalla. What better way to loot an unsuspecting colony than to simply pop a small team in from layer ten, grab the goods, and then pop right back here?"

Tara was silent for a long moment before she said through clenched teeth, "You'd better tell me it isn't true, Wade." Her voice was bitterly angry, her face white. Her reaction made it seem she was angered more by his destination than by what he had already accomplished.

Wade Midsel sighed. "There wouldn't be much point, my dear. The man has pieced most of it together."

"But how?" she asked, obviously asking how he had set this plan into motion, not how I had made an educated guess.

He looked at the time before he replied. "Marj Lendelson. I don't know that you've had the pleasure of meeting her, but I gave her one of your recruiting passes to send in. She must have been contacted while we stopped at Tangent, because she didn't get back aboard, and her transmissions began a few hours later. She really is a convincing actress."

"She couldn't be any more proficient than you are," Tara said. I couldn't decide how much control she had left. Her voice sounded on the edge of breaking up, but her eyes were wide open, filled with a vitality I hadn't seen in many people. Wade might seem capable of taking any action required to get him to his goal, but at that moment it seemed to be much safer to cross him than to get in Tara's way. A weaker person might have been calling him names or spitting at him. I admired her strength.

"You usually see the bright side of everything, Tara. Don't worry about your friends on Xanahalla; we won't hurt them. You should be rejoicing now that you're rid of me. You'll be inconvenienced during the next few days, and then I'll be gone and you can go on with your life."

I didn't believe him. If I were about to steal an enormous accumulation of wealth from a large group of potential religious fanatics, I wouldn't want to leave alive several witnesses who could identify me. At least some of the Xanahalla residents were bound to keep looking for the pirates long after the authorities gave up.

And even if I did believe he was sincere, I couldn't trust that nothing would go wrong, or that one of his subordinates might not try to arrange a share larger than planned for. There had to be a way out of this.

"That's enough casual conversation for now," Wade said. "Mr. Kraft here has necessitated some changes in our plan." He looked back at me. "I understand that you and Ms. Luxon are the best navigators on your crew. As you managed to dispose of some of my talent, I'll need to get the two of you to perform some services for me."

"They will do no such thing," Bella said.

"Oh, but they will. You see, I'll get two opinions on every projected action. If those opinions disagree, I'll toss a coin and kill one of the two. Then I'll get your next-best qualified navigator and start again. If either of the two refuses to give an answer, I'll kill one of the crew for each ten-minute delay. Is all of this perfectly clear?"

I said nothing. It was all too clear.

"One more thing. No messages between Mr. Kraft and Ms. Luxon. Or maybe I should say between Jason and Razzi. It is Razzi, isn't it? Good. We've got a lot of work to do together, and I think it will just slow us down to be too formal. Anyway, no messages. We'll keep you separate and I'll be watching closely when you're on the bridge. If I find any message, I'll have to assume collusion. And then I'll have to flip my coin. Heads, you die, Jason. Otherwise, you die, Razzi."

Wade's voice was perfectly unruffled as he calmly explained the rules. The fact that those rules could decide life or death for crew-mates and passengers wasn't enough to change his expression from calm and mildly attentive into deadly earnest.

I would rather have been dealing with someone who felt the need to pound his fist to make points, someone who was newer to this life-or-instant-death business. Obviously Wade was a good actor, but I didn't doubt for a moment that he would follow through with what he had just told us. I had seen how little effort it took for him to get one of his subordinates to accept the fact that six of her compatriots had just been killed by someone who was still available for revenge. He must have already proven himself to them somehow.

Bella, her tone just as calm and matter-of-fact as Wade's had been, said, "Mister, you'd better hope and pray you don't make one tiny little slip-up. You won't get two." She said exactly what I was thinking.

"I'll leave the hoping and praying to Tara. She's good at it. But don't waste your time hoping or praying. Just do as you're told and you'll all be healthy and free shortly. One tiny little slip-up and some of you won't be so healthy."

Bella said nothing but she gave me an intense look that was entirely transparent to me. It said *I'll race you, Jason. One of us will find a way to get this bastard.*

The door to the bridge sounded again and another black-suit entered. I looked back, and through the opened door I could see a guard stationed outside.

"All finished," the new arrival said. He was a tall muscle-bound man with graying sideburns.

"Good. Escort those two to the office next door." Wade pointed to Bella and Razzi. "Their collar numbers are five and two. Use your control with only the slightest provocation. Ladies?"

The newly arrived guard made adjustments on a small black control box strapped to his wrist. Bella and Razzi got up slowly to avoid making anyone nervous, and followed the guard into the hall.

The door closed behind them and Wade turned to me. "Time for you to earn your keep."

I joined him at the console. Arguing about it would only lead to renewed threats against the crew or passengers, and being cooperative now could conceivably gain me some critical time when it might be essential.

Wade said, "The transmitter Marj is carrying is fairly exotic. It doesn't generate any signals in normal space. Instead, it periodically shifts part of its internals to layer fifteen, where they transmit a very short burst. Those blips should be discarded as noise by anyone monitoring normal transmissions in layer fifteen."

"How do you know Lendelson still has the transmitter with her?"

"I don't actually, but the odds say it's with her. When Tara went to Xanahalla, she kept a small bag with her for the whole journey. They provide new clothes and all the standard conveniences, plus a complete library. Small mementos are allowed, however. Marj has a picture cube with her—one that's very special to her." Wade grinned at me conspiratorially, as though we were on the same team, but I wasn't wearing a black suit any longer.

While he talked, I glanced surreptitiously at the control unit on his left wrist. On its surface were six recessed switches, presumably one for each collar, and a larger master button, also recessed. It seemed to me that if Wade were to accidentally bump the control against something narrow enough to fit the recessed area, whoever's individual switches were turned on would die right then. The unit itself looked too small to have its own protection field, so it must have taken advantage of the field that bled out from Wade's own lifebelt.

"Here's the last transmission we received," Wade said. He knew enough to display the characteristics on the screen.

I sat at the console and calculated our change in position. We had been traveling for almost a half-hour since they'd made a fix on the transmission. Normally, that delay would have required me to know the range as well as the relative direction, but we were already headed in generally the same direction and the ship was moving slowly since Wade knew that keeping up with a layer-zero craft would be easy.

"You want me to make the course correction?" I asked.

"No. Just tell me what you would do to keep us on track. And tell me very carefully."

I understood the implication. He would have Razzi come back and make the actual correction. And if my answer varied too much, there would be trouble. "Assuming you get your second opinion within fifteen minutes, here's what you do." I gave him the commands, and made it a point to give him error tolerances, so Razzi's answer differing from mine in the second decimal place wouldn't cause a needless death.

We were now moving at an angle of almost sixty degrees away from the course that would have taken us to our next scheduled stop, Leviathan. Ahead of us lay the almost solid whiteness of a dense star field.

I casually moved my hand toward a dark button marked with a crosshatch.

Wade's voice changed from casual to too casual. "What does that button do?"

I almost told him that it controlled automatic display generation in the event that we got too close to another craft, or some other nonsense, but I saw his grin widen. "It turns on our emergency beacon," I said.

"Indeed," he said, obviously aware of what it was. "Off limits, Jason. Touch anything you don't have permission to touch, and you get the penalty I already discussed."

Call them Freudian slips, call them subconscious insights, call them precognition, but at times in our lives we say or do something that seems to be illuminating in a way we never fully realize until afterward. Responding to Wade, I said, "That's the story of my life. I can look but I can't touch." But as I said it, completely without conscious intent, I glanced directly at Tara.

7

Captives of the *Redshift*

"The *Redshift* can't just drop out of sight without a ripple, you know," I said to Wade Midsel. The hand I had casually reached toward the emergency beacon switch was now stuck firmly in my pocket so I didn't get tempted to do anything else Wade might find objectionable. "Obviously the network controllers already know something's wrong. That blinking box at the upper-right corner of the screen says we have pending messages from them."

He smiled broadly, obviously unconcerned. "I know. But I also know how long it will take them to get another ship out here, and how long after that before they have any real hope of being able to find us. We'll be comfortably docked at a safe jumping-off point before they can even expect to get a radar return back."

He must have been feeling euphoric after having had me come so close to ruining his plans and then being so obviously under his control. Maybe he thought every plan would encounter at least one unanticipated event and he was lucky enough to have his out of the way already. I had to admit that right now I didn't see any other flaws in his preparation. And having a man outside exploring the hull when the gas was triggered was the kind of thing that would be quite difficult to anticipate.

Even the fact that I had been outside the ship was necessitated only by the previous mistake, that of allowing Jenni Sonders to notice something amiss. As far as I knew, all of Wade's problems had rippled out from that single deviation from the plan: a passenger who liked to explore cargo bays. And now all the ripples had died out; all looked smooth for the black-suit team. I was dejected that everything seemed to be under control, but hopeful that where there was one flaw there could be another.

Tara tightened her bathrobe around her. Some of the anger in her eyes had faded, and numbness seemed to be settling in. She had even more to adjust to than I did.

Wade was apparently oblivious to Tara's condition. He turned to Daniel and said, "We'd better get our second opinion on the course correction before the coordinates change too much. We wouldn't want anything to happen to Jason or Razzi merely because we were slow. Let's get the other two in here."

Daniel's expression said he wouldn't mind in the slightest if something needed to happen to me, whether it could be avoided or not, but he gave orders to one of our guards. Daniel preceded Tara and me into the corridor, and the guard followed, maintaining a prudent distance. I hoped they would simply have us trade positions with Bella and Razzi so I could somehow leave a message, but they eliminated that possibility. And by having Tara stay with me, they eliminated her usefulness for passing messages.

We passed the door next to the bridge, a door which led into a small room that was normally used, during less exotic emergencies, for cat-naps between extended shifts. A hole had somehow been cut or burned into the surface of the door near where it slid into the wall. A sturdy peg inserted in the hole kept the door from opening. No doubt that's where Razzi and Bella were.

Tara and I were escorted to a door farther down the hall, a door to which the same procedure had been applied. "After you," Daniel said, politely gesturing first to Tara and then to me. I followed Tara through the door, and, as I was about to turn to watch Daniel close the door, he kicked me solidly in the small of my back. His foot hit the back of my lifebelt, but the lifebelt was too thin to provide much protection.

Even as I stumbled across the room and careened into a table, I heard the door begin to slide shut, cutting off Daniel's laughter. I hit the floor before the laughter completely died away.

"Are you all right?" Tara asked. She moved toward me and gave me a hand up. The concern in her voice and the tingle I felt when my hand touched hers more than made up for the soreness in my back. I was still open to the possibility that Tara was actually working with Wade, the way he had included himself with the captive passengers, but I couldn't actually bring myself to believe it.

"I'm fine. Thanks." I surveyed the room quickly, already sure there was no way out, no access panel, no emergency exit. I was right. We were in another extended-shift break room, with nothing more than six bunks inset in the walls, four chairs, a table, a bathroom beyond, and a meager food supply.

When I completed my brief inspection, I looked back at Tara, who was staring at me with a puzzled expression on her face.

"I don't understand you," she said. "He just kicked you, really hard from the looks of it, and all you do is examine this room. You don't show your anger at all. Why do you wear such a thick mask?"

I looked back at her, sorry that she had to be one of Wade's victims, too. "I don't look angry, because I'm not angry. Not about that anyway. I've taken a lot worse than that in the past. Besides, it's to our advantage to have Daniel on the team. If they were all like your—like Wade, all cool, calm, professional, then we'd have even less chance of stopping them. As it is, we have a weak link. So that's good news."

"Stopping them? What chance do we have?" Tara's blue eyes were wide, incredulous. "I can't believe all this is happening. Everything is going too fast. And you actually killed six people in the last few hours? Doesn't that bother you?"

"This whole thing bothers me. Sit down a minute and relax." I waited until she took a chair, and then I sat down across from her. "I'm not going to spend a lot of time justifying what I've done. I believe that anyone who puts innocent people's lives at risk, or actually kills, has forfeited the right to live. Believing that doesn't make it easy or painless to follow through. I'm not going to try to convince you that's right, and you're not going to convince me otherwise. End of topic. Now I know you've got even more to adjust to than I do, so if you need a minute or two to clear your head or use the bathroom, do it now. And then I want you to tell me everything you know about Xanahalla. And about Wade."

"You're joking."

"You've got two minutes."

Tara looked at me and took a deep breath. Without another word, she got up, went into the bathroom, and closed the door. When she returned, she calmly sat down and said, "Tell me why you want to know and why it has to be now. This ship may take a few days to get there."

"I want to know everything that may give me an edge, anything that I can conceivably take advantage of to overcome this gang. Knowledge is power—you've surely heard that a thousand times. We need all the power we can get. I need it now because for all I know we'll be separated in five minutes and I won't have another chance. You're the one person on our side who knows Wade and who knows Xanahalla."

"I'm sorry." Tara looked down at her lap. I noticed that she was barefoot. "This is all my fault. If I hadn't been to Xanahalla, if I hadn't told Wade—"

"Stop it."

"—if I hadn't—"

"Stop it! This is no more your fault than it is mine. I'm sorry it's happened, too. But it's a fact, and we're not responsible. The only failure we can be responsible for is inaction, if we just sit here and let it happen. Now tell me about Xanahalla."

"No. It's hopeless. We'll never stop him."

My voice rose. "Don't you say 'no.' I don't *ever* want to hear 'no' again. I've heard it enough to last a lifetime. We're going to do something about all this. I don't know what yet, but we're not going to say 'no.' Is that perfectly clear?"

Tara stared at me. I almost expected her to say 'no' again, but she surprised me. "I'll tell you everything you want if you'll tell me about yourself when we're finished."

"What could possibly—we're wasting time."

"Promise me." There was no mischievousness in her clear blue eyes, just a stubborn intensity that I could easily relate to.

"Whatever you want, as long as you talk now. Where are newcomers brought in?" I was sure I could talk about myself long enough to bore her and never have to bring up Redwall.

Tara took a deep breath, as though preparing to talk for a long time on one lungful. "Xanahalla has an small orbital station, like on any planet off the main hyperspace net. I'm getting this out of order. I was contacted during a layover and led to a docking station where I boarded a small hyperspace vehicle—a zero-gravity model just large enough for a few people. We traveled for what I estimated to be eight hours. After that they translated us to a larger conventional spacecraft.

"The larger ship took us to a docking station in orbit around Xanahalla. The planet rotates fast—a complete rotation is only about eight hours—and we were low. Low enough that the Tower of Worship was visible from orbit. It's roughly at the center of a circular, deep-green area that looks like it must be less than five or ten percent of the planet's surface. As far as I know, the rest of the planet is unoccupied. From there, we went down to a surface spaceport in an atmospheric shuttle, a twenty-passenger job.

"We traded clothes on the orbital station. They insist that everyone wear a robe, rather than normal street clothes. I'm still getting this out of order."

"That doesn't matter," I said. "Just tell me everything you can remember."

"I noticed one other thing from the station. There was really no way to avoid missing it. They asked us not to tell any outsiders, but I suppose it can't hurt now. Xanahalla is a ringed planet."

"How appropriate."

"I beg your pardon?"

"Nothing. It's just that the halo image seems well suited to make people feel that somehow this place really deserves to be the home of a large religious institution."

"You make it sound like a business decision rather than simply a fact of life."

"It doesn't matter. What about all these people who go there? Are they all members of the same religion?"

"No. Xanahalla's open to anyone from any religion. The only thing in common is that they accept only those people who believe in the Third Coming."

I must have frowned, because she said, "And what's the matter with that? I'll tell you anything you want to know about Xanahalla, but you don't have to pass judgment on it just because the people there don't believe the same things you do. What *do* you believe in?"

I got up to check the door, just on the remote chance it wasn't properly secured. It wouldn't budge. "What do I believe? I think at times we believe what someone else wants us to believe. Sometimes we believe what we want to believe. And once in a rare while, we get a glimpse of the truth."

"And you believe in yourself." She made it a statement, almost daring me to disagree.

"Yes, I suppose I do. But let's get back to the topic. What happened next?"

Tara hesitated, as though she'd rather have talked about other things, or she'd rather have been catching up on her sleep, but she went ahead. "All right. We landed at a small spaceport on Xanahalla. By the way, do you know where the name comes from?"

"No."

"It's a merger of 'Xanadu' and 'Valhalla.' "

"Oh," I said, perfectly unenlightened.

My face must not have been the opaque mask Tara had complained about, or she must have been getting better at reading whatever small signs were there, because she said, "Some things you say make you seem well read, but you've got a few gaps in your education if you haven't heard those words before. Xanadu comes from an old poem; it's an idyllic place of beauty. Valhalla is an older name; it's a mythical place where honorable warriors went after their final battles."

"Meaning that Xanahalla is a beautiful retreat available to people who have waged the battle against sin? That they're through fighting and it's someone else's problem then?"

Tara nodded as she heard my first sentence and then shook her head abruptly. "Maybe we should get back to the topic." And a weak version of that mischievous smile I had seen earlier touched her lips.

I said, "I must say you're coping better than I would have expected from someone whose husband just turned on her." I would have added, "and whose expected life-span might be only a week more," but having her worry about Wade's probable plans for the *Redshift* wouldn't serve any purpose.

"I guess I am." A wistful expression came over Tara's face. It was there only a second or two before it faded and she shook her head lightly. "To tell the truth, things weren't going all that well between us."

"But you kept trying because you didn't want the responsibility for being the one to end it?" I thought about how happy she had looked with Wade, about how she had defended his actions even when he was clearly wrong, and I thought that Wade must be an incredibly stupid man in some ways.

"Maybe. What I'm sorriest about is that Jenni had to die because of all of this."

"Let's just make sure it wasn't for nothing. Tell me about the spaceport. What kinds of ships did you see?"

"Just three conventional ships, all small ones like the one that landed me there. The spaceport is at the edge of the green circle around the Tower of Worship."

"But there was no hyperspace dock in orbit?"

"Nothing that looked like one where we were. Someone once told me the translation process between normal space and hyperspace generates some disruption that can be picked up by someone who's looking for it. I suppose they use only conventional ships near Xanahalla itself to keep from attracting too much attention."

I nodded. "So it's not simply a casual little out-of-the-way retreat run by some naive priest; they've thought things through."

"I guess they haven't thought everything through. Can Wade really just move the ship so it's superimposed on whatever they want in real space, zip over and grab it, and zip back to the ship?"

"The process is harder and more dangerous than it sounds, but yes. Normally, docking is the only time anyone translates, and the ship is instrumented to keep pace with the dock. When you're out in space, you can translate back and forth without much worry. But when you're around masses in normal space, it's not all that hard to translate directly into a solid. That can be real painful."

"I assume you're joking."

"Yes. It's actually lethal. The translation process pushes light materials, like atmosphere, out of the way of the traveler, but it can't do anything about liquids and solids. The atoms in your body force their way into the matrix of atoms in your path. Once that's done, you're not only dead, but there's no way to reverse the process. The sensors scanning back and forth between here and normal space can be destroyed the same way, so you would have to move the ship very carefully."

"But what about other places—like banks or art museums? How do they protect themselves?"

"With disrupters. We try not to talk about them much, to keep people from thinking about other possible uses for a ship. Disrupters set up a field that scrambles the molecules of anything moving to or from normal space. I assume Wade feels your friends don't employ anything that sophisticated, or he just plans on dropping a heavily armed team somewhere close enough for them to blast their way in."

Tara leaned forward and put her hands on her knees. "But no one there is armed. They would just be cut down like school children sent to war."

"That's one more reason we've got to find a way to stop them. Let's get back to your description. Where do newcomers go once they arrive at the spaceport?"

"Several underground tunnels radiate out from the spaceport. One goes directly to the Tower of Worship. The others go to points spread around the residential areas. A network of underground corridors interconnects almost every building, so people can get around during bad weather. Most everyone uses the walkways on the surface whenever they can though. The view of the rings—"

Tara stopped in mid-sentence as the door to our room opened. Whoever was there would hear her last few words, but there was no help for it.

Daniel stood in the doorway, flanked by two of his compatriots, one male, one female. Both of his aides were enough taller than he was to make the eye tell the brain that Daniel should have been standing far out in front of the other two for the perspective to be right. Daniel smiled and opened his mouth for one word. I was beginning to dislike that smile intensely. I was surprised at the word, though, because he had said merely, "Mealtime."

I said, "And they say room service isn't friendly. But I don't see our plates. What did you order, Tara?"

Daniel cut in. "We didn't bring you anything. You're going to *fix* the meal."

Great. I hated cooking.

Cooking for two to three hundred people wasn't what I'd really call cooking. In this case, one description that came closer was "pulling, pumping, and pouring." On nearby counters were the remains of whatever food was being prepared when the gas had reached the galley. Containers stood open, their integral subjective-time countdown timers showing their remaining useful lifetimes.

Layne Koffer would have been mortified if he watched us as we prepared the meal. With Daniel and his two colleagues "supervising," Tara and I used a handcart to roll a large cylindrical container from one of the black-suits' crates on level six into the elevator, went down to the galley on level five, and poured the contents into a large heating vat to which we added water.

"What is this stuff?" I asked. "Dehydrated liver?"

Tara wrinkled her nose without offering a guess.

"It's what Confederation Marines eat when they're on R and R," Daniel said, from a safe distance. Safe from me, that is. Not safe from the odor. "It's nutritional and easy to fix. We don't have time to run a standard galley."

"What's 'R and R' stand for," I asked. "Raw and rank?" This was one watched pot I hoped would never boil.

"Shut up and keep busy."

"Why aren't you people doing this? It's taking more of you to guard us than it is to do the work. This is worse than the government."

"We're saving our energy." What Daniel didn't say was that this was probably also designed to minimize our talking or resting.

"My collar is beginning to chafe," I said. "How about taking it off for a while?"

"Keep it up, Jason, and I'll *really* take it off."

I turned back toward the heating vat and said to Tara, "I wonder what's for dessert. Chopped rodent parts?"

Tara shook her head and grimaced.

"What did you say?" Daniel demanded suspiciously. Either he wanted me to speak up or he didn't. There was no keeping the man happy.

"I said this should really stick to everyone's stomachs." I turned back toward the vat, and added, more quietly, "Or to the roofs of their mouths."

"Would you stop it?" Tara said. "I'm going to need a c-sick bag pretty soon." I looked at her to see if she was serious, but she seemed to have adopted the same defense I had: don't take it too seriously or it will get to you. She gave me a wan smile.

While facing the vat I said quite softly, "What's the housing like?"

Instantly she was on the same wavelength and she replied. "Individual houses. People move once in a while, because the longer you've been there, the closer you can live to the Tower. More like moderately fancy apartments than houses, though, because they don't have any storage places for vehicles. Just a kitchen, bedroom, bathroom, living room, often with an atrium. Lots of outside walls have clinging vines on them."

As I was formulating my next question, I realized that somehow, in a matter of no more than a few hours in Tara's presence, I felt more rapport with her than I had ever felt with anyone before.

"Where are the valuables kept?" I asked, but before she could reply, Daniel said, "Isn't that stuff ready yet?"

"How can you tell if this stuff is done?" I asked. "Does it start smelling like food?"

"What's the temperature?"

I told him.

"It's done."

If the passengers who woke up in their nightclothes and found themselves massed around the swimming pool weren't irritated yet, this gruel would certainly accelerate the transformation. If I were a passenger, I'd demand a refund. And my clothes.

While the guards kept their positions, Daniel retrieved two large wheeled carts with deep food trays mounted on top. "Let's pour two-thirds of it into this one," he said

The gruel had become significantly heavier after adding all that water, so Daniel and I lifted the heating vat to pour its contents. I try not to underestimate people, but I was surprised at the ease with which he supported his end and helped pour the contents without trembling because of the weight. With his short, wiry frame, he must have given quite a surprise to any kids who had tried to pick on him when he was younger. I wondered if *he* had ever killed one.

We poured about two-thirds of the remainder into the second tray. The balance, we put in a large bowl and left it on the counter.

"Just like the three bears," Tara said.

"What?" I said.

"Goldilocks. The three bowls of porridge. Oh, skip it," she said when she looked at my genuine puzzlement.

Daniel said, "Maybe the first officer doesn't read the same kind of books you do. Maybe he reads the classics."

I still didn't understand Tara's allusion, but there was no mistaking the condescension in Daniel's voice. Briefly I wondered if one had to be condescending to women to be on Wade's team, but a glance at our guards reminded me that there were women actually on the team.

This woman, a blonde with short, straight hair plastered back like a textured shower cap, showed no sign of being disturbed by Daniel's comments to Tara. Maybe she viewed them simply as remarks from captor to captive rather than from generic man to generic woman. Maybe it was only me imagining sexism. She returned my stare with a dispassionate air of duty.

Daniel loaded a tall stack of nested cups on the lower shelf of the tray. "All right. Let's go next door and feed the hungry masses."

So now I knew where the remainder of the crew were being held, but the knowledge did me no immediate good. We wheeled the medium-sized container down the corridor to the door to the dining hall. This door was blocked with the same mechanism they had used on the other doors: a hole cut in the outside surface and a peg inserted. In addition, the hijackers had cut another hole all the way through the door, to allow inspection from outside.

While Tara and I looked on, and the two guards watched us, Daniel spoke through the hole. "Everyone, get well back from the door, and lie down on the floor. Everyone. Do it now if you want to eat."

He was taking the same precautions I might if I had been in his position. With everyone reclining, they wouldn't be able to perform a speed-of-light run and surprise the person opening the door. That was the *Redshift* equivalent of making a suspect stand well out from a wall and lean against it.

Evidently everyone complied, because a moment later Daniel gestured for me to approach the door and bring the cart. "Go in and leave that tray. Explain to them that anyone with a collar gets killed if we have any trouble. Tell them this stuff is concentrated, so not to eat any more than they have to. That's all they get until we let them loose. And in this environment, it won't spoil, right?"

"Looks a little monotonous," I said.

"Get used to it. That's all any of us are going to have."

"Maybe we could save some time and just mix in some stomach-settler right now."

"Get inside. No wait. Just a minute." Daniel took another look through the hole. No one poked him in the eye. "All right. Now go fast." He pulled out a peg and slid the door aside quickly.

Tara stayed outside as I went into the crew's prison. Daniel slid the door closed behind me and I wheeled the cart to the center of a semicircular area cleared of reclining crew members. Around the edges of the large room, beyond the neatly set dining tables, were four doors, all no doubt sealed securely. The ventilation ducts high on the walls were too small to admit a person trying to escape. The array of prone crew members looked more like an aerobics class than the professional staff of a hyperspace liner.

"What's going on, Mr. Kraft?" was the first question I heard. Bensode lay on his stomach, looking up at me from his resting place. Around his neck was another collar. Bensode looked even more than unusually unhappy about all this, a feeling I shared. Near him was Rory Willett, one eyebrow cocked. Rory also wore a collar, but I saw no others. Mostly I just saw an expanse of puzzled, irritated, and unsure expressions.

"The ship's been taken over by Wade Midsel, Daniel Haffalt, and a group of people smuggled aboard in shipping crates. Tara Cline, Wade's wife, is not part of it." I wasn't doing a good job of telling the basic facts in the news-style descending order of importance, but the fact that Tara wasn't involved was surprisingly important to me.

"Are you all right?" Rory asked. He seemed to be looking at my bloody uniform sleeve.

"Compared to what?" I flexed my cut arm. It didn't hurt too much. "I think so."

I had just finished explaining the purpose of the collars and the limitation of the "food" supply when Daniel called through the hole, "All right, Jason. Come on out." Before I responded, one of the crew said, "Where are the passengers? Has anyone been hurt?"

"So far as I know, none of the crew or passengers has been hurt." I explained that Bella and Razzi were being held separately for navigation purposes.

"You're not helping these bastards, are you, Jason?" Rory asked.

I turned to face the group. "Yes, I am. To a limited degree. It's either that or they come in here and kill you one by one."

"Maybe they're bluffing. Maybe if you totally refused, we'd all be free," said a voice from farther back. He sounded unhappy, and he probably hadn't even smelled the "food" yet.

"That's a risk I would consider taking myself. It's not one I'll take for anyone else." I didn't add that I had encountered a few men like Wade before, men so obviously calm despite the adrenaline high they had to be on that you knew intuitively they would freely do whatever they thought necessary to maintain control of a situation. And, if intuition wasn't enough, I'd seen what happened to persons who attempted unsuccessfully to block their efforts. There had to be a way to depose Wade, but it wasn't obvious to me yet.

The smell of the gruel must have reached one of the crew, because a voice said, "That's what they brought us to eat? How can we eat that?"

I said, "Don't worry about it. It's on the house."

"Get out of there right now, Jason," Daniel called through his peephole.

As I moved toward the door, I realized that, in addition to wanting to keep me busy, Wade and Daniel must have wanted me visible to the crew and passengers, in an obviously powerless capacity, to keep them from fostering any optimism and to discourage the inevitable escape plans.

I waited at the door while Daniel verified it was safe to open and then it slid aside abruptly.

He forced the door closed. "Next time I give you an order, follow it," he said angrily.

In other circumstances, I would have said, "Next time you give me an order, you can shove it," but at the moment I was still grateful that the team included a hothead we might be able to take advantage of. I needed a calibration on him, though, so I would know how far I could push him when the time came. I said, "You forgot to say 'sir.' "

Daniel grabbed me by the throat, under the collar, and pushed me back against the wall. "Listen to me, you son of a bitch. Your rank doesn't mean anything at all right now. This collar means I outrank you and that's all you need to know. And don't you forget it for one minute." Tara and our two accompanying guards stood absolutely still.

"You also forgot to say 'please.' "

Daniel looked apoplectic for a second as his face turned red. He pushed upward on my collar, hard, so it bit into my neck and chin. With his other hand, he punched me in the stomach.

His fist could travel no faster than ten meters per second, but it was mass-shifted so he could still deliver the same impact as in normal space. It was a forceful blow. Fortunately I had tensed my stomach muscles so it didn't bother me so much.

I had learned enough for the moment, though, so I doubled over as if Daniel's blow had been more effective. The reaction was evidently satisfying enough, because he took no further action.

"I have a knife, too," he said when I stood up straight. "So don't get any silly ideas about me holding back because we need you alive to navigate." His dark eyes narrowed and he stared up at me for a long moment.

"Message received."

Daniel stepped back from me. He tugged at his cuffs to pull them back out to his wrists and he thrust his shoulders back. "Let's get back to the galley."

The five of us started back down the hall, the guards ahead and behind, Daniel walking well ahead of Tara and me.

Tara leaned toward me and said softly, "You shouldn't antagonize him."

"Yeah. I know. Don't tease the animals."

She stifled a sudden nervous laugh. Even before Daniel turned around to see what the sound meant, she was coughing to conceal her action. Daniel scowled suspiciously for a moment and then faced ahead. The guard in front of us looked at me as if I had just called the Confederation president by her nickname, to her face.

In the galley, we retrieved the largest tray of gruel and wheeled it out on the other cart, accompanied by a much larger supply of cups.

As the elevator took us up to level five, the guards in either corner of the enclosure had their fingers poised on the buttons controlling our collars. I was careful to avoid nudging anyone.

The doors to the swimming pool had been equipped the same way as the galley. Daniel gave directions for the passengers to clear the entry way. When he was satisfied, I wheeled the tray in and Tara brought the large collection of cups.

As the door slid closed behind us, I turned to Tara and said, "We make a good team, huh?"

That familiar mischievousness returned to her blue eyes for an instant and she said, "Yes, we do. Just like Jekyll and Hyde."

8

Hyperspace Voyage

I pushed the "food" tray through the swimming pool foyer and beyond, into the next room. Tara followed me, carrying the stacks of cups. Passengers in nightclothes crowded around the end of the hallway. Some people looked frightened, others looked sleepy. Most looked irritated. Not one had a life preserver or a squeaky duck.

Someone had fished the black-suit body from the pool. The white water was calm, undisturbed, inviting.

Once the passengers saw Tara and me, they crowded forward and the flood of questions began.

"What's the meaning of this?"

"Why are we here?"

"Who's responsible for this?"

"What *is* that stuff in the tray?"

I held up my hands to reduce the flow of questions and to indicate I was ready to answer some of them. One of the faces in the crowd was that of the elderly man I had dragged and bounced from his cabin to here. I was relieved that he seemed to be okay.

At the side of the pool sat two youngsters I recognized, both dangling their feet in the water. Becky, the runner I had warned, was wearing a long, lime-green nightgown. Becky looked like she could have been at a normal pool-side party, wondering when the food would be served. Would she be surprised. Beside her sat Merle Trentlin, looking somber and attentive.

"I apologize for the situation you have found yourselves in," I said when the crowd quieted and the loudest echoes stopped bouncing around the cavernous room. "The ship has been taken over by a group of people who intend to use it for their own purposes for several days, after which they intend to release everyone and let us resume our trip."

I was interrupted by a blustery, double-chinned man near the front of the crowd. "They intend to release everyone? Oh, that's so very accommodating of them. But maybe instead of standing around talking about it, you should *do* something about it. I've got an important meeting on Leviathan three days from now." The man's bathrobe sported the letters FDK in flowery script.

As I considered my reply and was about to tell him how his meeting stacked up against the harassment of, and probable danger to, the rest of the crew and passengers, Tara animatedly came to my defense. "For your information, *sir,* the first officer has been doing far more than just standing around and talking about the situation. So far, six of that group are dead, all at the hands of the man you're so quick to criticize for doing nothing." That moment was the first time being defended by someone felt that good.

Both Becky and Merle were instantly wide-eyed. A brief ripple of murmurs spread across the crowd.

"Is that true?" the man asked abashedly, apparently flustered into repetition. "You killed six of them?"

At a younger age, I might have replied, "Yeah, so don't make me angry." Instead I said, "Yes. But obviously I didn't get enough of them." I explained the collars Tara and I wore, and a little more about the situation and the "food." I don't think people were greatly encouraged.

I also gave them the current master combination to the weapons locker, just in case anyone managed to get free.

The self-appointed group spokesman seemed more considerate since he'd been chastised by Tara. "But if we get free, won't that endanger your lives?" Maybe he wanted an excuse for inaction.

"Possibly. But you have to assume they're already at risk. Even if this team fully intends to honor their word, there are too many possibilities for error. We could even be killed accidently if one of them inadvertently pokes a button on his wrist controls. We'll all be better off when this situation is over." I didn't like mentioning that possibility of death in front of Tara, despite the fact that she must certainly have come to the same conclusion long ago, but keeping all the captives too scared to try to escape helped no one. Although I viewed reversing the situation as the crew's responsibility, we would be foolish to eliminate any potential help.

I answered a few more questions before a series of thuds came from the main door. Daniel was getting impatient. If my attention span was as short as his, I probably wouldn't have been able to dress myself in the morning.

"There's someone at the door," I said to Tara, with a fake air of boredom and the lazy acknowledgment of an annoying interruption.

"There's never any peace and quiet, is there?" she said, in the same tone.

For just an instant, looking into Tara's eyes, I imagined she and I were light-years away from here, with not a problem in the world.

As I turned to leave, I caught sight of Amanda Queverra. She still wore the thin negligee she had worn when I searched her cabin. It seemed to be getting her even more attention than the low-cut dinner dress, and she appeared to be enjoying herself. She and the three men near her were already going back to whatever conversation had been underway. It was an uncharitable thought, but I wondered if Wade's towing crew had brought a bathrobe with her, but on waking up and realizing some of what had happened, Amanda discarded the bathrobe.

We extricated ourselves from the crowd of irritated, poorly dressed passengers, cautioning them to stay clear of the foyer until we were gone. Despite the severity of the situation, a few in the crowd were certain to be in fact irritated by being held there without swimming outfits. But even those fortunate souls who could enjoy the adventure would probably be incensed by the cuisine.

Wade's team received no special treatment when it came to food. We took the third and smallest portion of gruel to the bridge, and almost everyone there had some immediately. If I hadn't already thought Wade's crew was dedicated, the absence of complaints would have made me a believer.

After all my disparaging remarks about the gruel, it turned out to have restorative powers which enormously exceeded its appeal to the senses. I didn't feel bad at all, even though I had been up all night and all of the previous day. All night, that is, except for two periods of unconsciousness which I chose not to count as sleep. My eyes felt fine, but the lighting on the bridge had acquired the harshness that accompanies the late shift.

Wade had apparently caught a little sleep since Tara and I had been on the bridge, and now it was Daniel's turn, wherever he was. Two guards occupied chairs propped against opposing walls while Tara and I sat in chairs facing Wade. Behind Wade, the primary screen showed a view centered on our direction of travel. The dense star field image generated so much light we could almost have turned off the normal indirect lighting on the bridge.

Tara yawned. I yawned.

Wade looked up from the calculation pad he had balanced on his knee. "I need some lessons, Jason."

"Human relations? Love and loyalty? Maritime law? The culinary arts?"

"Driving. Piloting."

"Oh, sure. It may take five or ten minutes, but you'll be great. Of course you'll probably translate us directly into the core of a sun, but we won't suffer long."

"Your sarcasm is wasted, Jason. I know this won't be trivial, but, as you've probably figured out by now, I happen to be missing the two people who had training in that field. But you don't need to concern yourself. There's a way out of this dilemma. You and Razzi will give me lessons, which I will compare closely. Deviations will be handled the way we discussed earlier."

"That sounds easy enough in theory," I said. "But the reality is that piloting a hyperspace craft is something that people train for months to be able to do safely. And that's after they can handle layer-zero ships. Besides, you don't need to pilot; you've got me."

"But I don't trust you. Oh, don't look so shocked. I know your type. You'd probably feel honored to die if you thought your death would somehow ensure the safety of your crew and passengers."

From the corner of my eye, I saw Tara, who was paying close attention to our exchange. "If that were true, I'd go for you right now so one of your two helpers would have to activate my collar. If you learn enough about piloting the *Redshift* to think you can handle it, then we'll all be in far more danger than we are already."

His two helpers leaned a few centimeters forward.

I went on. "Anyone with the bad judgment to throw away someone like Tara certainly isn't going to make a good pilot." Even as I spoke, I realized this wasn't as well reasoned as most of my arguments, but it was hard not to let my irritation show.

Wade looked at me, amused. "You probably didn't start out like I did. I had things rough. There was never money to buy the things I wanted. I've made some progress since then, but it seems that each new level of wealth brings some new goals that are a bit farther away. With Xanahalla's treasury, I can do anything I want. I can have ten Taras if I choose."

I was already starting to think he couldn't find another Tara no matter how long he looked, but if he wanted ten women, he wouldn't be talking about women like Tara. I said, "You sound like a drug addict who's decided to try ten times the normal dose."

Wade frowned. "Show me the controls, Jason." He swiveled his chair and pushed himself to the control console. He motioned for me to join him.

I sat there, considering. It took only a moment to decide the best way to convince him of the difficulty was to go ahead and teach him some fundamentals. I pushed my chair over next to his. "All right." I pointed out the location and use of several of the primary controls and then moved into a more detailed discussion of indicators on the screen. Wade sounded as though it was all making perfect sense to him.

"Let me give you a little test," I said after he gave me several indications that this was simple after having flown a shuttle. "Suppose that just ahead of us in layer zero is a planet. Two of your team, say these two—" I pointed at the two guards who were watching us quite closely now "—are equipped with suits and atmospheric backpacks. You want to drop them maybe a kilometer over the planet's surface so they can maneuver easily to their destination and you don't have to too accurately get a fix on your altitude. Is this all making sense?"

Wade nodded.

I expanded the center display. We were coming up on a planetless sun. It was a yellow, G-type star; I could tell from the temperature indication, not because I could see the color. "All right. Suppose that sun ahead is the planet. All you have to do is maneuver to a safe drop height and then when you're ready just tap this blank section on the console. That will be the signal to your two friends to step through a translator portal. And if this were real, they'd be on their way. Since this is a star instead of a planet, determining the right altitude is going to be a little difficult, so just get approximately a hundred thousand kilometers off the photosphere and we'll say that, by definition, you're in position. Do you think you can handle this, or is it a bit premature?"

"Come on, Jason. This is easy. Trying to scare me isn't going to do you any good. Let's do it."

The two guards were even more attentive than when I had suggested that sacrificing myself might be an effective strategy.

"All right," I said. "Do it."

Wade eagerly reached for the controls, like a kid reaching for a timed test that he had studied hard for. Instead of passing the sun on our original course, we began to slow, veering toward the star. Its disk began to grow dramatically in the view-screen until we could see nothing more, and Wade expanded the viewing ratio so we could once more see the arc of the sun's surface. Our speed relative to normal space dropped low enough that the screen switched from network-provided views to actual views taken from the navigation system aboard the ship. The brightness did not increase, thanks to the automatic light-level controls, so we could see mottled sunspots. A large flare reached almost as far out as our ship, but in a different direction.

Finally Wade was at approximately the right distance and he asked me to confirm.

"You want a co-pilot or do you think you can do this yourself?" I asked.

"I can do it."

"Then let's see you."

Wade nodded. He began slowing the ship still more until finally he said, "All right. This is it." And he tapped the console to indicate the start of the imaginary journey for his friends.

I glanced at Wade's two guards. Their attention was firmly on us. "So that's when you would have given your friends the order to jump?"

Wade frowned at me. "You heard me say so. What are you implying?"

The sun's disk began to shrink in the viewer. I said, "Look at the upper right indicator, there."

"All right. It says, 'Layer Zero .010227.' "

"Right. Our translator gear is matching speeds with an object in layer zero traveling at one percent of the speed of light there. Corresponding distances in our layer are a lot smaller, so here we're moving at well under .01 c."

"All right. I slowed down to make maneuvering easier. What's the problem with slowing down?"

"No problem. You just didn't slow down enough. If we're matching speed with one percent there, anyone translated to layer zero will be doing that speed."

"Go on." Wade's voice was suddenly cautious, subdued.

"One percent of c in layer zero is about 3000 kilometers per second. If we estimate the speed of sound at 300 meters per second, you just ejected your friends at Mach 10,000. In an atmosphere. So if they had been actually translated to a typical atmosphere about a kilometer off a real planetary surface, they would have been burned to cinders before you could hear their screams.

"Not only that, but if somehow they were shielded against all that heat, you sent them in there doing something faster than escape velocity. Escape velocity high enough for a typical small star, let alone escape velocity for a meager planet. So the carbon cloud that would be their only remains would be ejected from the atmosphere. Unless of course, they were pointed toward the ground, in which case their remains would impact in something under a half a millisecond. You know, that's an interesting question. Would half a millisecond give them time to be incinerated, or would they hit the ground still intact?"

I glanced at Wade's companions. They appeared distinctly unhappy before they reacted to me looking at them. Then they leaned back against the wall, their faces unreadable once again. I went on. "If you'd been trying to deposit them in a hallway on the planet's surface, and you had lined up their motion along the hallway, they'd kill everyone else in the hall before they smashed through the wall at the end. In fact if you'd—"

"Enough!" Wade said, with more emotion than I had so far heard from him. "I get the point. So it will take me a while to learn. That doesn't mean it's impossible."

"My real point is not that you would have just killed your friends. It's that piloting a hyperspace craft seems deceptively simple. You can convince yourself a hundred times you know what you're doing, when in fact you don't, before your common sense and instincts are converted into responses that are valid and useful in this environment. Think about it. You can't even carry a full glass of water across the room without spilling it unless you avoid looking at it."

"I've heard enough." Wade's words were more distinctly enunciated than usual, the only indication that I was getting a measure on his tolerance. I knew he would be tougher to deal with than Daniel, but at least he wasn't an unreachable automaton either.

"You haven't heard nearly enough," I said. "Unless you're prepared to spend months of training time, you're a danger to all of us, including your own people."

Wade turned to one of the guards. "Get him out of here." His words were slowly spaced and quite clear. He could have been giving diction lessons.

"Tell me more about the valuables on Xanahalla," I said as the door slid shut behind us.

Tara gave me a disbelieving glance. She and I had been escorted back to the break room. Presumably, Wade intended to get lessons from Razzi and Bella.

The look Tara gave me was her only concession to her obvious fatigue. She took a seat, breathed deeply, wrapped her bathrobe more tightly around her, faced forward, and began to talk. "As far as I know, everything of exceptional value is in the Tower of Worship. I think I already mentioned communion cups made of pure gold. They're just one example. Walkways reach around the four sides of the tower, and five elevators on each wall. They go all the way up to the apex. The bottom ten levels are partial floors, not just walkways. They're open in the center, so if you stand in the middle of the ground floor, you can see all the way up. Suspended in the open space, held in place with wires, are ornamental solid shapes—cubes, pyramids, spheres. They're all edged with gold, too.

"Pews are on the main floor and the ten cut-away levels. An armrest divides each pair of seats, and on every armrest is an inset gemstone. On the main floor, they're rubies. On the second level, they're Eyes of Ramah. On the tenth level, they're all diamonds."

"How large?" I asked, hoping we wouldn't be interrupted soon. I took a seat near Tara and watched her as she spoke. The nervous humor she had shown earlier had fled now that she was undoubtedly thinking of what would happen when the *Redshift* reached its new destination. Her face was serious, even sad. I wondered how much pain she'd felt before she'd even met Wade.

"A few carats each. The front of the pulpit is a mosaic of gemstones. All those stones are worth a lot of credits, but they're only a small part of the wealth. In the exact center of the main floor, there's a circular vault cover at least five meters across, bearing a large stylized 'X.' In the vault is the main treasury." She looked directly at me suddenly, as though she was aware that my thoughts weren't as impersonal as my spoken questions.

I moved quickly to a question, uncomfortable with the idea that someone might be guessing my thoughts, or able to see inside me that clearly. "Why is the Tower so ostentatious, and how do you open the vault?"

"The Tower of Worship was built to honor God, to show Him how important He is in our lives. Even so, less than five percent of Xanahalla's funds have gone into the Tower. The bulk of the assets are either in the vault, awaiting a major emergency, or they have already been spent on emergencies. A lot of very rich people have donated. And lots of them have gone to Xanahalla to live out the rest of their lives, so they brought their entire fortunes." Tara looked away and rubbed her forehead. "What was the other part—oh, yes. How to open the vault.

"Opening it requires the presence of ten church elders, each with a part of the overall combination. When the door is unlocked, it slides sideways far enough to expose the opening and the steps leading down into the vault. Small deposit-chute openings ring the perimeter, so the vault itself doesn't need to be opened frequently. How do you suppose Wade intends to get access? Wait until it's opened and then pop in a few people with weapons?"

"Could be," I said. "Or, if he's lucky and the vault isn't protected by a disrupter field, he could just deposit someone directly inside the vault and then just grab the valuables as his helper sends them back. What's actually in the vault? Credits, precious metals? And why isn't it in banks, earning more for the church?"

"I'm told it's a mixture—whatever the elders think is a good balance between funds immediately available, versus tangibles that take longer to turn into something spendable, but will supposedly be a hedge against inflation rates. They don't use banks, partly because of that, and partly because, given the size of the treasury, they'd have to split it among way too many banks—and make it that much easier for someone like Wade to find them."

"How long will it—"

"Is this really—" Tara began. We had spoken at nearly the same moment.

I gestured for her to proceed. Just after I finished, I saw her make the same gesture.

Knowing that we had responded at about the same time and that she had just seen my gesture, I waited. She did the same thing.

Finally I said, "How long will—"

And she said, "Is all this really—"

We laughed.

Syncopated observations in this bizarre slow-motion environment made too many things seem random. I moved my chair closer to Tara, to reduce the communications delays. Once I was settled, I looked up at Tara. She was looking at me quite intently. For just a second, I felt that discomfort associated with being examined beneath the surface, and then the discomfort vanished. I noticed that Tara's blue eyes were flecked with gold and green.

Blue and violet were the colors that usually meant an object was approaching rapidly. For just an instant, as I looked into Tara's deep-blue eyes, her face seemed to be rushing toward mine. She was getting too close.

I looked away and said quickly, "How long would it take them to get all the valuables? And are people around all the time or just parts of the day?"

Tara didn't answer the question. She just gave me a slow, amused grin that I felt more than saw. Then the grin faded and she said, "I'm still having trouble adjusting to the fact that this shy-little-boy person just killed six people. Who are you?"

"Jason Kraft, First Officer of the *Redshift,* Confederation Maritime Service Number CO3E8MPS."

"Name, rank, and serial number. You're hiding behind that, aren't you?"

"I don't know how to hide from you," I said without thinking. That impression of being closely examined had returned, but without the threatening feeling. Once again, this woman had forced an admission that I would never have made to someone else.

"Who are you, Jason? You're capable of killing, yet you're shy when someone gets close. You don't know a common children's story, but you're obviously intelligent and well-educated. You've got a hard shell around what I think is a vulnerable interior. You see a lot in other people, but you're more like an observer than a participant. And sometimes you don't seem to know yourself very well at all."

I stared at the far wall. "I need to know if people are in the Tower of Worship at all hours or not."

"No, they're not. Even though the light period is short, people are urged to adopt a near-normal day that includes light and dark periods. And that's the last question I'll answer before you tell me who you are."

When I looked at Tara, she appeared absolutely serious. In answer to my unasked question, she said, "I'm not kidding. I'm tired and worried and irritable. And curious. I'm not answering another question until you tell me who you are. If we might be dead in a few days, you can at least tell me that much."

I considered what I might have done earlier in a similar situation, thinking that anything I could hold within my emotional event horizon could avoid influencing anything or anyone outside. I fully intended to say nothing, but in the next instant I heard myself say, in hardly more than a whisper, "I grew up on Redwall."

If any one thing had made me what I was, it was Redwall. And Redwall was the one thing I had told myself earlier that I wouldn't mention.

She was silent, but her expression said she didn't know what I meant. I wished she knew about Redwall so I didn't have to explain anything else.

"Go on," she said finally.

"My earliest memories are of 'the dormitory.' It was an enormously long, barracks-like building, wide enough for a center aisle and two pairs of bunk beds, one set on either side, heads to the wall. Two storage trunks sat under each bottom bed, one for the person on top, one for the person on the bottom. My trunk was about this big." I gestured, spreading my hands approximately the width of my shoulders. I stared at my hands without seeing them. Instead I could see the scratches next to the lock on the trunk, scratches from uncounted attempts to redistribute what little wealth existed at that point in space and time.

"I—I've never talked about this to anyone before," I said, my throat incredibly dry. "I managed to get out of there and I never looked back. I—I—"

Tara's hand touched my arm. Her hand felt white hot through my sleeve.

I drew a deep breath. "I had the combination to the lock on my trunk. And so did the sentries. They could take whatever they wanted whenever they wanted, but at least the other kids couldn't."

When I paused, Tara asked, very quietly, "What is Redwall? A reform school?"

"Don't I wish." I heard the bitterness in my voice, bitterness that I had strived so hard to leave behind me. Behind me with Redwall and my parents. "Redwall isn't a reform school. Redwall was—is—a pleasure planet. I guess everything's relative, because it was never a pleasure planet for me."

"Dear God," Tara said. Her voice caught, and I heard her quick intake of breath as I continued to stare straight ahead.

I went on. "On Redwall, you're never too young. Oh, for a while you may be too young for the paying visitors, but you're not too young for your compatriots, your fellow victims. The six-year-olds took advantage of the four-year-olds. The eight-year-olds took advantage of the sixes. And so on up the chain. At ten, you were old enough for the paying visitors." My breath was ragged and my words were shaky. I wanted to quit talking, but somehow, now that I started, I couldn't stop.

"I killed for the first time when I was fourteen. A boy a year older than me, who lived three bunks up from me, was working out his frustrations on a nine-year-old girl who lived ten bunks down. I didn't —interrupt him in time. Rissa died a couple of days later. But the boy died as I watched him. With my—bare hands I killed him. And the gratitude I saw in that little girl's eyes—that pitiful, helpless, little girl —her gratitude left me no doubt that I had done the right thing."

I clenched my teeth, breathing heavily through my nose, struggling hard to maintain control. I hadn't consciously thought about that boy in a long time, but I could still see his anger as it faded into a puzzled, vaguely worried look before his features relaxed still farther into uncaring oblivion. Obviously my subconscious must have been making frequent trips back to the scene of the crime; the boy's image was as sharp and clear as the picture of my father.

"Jason," Tara said. "I never meant to—"

"It's all right. In fact, maybe it's better if I talk about it. I've been storing all this inside for a long time now. It seems to get a little tighter in there every time someone prods me. Sometimes I feel like I'm going to implode. No one's ever been able to get me to talk about this before."

"Yes. I realize. I'm glad it was me."

I let my thoughts wander for a moment, deciding whether to continue.

"It sounds to me," she said, "like that incident with the girl is where you started to feel a need to defend women."

"Maybe so, but I don't think the feeling is restricted to women. Anyone who's been victimized or taken advantage of." I rubbed my hands together to warm them. "She died without ever telling them who killed her attacker. By doing that, she violated one of the most important rules on Redwall. Kids who damaged the merchandise were dealt with harshly, because that meant lost income. Theft and harassment were more common than outright physical violence. But most of the kids knew that if they turned in anyone who gave them problems, they'd get worse than the person they turned in. But she had nothing to lose by telling. Her attacker couldn't retaliate."

I switched topics because the first one hurt too much. "The sentries gave us a cut of what the customers paid. We got what probably amounted to a tenth of a percent of the money they received. Just enough to make it actually seem possible that one day we could buy our way out, as long as we stayed cooperative." My voice turned hard.

"We even had a say in what kinds of services we preferred. Most of the customers, male and female, requested sex in a variety of forms. Some of the more honest customers made no attempt to pretend they wanted anything other than raw violence. Redwall fees were determined by how happy the customers were with us, and how long they put one of us out of the job force and into R and R. I had sex with women and men old enough to be my grandparents, and I received beatings from people who probably went back home in the guise of model citizens. After I learned about both 'pleasures,' I opted for the beatings."

My voice turned ragged again. "A beating let you have a longer time off before you had to deal with customers again. And it didn't come with the pretense that you were somehow being done a favor." I had to stop talking so I could keep control. I had to force air into my constricted lungs.

"Jason, how did you—" Tara shook her head abruptly and compressed her lips. She looked away.

"How did I what?"

"No. I've asked far too much already."

"How did I what?"

Tara turned toward me. Tears glistened at the corners of her eyes. "How did you get there? On Redwall. How did you come to be there?"

I considered lying to her at that point, but, where I could lie to someone else, I found I couldn't lie to her. "I was sold. By my parents."

9

Destination Xanahalla

"Your *parents* sold you to those people on Redwall?" Tara asked after a moment of speechlessness. Pain squeezed tiny vertical wrinkles between her eyebrows. "But that's not possible. Aren't there laws?"

"Not many laws don't have loopholes," I said. "According to Redwall's charter, they operate a boarding school. Their students supposedly make enough money for the school by performing extracurricular jobs that the school officials can afford to give parents a finder's fee."

"But that's inhuman."

"But it happens. Especially in regions of the Confederation where the public officials are the cheapest to buy."

"How did you learn all this? Surely the people who ran Redwall didn't just tell you."

"No. In fact, they found it was to their advantage to tell us we were born there, that we were leading a normal life for people like us. Whispered rumors were generated from casual remarks made by customers and passed on to the rest of us, but we didn't know the truth. When I was sixteen, I had taken all I felt I could take. I had to either get out of there or kill myself.

"I managed to get out. I killed three sentries in the process, and I badly injured a customer, but I had no regrets. On my way, I managed to copy a portion of their records."

"But why would you—oh, you wanted to know where you came from." Tara's expression was transparent as she reached the next logical conclusion, and her face paled still further. "Oh, my God. Jason, what did you do to your parents?"

"Their names were in the records, so, after educating myself about the real world, I decided I would go find them. But I didn't have the money to afford a hyperspace trip. Working my way onto a maintenance crew led to being able to go where I wanted before I could afford to be a paying passenger, and eventually led to my current job.

"It took me almost three years to get to the planet the records said they had lived on, Transom Five. It took me several weeks on the ground before I was able to trace where they currently were. Late one afternoon, I finally reached the building they lived in. It was more depressing than the 'dormitory.' Graffiti obscured almost the entire area a person could reach from the ground or from standing on someone else's shoulders. The building had apparently been in a war zone at one time, because the outer walls were scarred, and they'd been sloppily repaired with mud and leaves. The stairs up to the level listed in the address were missing almost a third of the steps.

"At first I had been worried about carrying a gun, but in that neighborhood I would have looked out of place without a weapon. The kids playing outside watched me just as warily as I would have watched a sentry on Redwall. Anyway, I went up to the apartment door and knocked on it. At first I thought no one was home, but finally my father opened the door. I knew he was my father, but not from the features that most people would notice first.

"He looked like an untreated radiation victim. His hair was falling out—had fallen out—in clumps. His teeth were yellow. His cheeks were pock-marked and one eye was swollen shut." I had to take another few deep breaths before I continued.

"Beyond him, I could see the woman I assumed was my mother. She was sitting on a ragged reclining chair so ripped up the frame showed through most everywhere. She was watching a screen a meter away. The image was black and white, and the forward dimension had shrunk so far that all the proportions were distorted. She stared at the screen like she was in a coma. She never looked toward the door.

"My father said, 'yes?' He obviously had no clue who I was, so his mind must not have been functioning any better than the rest of his body. My hand was in my pocket, and I felt my gun, but my fingers were numb. I couldn't do it. I couldn't do anything except mumble something like, 'Sorry. Wrong apartment.' And then I went away.

"I came back the next morning and waited all day for him to come outside. He never did. I came back the next day and waited again. He finally came out that afternoon and walked down to a neighborhood bar. On his way back, I took his picture."

After I was quiet for a long time, trying to retrieve my strength, wondering why I had told Tara all of this, she said, "Why?"

"Why the picture? You know, I'm still not really sure. Maybe to help me keep the hate alive no matter how old I get. Or maybe to help convince myself that whatever they did, they did because they had no choice. Or maybe to see what I could become if I'm not careful. Maybe to convince myself that even though I've killed, I'm still a decent person —you know, that I didn't take revenge when I had the opportunity. I just don't know. I just don't know."

My awareness lurched from that gray day back to the present and I realized I sounded like a little boy. I took a deep breath and drew my shoulders back. I rubbed my hands together nervously.

Tara said, "If I'd had any idea how much telling me this would put you through, I wouldn't have asked. But I'm glad I know."

"Why? What am I to you?" I looked at Tara's hand still on my arm and then looked back into her eyes. Those deep-blue eyes didn't contain the slightest trace of mischievousness, but rather seemed to reflect the hurt I realized I still felt after all these years.

Tara withdrew her hand. "What was that little girl to you? The one who was so grateful."

"Just someone in pain."

"Does it need to be anything more complex than that?"

"I suppose not. But I didn't think my pain showed that much."

"With the way you hold yourself back from people, even though you're perceptive and you obviously care about what you see?"

I forced a grin and I said, "I'm tough. I'll survive."

Tara nodded slowly and she gave me a weak, wry grin. "Yes, but keeping it all inside is just going to turn you into a burned-out hulk. Kind of a human black hole."

"I'm fine. Really." I put on my reassuring expression. But I didn't feel fine. I felt lonely. And I realized that I had felt lonely for a long time, without realizing precisely where the source of the pain was.

"You're not fooling anybody, you know. But if you want a shoulder to cry on sometime, I'll be around."

I was well aware of how strong my inhibition against crying was, and I was also belatedly aware of how close I had come to actually crying in front of her. Somehow, she gave me the feeling that crying didn't need to be a sign of weakness, but rather simply a product of pain. "I'll keep it in mind. I—"

"What?"

"Nothing."

"What were you going to say?"

"Just that—that Wade must be a very stupid person."

Again she instantly followed the twisted path and caught up with my thoughts. "Well, if he is, that's his problem, isn't it?"

"Maybe you're the one who could use a shoulder to cry on."

She shook her head lightly, her hair brushing her shoulders. "If you're all right, I'm all right." But as she said it, I could see the pain in her eyes and the tiny furrow in her brow, and I wondered if I was just as transparent. Or whether she even expected me to believe her.

"You know," Tara said suddenly, as if deliberately trying to switch the subject. "I'll bet you see yourself as a logical person. With logical reasons for doing most of the things you do."

"I suppose so," I said, unsure where she was heading.

"I'd also be willing to bet that you make more decisions based on feelings than on logic. And then you backfill—you look for logical rationales you can use to back up those decisions in case anyone questions them."

"That's ab—" I stopped in mid-denial, slowed by thinking about how accurate some of Tara's other perceptions had seemed. And, as I sat silently, I realized I felt intuitively that she was correct once again. Finally I said, "Maybe. Maybe you're right." And even as I spoke, I felt the conviction that she *was* right.

"Jason," Tara went on, "I'm not sure why—"

She was interrupted by the door sliding open. "You're not sure why what?" Daniel asked. Apparently he had finished his nap. He looked clear-eyed and more alert than before.

"She's not sure why everyone's convinced that homo sapiens evolved from apes," I said. "Some of us seem to have evolved from snakes."

Daniel's nap must have also restored some of his tolerance, because he didn't react. He just said, "It's time to go back to the bridge."

At least we didn't have to go back to the galley.

"The transmissions have stopped," Wade said.

I wondered if Wade thought that meant the transmitter was dead. From Tara's comments to me earlier, that probably only meant the ship carrying Marj Lendelson had translated to layer ten for a hyperspace jaunt long enough to make things difficult for potential followers. I said, "The chime never sounds when you're waiting for a call, does it? Does that mean we're free to go?"

"Not quite yet. It means I want you to maneuver us into the position we received the last transmission from. Their ship must have entered hyperspace. When they come out and the transmitter starts functioning normally again, the first transmission should give us an accurate course to Xanahalla."

I moved to the console and reached toward the controls.

"Not so fast," Wade moved to my side. "I want you to explain each step before you take it."

"Why don't you just do it yourself? Not that I'm trying to talk you into that. I'm just curious."

Wade stared at the star chart for a moment before he said, "You and Razzi have managed to convince me how easy it is to make mistakes. I'm not one to butt my head against the same wall for very long. But don't assume that gives you licence to stray from what I tell you to do. I have Razzi's directions for this next maneuver, and they'd better exactly match what you do, a step at a time."

Carefully, I guided the *Redshift* to the coordinates of Marj's last transmission. Before each step I told Wade what I was about to do, and why. Before some of the steps I told him a few of the common errors that trainees frequently made, and their results. Even though he had said he was convinced he wasn't ready to be a pilot, nothing could be lost by driving the point home.

Minutes later the journey was complete and Wade looked satisfied. He gestured overly politely for me to have a seat. He took a seat and leaned back. "Now we wait."

I sat next to Tara. She seemed to be taking the day in stride. At the moment I couldn't think of anything I wanted to ask her that I didn't mind Wade overhearing. With no external situation to respond to, I suddenly realized how tired I was. I closed my eyes.

I dreamed about what it would have been like to be living in the apartment on Transom Five where I had found my father and mother. The dream no doubt distorted reality in more ways than I realized upon waking later, primarily because the only information I had on what family life was supposed to be like came from overheard conversations; I had never asked anyone direct questions about normal childhood from fear of having to explain why I had asked.

My father wore the uniform of a sentry on Redwall. My mother sat mesmerized before a dim, flickering screen. My father stood up and said, "Go get me a case of five-star from the bar." He belched loudly and unabashedly.

I said, "You want a drink, go get it yourself."

"Get me a drink, you lazy brat, or I'll sell you to Redwall. You'll pray for a day you only have to do things as simple as fetch me a drink."

I rose from the chair I had been slouched in and I moved wearily toward the door. I turned the knob and swung open the door. There in the dim hallway was the kid I had killed on Redwall, risen from the grave, twice as massive as before, four times as ugly, with yellowish-brown slime dripping off his wet hair, down his cheeks, and onto his jacket. His glazed eyes stared sightlessly at me.

He held something concealed behind his back. The tip that showed over his shoulder reminded me of the whips. He smiled at me, a vile, chilling mockery of a smile. "Can Jason come out and play?" he asked sweetly.

"Jason. Jason, are you all right?"

My eyes flashed open and I realized Tara was shaking my shoulder. I was back aboard the bridge of the *Redshift.*

"Sure," I said, wiping grit from my eyes. "Just reminiscing."

"Just—" She stopped and swallowed. "You sounded as though—"

"Pleasant dreams?" Wade interjected, looking at me smugly. Probably he never had bad dreams.

"Yeah," I said. "I dreamed I was in an alternate universe where I was in door-to-door sales."

Wade lost his smug look and his expression turned thoughtful. "You know, that reminds me of an idea I had and then forgot about. The ship we're following is probably going to be in hyperspace for another day or two if it's on about the same schedule as the one that took Tara there. What's to stop us from accelerating to near the speed of light, to slow down our rate of time? That way we could reduce the wait to a few minutes or hours."

I took my time in answering. I had thought about that possibility earlier, but had decided against mentioning it so I could have as much time as possible to think of a way out of this mess. So far I had thought of nothing that seemed to hold out hope. And I was still groggy enough from my sleep that I couldn't think of a convincing lie. I hesitated.

Finally I said, "Nothing, I suppose, except energy. We normally do between .8 and .9 c to minimize time dilation, and to conserve energy."

"How fast could we go and still keep an adequate energy supply?"

"It's not just how fast; it's also how many starts and stops. They're what cost energy. We could probably get up to .99 c and stop again a few dozen times before we started to significantly reduce our available power. And .99 c gets us down to about a seventh of normal time."

Wade thought about it and then said, "So a half-hour out at that speed and a half-hour back puts us right here in an hour of our time, but seven hours will have gone by for stationary observers?"

"Assuming we don't smash into another ship while we're zipping along." I looked around the bridge. Tara still sat next to me, and Daniel sat on her other side. Daniel looked confident, his arms crossed on his chest. The guards had been changed. Of all the people nearby, the guards were undoubtedly the ones Wade most wanted alert. One of the replacement guards was the stern woman from our galley tour. She looked disapprovingly at me, as though one of the dead black-suits had been more than merely a professional associate.

Wade said, "Everyone always talks about how vast space is. I hope you're not trying to tell me it's actually likely that we would have the incredible misfortune to actually run into another ship."

"Hyperspace layer ten is a lot smaller than normal space. That's why we can make good speed even at only eight or nine meters per second. The speed of light gets slower as you get farther from normal space, but the fact that corresponding distances shrink even faster is what makes travel here worthwhile. Speed-of-light travel effectively doubles its pace for each layer you move to. Here in layer ten, the improvement amounts to a factor of 1024. So we're probably at least 1024 times as likely to run into another ship. Of course the initial odds are small enough that the new probability is still fairly small."

"Pick a direction you think is the safest and let's go."

I still could think of no major objection, so I pushed my chair to the console and locked it into the floor sockets. While Wade watched over my shoulder and I kept him informed of each step, I called up a display of all scheduled hyperspace routes. Wishing we could use holograms instead of the flat screen, I plotted a sphere around our current location, a sphere with a radius of three and a half light-hours.

"This sector looks the cleanest," I said, after I had rotated the display enough to get a good feel for where we were.

"Fine with me," Wade said. "Go ahead. We'll start a pattern. One hour traveling, one hour back here, waiting for a signal. We'll repeat until we hear from Marj."

I added a vector to the plot, showing our intended route, and turned on the drive. The display that had read zero rose rapidly to .8, and then began to slow, asymptotically approaching .99. "We're on the way."

Wade said, "I still have a hard time getting used to accelerating without feeling it."

"We're moving, whether you can feel it or not. You see the velocity display. And you can see the clocks." I pointed above the large star chart display. Our subjective-time ship's master clock counted its normal leisurely pace, second after second, but the time displays for the ports on our original route were decidedly fast. The second's one's digits flickered, and the ten's digits counted almost as fast as the one's digits normally did.

Time flies by when you're on the run.

"What happened after I left you at the pool?" I asked Tara. "When you were just coming around?"

Tara and I had been shuttled back to the break room, while Wade presumably asked Razzi to confirm what I had done on the bridge. I had told him the truth. There was no point in lying until I could see an advantage in doing so, and I might have a better chance when I needed it, if I could build up at least a moderate sense of security.

"Don't you ever quit?" Tara asked, but she had apparently adjusted to my string of questions, because she gave me another weak grin and began to talk with no prodding. "While my head was still clearing, Wade was beginning to come to. I showed him the knife you gave me, so he wouldn't try to fight his way out unarmed, and I told him what you had told me. I stood up and it was then I saw the man in the pool. I suppose I was a little slow in reacting, because I was just realizing that the man in the pool must have been dead when Wade took the knife out of my hand and went to a comm panel. At the time, I thought Wade was adjusting to it all faster than I was because the drug's effects had left him earlier than me.

"He called the bridge, I think, and said something like, 'We've got a problem at the pool. Send everyone up here.' Whatever he said didn't feel exactly right, but I was still confused enough not to spend time worrying about it. Several of the other passengers were coming around, so I helped some of them.

"Wade waited at the door. When the others arrived, several of them made for the rear door. Do you remember what happened when you opened the door?"

"Yes. I suppose he had sent someone around the back way to cut off my escape path, but I never found out."

"Anyway, as soon as they knocked you out, everyone on the team but Wade went through the door. When some of the passengers finally thought about trying the door, it wouldn't open. But even as they were finding that out, Wade was pushing me toward the front door.

"I suppose I realized before he got me out of the room that he must be involved in whatever was happening, but I didn't want to believe it. So I went with him, wishing this was all some terrible dream. When we reached the hallway and someone I didn't recognize, wearing a black suit, let us out and then locked the door on the rest of the passengers, I couldn't pretend any longer. But I was also in no position to get away. Of course I tried, but Wade and two of his friends were too strong for me. Probably I was still a little stunned anyway."

"Do you have any idea why Wade was there? Why he wasn't taken to the bridge?"

"I think it was just his way of being thorough. I heard them talking later, and I assume he wanted someone on his team to be there when people woke up so he could listen to initial reactions and find out if he was overlooking anything. The person needed to be one of the team who was also a passenger. That meant him or Daniel, and apparently he decided to be the one. I assume he would have got the two of us out after a little while. You just accelerated his plans."

"Just like I did again."

"You mean speeding to cut down on the waiting time?"

I nodded.

"Why were you so cooperative? Wouldn't it be better to have as much delay as possible?"

"Maybe, but this way gives us one small possible relief. We're traveling one hour on and one hour off. With the seven-to-one speedup, that means, for seven hours out of every eight for an observer at slow speed, we won't be listening for Marj Lendelson's transmissions. That also means that, if at some point after their ship comes out of hyperspace the crew finds her transmitter and destroys it, we might be lucky enough not to hear another transmission. And if Wade has to search a sphere in space with a radius of—let's see—say two light-days times 1024 is over five light-years—a sphere with a five-light-year radius in a region of space this dense, he'll need a great deal more time than he's got available before people come looking for us."

"You must have played a lot of games where you have to bluff. When he asked you about his idea and you agreed that it might be possible, your expression made me think things had gone from bad to worse, but you were trying to keep your anxiety hidden."

"That's a relief."

"That Wade didn't understand?"

"That you didn't. No one before you has seen so clearly into what I am." I grinned. "A person likes to have a little privacy."

Tara looked at me for several seconds, and, as she did, the mischievousness I had observed earlier resurfaced. Her lips slowly formed a delicate smile and her eyes regained their animation. In a different environment, I might have guessed that she was searching for a practical joke to play, or looking for someone to tease. I found myself marveling at her resilience. And I found myself liking her more by the minute. My grin must have widened, because she said, "What?" and cocked her head at me.

"Nothing."

She shook her head lightly, indicating she didn't believe me.

I said, "Do you have a lot of friends on Xanahalla?"

She hesitated, no doubt considering pressing her question. "Some. One that I expected to be there left before I arrived."

"Anyone special?"

"Not that special. A girl I grew up with went there, or so I was told before I decided to go. I was looking forward to seeing her again, but I guess she must have reached the same conclusion that I eventually did: the real world is more exciting."

"So you've never wished you were back there? I somehow had that impression."

"Now and then I've thought about going back, particularly, I suppose, when things were rough between Wade and me. Maybe what you said before is true. Maybe I was looking for a way to check out, to avoid facing problems. It is a tempting alternative sometimes."

"Like suicide?" I still felt stupid for having misread what happened to Jenni Sonders.

"Perhaps. Or at least I can empathize with someone who might choose that way out when the world seems too intimidating. When it seems like there's never any way to be happy. But you've never been tempted to give up, have you? You've struggled out of a pit that most people would keep falling back into."

"Yeah, and look how happy I am."

"Sure, you may not be all that happy right now, but I bet you get a certain satisfaction from your job. And you probably keep hoping that you'll be happier someday, don't you?"

In another of those unconscious admissions, I looked directly into Tara's deep-blue eyes and I said, "You've got me there."

Back on the bridge, I piloted the ship back to the point where Marj Lendelson's last transmission had originated and we stopped. In the hour we waited for a signal, we detected nothing. As they say, no news is good news.

. . .

Two subjective hours later, or about eight real-time hours later, we had still heard nothing. Too bad I couldn't get the ship up to .99999 c without Wade noticing. That way we'd skip about nine days for each travel hour. Maybe Marj's transmitter would be discovered by then. Of course the paying passengers would be even later when they finally reached their destinations. Anyone currently drawing a real-time salary might not be too disappointed, though.

After three more cycles of leave-return-listen, I was starting to believe there was cause for hope that the transmitter had indeed been found and turned off. I was also starting to feel like a yo-yo.

"Maybe Marj forgot to take the transmitter with her," I suggested. We were listening during our seventh rest period, still with no results. "Is she a forgetful person?"

"Hardly," Wade said.

"Well, you know how it is when you pack in a hurry sometimes. I know once I forgot to pack my—"

"That's enough, Jason."

"Or maybe she packed a transmitter, but not the one you planned on. Maybe Marj is really working for someone else. Maybe right now some other team is on their way there, homing in on the—"

"Stop it!" Wade rose suddenly from his chair and moved toward me. He curled and uncurled his fingers agitatedly, and I realized I had a hit a sensitive area. Either he really was worried about Marj Lendelson's loyalty, or he was worried about her safety. He calmed down even as he approached, though. By the time he stood next to me, he appeared relaxed again, and he said quietly, "I don't want to hear anything else unrelated to navigation until we pick up her transmission."

That was fine with me. I needed another nap anyway.

Less than four subjective hours later, the console beeped again—the distinctive long-short-long sequence that told all of us on the bridge that Marj Lendelson's transmitter unfortunately still worked. When the beep sounded, I could all too easily recall how I had felt when a Redwall customer expressed interest in me, and the chime by my bunk indicated that the lull was over.

= **10** =

A Hyperspace Odyssey

Under Wade's careful supervison, I entered the direction from which Marj Lendelson's transmission had come into the star chart and then plotted a vector from our current position. Until we moved the *Redshift* and got a second observation, I couldn't get a fix on the exact location, but we already had enough information to follow them and spot-check any planetary systems along the vector.

Wade knew all this, too, but he obviously wanted me to think aloud as I planned our next jump.

"All right," I said. "Worst case: they didn't care about time dilation. Even though I don't think they'd want to ignore it, they could have gone to hyperspace, pushed their ship as fast as their power allows, maybe seven 9s or better, and they would have reached their destination with very little subjective time having elapsed, but having lots of our real-time elapse. The fact that we received the transmission this soon puts a limit on their travel time and speed. Ignoring how fast their time went, given the fact that this last transmission was sent in layer fifteen, and transmissions are thirty-two times faster in layer fifteen, then the farthest they could have gone is the equivalent of—about forty hours at the speed of light in layer fifteen, which amounts to—150 light-years in normal space."

Wade whistled.

I said, "Maybe even more, if they were going downhill."

Wade said, "What?"

"Joke. Never mind. If instead they went to hyperspace immediately after the earlier transmission and exited just before this one was sent, but they ran at .9 c, then they would have gone only a little over ten light-years. Or they could have dawdled and gone only a couple of light-years. If we head for a point about ten light-years in their direction of motion, and about ten light-years off their course, we should be able to get an easy fix."

"Sounds reasonable to me," Wade said. "How long will that take us?"

"Fourteen-plus light-years at 1024 times c is—about 120 real-time hours. How long do you want to spend?"

"I'm still adjusting to this. Tell me the options."

"All right. Our typical .9 c compresses time by 2.3 so it would take us —fifty-plus hours. Two 9s brings it down to—seventeen hours. Three 9s —a little over five. Four 9s, about an hour and three quarters." I didn't point out that no matter how slim we cut our subjective time, real-time would still advance the full 120 hours, giving us that much more opportunity for Marj Lendelson's transmitter to be discovered and eliminated. And that much more time for anyone searching for the *Redshift*.

"Four 9s, which I assume means .9999 c, sounds good," Wade said. "That won't cut our energy reserves too close?"

"We'll be fine."

"Let's go." This time, Wade didn't get Razzi back to double-check.

We screeched to a halt, figuratively speaking, less than two subjective hours later, and began to listen again. I was glad their receiver couldn't hear transmissions whenever we traveled fast enough to make subjective time less than half of real-time, but that fact turned out not to be very helpful. Not more than ten minutes after we stopped, we heard Marj Lendelson's transmitter again.

"Terrific," Wade said. He looked around at his team and rubbed his hands. I couldn't believe he actually rubbed his hands.

Apparently the entire team, or at least what was left of it, was on the bridge. Besides Wade and Daniel were six other people all dressed in black. I felt like I was at a funeral, and I didn't want to think about whether the funeral was past or future, or whose it was.

I plotted the new vector on the screen. Apparently Marj Lendelson's source of transportation had stopped, because the old and new vectors intersected near a star system about twenty-five light-years away.

From force of habit, I said, "Bearing three five zero lateral, four two up. Range oh two four point seven oh," but there was no one on the bridge capable of confirmation.

I indicated the coordinates to the ship's computer, and a full-page summary came up on a nearby screen.

G-type star, four planets, one ringed, controlling interest owned by Third World, Incorporated, cataloged over a hundred years ago, no population except a mining colony, no facilities for repair of large spacecraft. No services.

Presently Wade said, "Let's go, Jason. Four 9s." He had been reading over my shoulder. I hate it when people do that.

The three-hour journey went fairly quickly for us. Marj Lendelson, on the other hand, would probably be wondering why we were taking our time; for her about thirteen days would have passed—four on our position-fixing run and nine more on the way from there to Xanahalla. Bad times go slower than good ones anyway, so she'd probably be really irritable when we finally showed up.

Since I had awakened the first time, Wade had always been in a fairly good mood. By the time I halted the *Redshift,* he was almost jovial. After a half-hour of low-speed navigation, he came down from his high.

By then we realized that Marj Lendelson's transmitter had stopped.

"Does that matter to you?" I asked Wade. "This has got to be the place." On our primary screen there was a large image picked up by our layer-zero scanners. The ringed planet in the screen's center was close enough that the flat sides of the screen clipped off part of the rings.

Wade lowered his voice slightly. "You have no call to be condescending, Jason. I understand loyalty as well as you. The transmitter failure will make it more difficult to locate Marj so we can get her back, but we'll do it." He didn't look in Tara's direction.

What I really wondered, and what Wade didn't mention, was what had caused the transmitter to stop or fail.

"Take us in for a closer look," Wade said.

We were far enough away for the rings to look solid, but two wide divisions and several more narrow divisions stood out. The left hemisphere was in night. The rings' narrow shadow split the right half of the hemisphere. I started us moving closer. Stellar images moved faintly behind the rings, like dim pinpricks of lights in distant rain. Finally, the planet's disk grew to the point that its edges almost touched the four sides of the screen.

Daniel broke his long silence. "Look, there." He walked to the screen and pointed at the planet's surface in the upper-right quadrant. He had to stretch to reach.

Where he pointed, a spark of light glinted from a structure on the surface. I assumed that from this distance the reflection could only be from the Tower of Worship.

"Take us closer to that point," Wade said.

The planet's surface began to turn under us as I changed our direction of motion. We were already close enough to the ground to be under the innermost ring, so I didn't have to worry about layer-zero scanners being smashed as they poked their eyes into layer zero and then whipped back to report what they had seen.

We came closer to the point where the reflected light had originated. Surrounding the general area was a roughly circular patch of land a darker shade than the outlying regions. Clouds were building to the north.

I glanced back at Tara. Even if I hadn't known from her description that we had found the right place, I surely would have known from her pallor and from her unblinking staring at the screen. I didn't even have the beginnings of a plan that would help her friends without harming the ship's crew.

By the time the circular area around the Tower of Worship filled the screen, the Tower was clearly visible, slightly to the north of the rings' shadow. It poked up from the flat terrain like a tack. I stopped the ship again, waiting for further instructions. As I watched the screen, the Tower and its surrounding land began to move off the screen.

"What's the problem?" Wade asked.

"You're going to need to be more specific," I said, sure of what he was concerned about, and fairly sure I could take another opportunity to convince him that he shouldn't try to navigate the ship.

"Is the planet turning under us that fast? Why is our view shifting so fast?"

"No. The planet's in orbit around its sun." I made a quick check. "It's doing about a hundred thousand kilometers an hour. Its rotation rate causes a point on its surface to move probably only one percent of that. To track a spot on the surface, we'll have to move in a helix. A curved helix traveling around that sun."

Wade grimaced. "But you do that all the time with orbital docks."

"Sure. Those docks are equipped with positioning beacons that the *Redshift* can lock onto. These folks probably didn't have your visit in mind when they decided not to equip the planet with docking facilities. Or maybe they did have you in mind. At any rate, we can program the *Redshift* to maneuver periodically to match orbit with Xanahalla. And we can program it to superimpose a smaller circle, to account for the planetary rotation, but if we get closer and you want the ship held accurately so it coexists with a specific spot on the ground then you'd better plan on an experienced navigator devoting 110 percent to the job.

And you'd better not interrupt whoever is doing the station-keeping. Otherwise, instead of translating onto a solid floor, you're more likely to find yourself with a ten-meter drop, or finding your legs commingling with solid rock."

Wade never looked away from the screen but when I stopped he said, "Point taken."

Daniel approached Wade and the two moved to a corner to confer in private. I tried to give Tara a reassuring look, but she was still staring at the screen with that troubled expression on her face. When the two men had finished their talk, Wade came back and said, "All right, Jason. Let's take her down for a closer look."

First I made an approximation for Xanahalla's orbital velocity and shape and then fed commands into the console. Next I gave the ship a rough guess for the planet's rotation rate. As long as I limited myself to navigation commands, Wade didn't object and he didn't require an explanation for every tiny action. If my hands had come near the communication panel, I'm sure he would have been more interested. Even then he might not have gotten too excited; he had taken the precaution of spreading tape over the control surfaces.

We hung approximately fifty kilometers over Xanahalla's surface, sitting comfortably in layer ten, looking out on the view from layer zero. Those on the ground would have no clue to our presence unless they had equipment sensitive enough to notice our tiny scanners as they made their oscillatory journeys to and fro between our layer and normal space. From up close, the only thing a human eye would see was a flickering grid of fourteen tiny dots, each as hard to make out as a centimeter of spider-web strand in dim light.

Satisfied with my initial approximations, I started the *Redshift* moving toward Xanahalla. The image on the screen grew quickly despite my widening the viewing angle. If the ship had trembled and shuddered the way an atmospheric craft did, the illusion of falling out of control toward the ground would have been complete. Conversation halted as I pulled the ship to a panic stop near what had been a white patch near the edge of the circle, no more than a half-kilometer in the air. In the sudden silence, I heard Daniel swallow.

Below us spread a spaceport with a pair of shuttle-landing strips in good repair, edged by low-lying vegetation. A taxiway connected the strips, forming a large "H." To one side of the "H," two modest rectangular buildings were the focus of casual activity. A shuttle rested on the taxiway near one of the buildings. Three people were walking slowly toward the shuttle. The scene was crisp. Features had sharp edges that our former distance had softened.

I moved us toward the ground at a more leisurely pace. A moment later, the screen showed a view of the shuttle from a perspective of a few meters off the ground. Except for the fact that the scene was flat and in black and white, we could have been looking through a window. I could see some minor heat discoloration on the shuttle's hull.

I refrained from moving the ship and just watched the screen. We began to drift away from and to the left of the shuttle. I made better approximations for keeping in sync with a point on the planet's surface and our rate of drift slowed. Finally I gave the *Redshift* a very slow spin, to correspond roughly with Xanahalla's rotation rate.

After positioning the *Redshift* so we faced the spire in the distance, I said, "I think this is your stop."

Wade said, "Tara, it's time you played a more active role. Sit over here, would you please?" Wade's phony courtesy was wasted. Tara probably wouldn't have looked any more displeased if Wade had said, "Get over here and help me find my lover." She remained sitting where she had been.

Wade tried again. "Tara, move over here now." He gestured to the chair next to mine. She ignored him.

He walked over and stood in front of her chair. I thought perhaps he would either threaten her or pull her by the wrist. Instead, his hand flashed red as it moved away from me and he backhanded Tara across the face, hard enough to knock her from the chair.

Her groan reached me a second later. By then I was moving toward Wade. He was offering her a hand up when I reached him and said, "Touch her again and you're going to have to activate my collar."

The guards at the edges of the room were totally alert. Daniel backed away so the guards could watch me carefully. Tara held a hand to her cheek and looked up at me worriedly. Wade's surprised expression gave way to amusement. After a moment he said, "Get her in that chair and we won't have a problem."

I offered Tara my hand, which she accepted. We went to the chairs at the main console and she silently took a seat to my left. A bruise was already forming on her cheek.

I was angry with myself for not going ahead and striking Wade regardless of the consequences, even though I knew intellectually that action would cost far more than it gained. And I was angry for exposing a potential weakness to Wade, a weakness he could conceivably capitalize on later. Then I saw Tara's grateful glance at me and I remembered the girl on Redwall, and my anger faded away like a disintegrating shadow.

I looked back at the screen as Wade sat down on the far side of Tara. We had drifted a few meters up from the surface, so I made another correction. Daniel took a seat on my right.

Wade looked back at the screen and said, "Why is this screen black and white? Is that a lot cheaper?" I heard faint anger behind the question, as though the limitation wouldn't have bothered him if he weren't irritated by something else. That was the only clue I had to indicate the scene just now had bothered him at all.

I said, "It's not a question of cost. It's a question of practicality. Since light increases its frequency as it drops, the hues on the screen would vary depending on how high your eyes were off the floor. No two people would be guaranteed to see the same view, and, if you optimized it for one person, the hues would be wrong for everyone else."

Wade absorbed that for a moment and then said, "All right. The first order of business is to locate Marj. What's the best way to do that?"

I thought Tara might refuse again, but evidently the act of locating Marj didn't seem to her as disloyal as helping Wade find the best way to retrieve the contents of the vault in the spire on the horizon.

"The Tower has a large wall map on the floor just below ground level. Beside it is a master directory of the residents. If Jason can pilot us there and we can look at the map, it will tell us where Marj Lendelson is living. She should certainly have been assigned quarters by now if she's been here over a week by their time."

"Well, Jason?" Wade said.

I made another correction to reduce our drift. "It's possible. Not trivial, but possible. The fact that matter exists in layer zero has no affect on us here in layer ten. The only real complication is viewing. The scanners oscillate back and forth between here and there. As long as they're going into vacuum or atmosphere, no problem. If they sense mass in layer zero, they don't go all the way, so they're protected. But if they translate into layer zero and a mass comes along while they're still there, they're gone. If you want me to navigate the ship while we're superimposed on a large enclosed room, I can probably do it. If you want me to follow a corridor, you'd better not distract me, and even then I might not be able to do it."

"It's a large room," Tara said. "High ceiling, walls far apart, with connecting tunnels leading out of it. The room is part of the hub that connects the underground walkways leading into the residential areas."

"All right," I said. "I'll give it a try." I proceeded to turn off all but one scanner. Having the normal array would just give me more equipment to worry about damaging. That way, if one got bumped into a wall in layer zero, we had thirteen backups. I told Wade what I was doing so he didn't panic.

I also put on command goggles. Maneuvering that tightly didn't allow for any communication lags. The viewer before my eyes gave me a color view of what I had seen on the main screen. Now the vegetation that had appeared to be dried out or dormant came alive in vivid greens, blues, yellows, and browns.

Most of the ground was covered with a grass-substitute from one of the outer colonies. Thick, short, yellow tendrils reached upward from a layer so dense it looked like carpet. To the right was a red-barked, thick-trunked growth that could have passed for a truly enormous cauliflower with a long stem.

I jogged the controls, pleased at the increased responsiveness, and we rose over the nearby trees. We began to move toward the spire on the horizon, the Tower of Worship. Through the clear air, I could see a rainbow arcing over the Tower of Worship. No moisture showed on the horizon, so the residents must have, for whatever reasons, been using an elaborate, high-power hologram.

Greenery and brownery flashed past as we glided smoothly toward the Tower of Worship. We traveled about a third of the distance without seeing any fabrications, and then we started seeing occasional dwellings nestled among large growths of exotic plants, many of which grew taller than the cottages.

About halfway to the Tower of Worship, interference began to show up in the viewer. The farther we went, the worse the distortion grew. I stopped the ship, removed my goggles, and looked at the black-and-white image on the main screen. It, too, was afflicted.

I moved us nearer the spire and the interference worsened.

"What's the problem?" Wade asked.

"Disrupter," I said, happy to find an obstacle in Wade's path. "I guess these folks aren't quite so unprepared as you thought."

"What's a disrupter?" Daniel asked at the same moment that Wade said, "Damn!"

This was interesting. Evidently Wade hadn't shared his entire knowledge with Daniel. I filed that scrap of information and answered Daniel's question. After I had told him the general idea, I added, "At this range, it's barely possible to translate safely. If we were close enough to the disrupter for the screen to be about half obscured by interference, anyone translating from here to layer zero would wind up with an expected lifetime measured maybe in weeks. Much closer in, and a translated body might still be recognizably human, but it wouldn't be living."

"You suppose the focus is the Tower?" Wade said.

"Seems likely," I said. "We can find out." I started the *Redshift* moving at right angles to our first course and tried to maneuver so that the amount of interference on the screen remained approximately the same. By the time we had traveled almost ten kilometers along a circle with the Tower of Worship at its center, the assumption was confirmed.

I said to Wade, "I'm sure that if you give yourselves up now, before any of the passengers or crew have been killed, that you'll fare better than if you let things get out of hand."

"Things won't get out of hand. We've got weapons aboard. But thank you for your concern. It's quite touching." Apparently Wade had totally recovered from the discovery of the disrupter. His voice was sarcastic and controlled, with just a hint of anticipation. Maybe, aside from the risk, he somehow preferred a direct confrontation rather than a quiet hit and run.

"Is there another roster?" he asked Tara.

"Several, farther out from the Tower. But they're all in the interconnecting tunnels. One's in the main tunnel between the Tower and the spaceport."

At Wade's request, I reversed our path, moving farther from the Tower to keep from destroying the scanner that was still shuttling in and out of layer zero. As long as we were above ground, I flipped on a second scanner directly opposite the main view and inserted a small image from it in an upper corner of the screen. After a short trip, the distant Tower was centered in the screen and the spaceport showed in the rearview image.

"All right," I said. "If you can show me the tunnel entrance at the spaceport, we can try to follow it."

Tara was silent for a moment. My goggles prevented me from looking at her to get a clue to her reaction. Then she said, "Passages to the surface are spaced out all along the main tunnel. I can't see where one comes out right now, but if you move slowly toward the tower I'll probably spot one."

I put us in motion and the ground below slowly passed under our view. No more than a minute later, Tara said, "There's one."

I said, "If you're pointing, it's not doing me any good. What quadrant of the screen is it in?"

"Upper left."

I saw nothing. "All right. Divide that quadrant into quadrants. What smaller quadrant is it in?"

"Lower right. It's at the base of that large Radalla tree."

"At the base of that monster cauliflower? All right. I see it." She had seen in a black-and-white view what I could barely make out in a color display.

I moved us closer until the large trunk of the Radalla loomed in the view screen. I said, "If you want me to go down there, you're going to have to avoid distracting me. I can handle 'left,' 'right,' and maybe a few others like 'stop' and 'surface,' but if you want me to respond to a large vocabulary down there, you've got the wrong person. What do you say?"

Wade said, "Let's go. All we want for now is directions to wherever Marj is staying. As soon as that's done, we'll come back up and figure out the next step."

I turned off the rear-view scanner and turned on video recording. "I'll have to shut down the scanner if we have to go through a door or wall, otherwise we may lose it." I moved closer to the door. Its rectangular outline showed against the brown-and-gray gnarled surface of the tree's trunk. The door matched the tree in texture and color.

"Just like Winnie-the-Pooh," Tara said softly.

"Is it important that I know the reference?" I asked.

"No. Just an idle thought."

I made a final correction to minimize drift, failing to improve it. I drew a deep breath and leaned forward. "Here we go."

I edged us closer and flipped off the scanner for what I hoped was the right interval. When I flipped it back on, we could see inside. A spiral staircase led downward into the planet. Fortunately, the center column was empty; I could never have navigated around that spiral and compensated for drift at the same time. Our scanner dropped straight down the column, the image of the stairs rising before our eyes.

We reached the bottom of the stairs and I kept my hands on the controls, constantly correcting for drift so we wouldn't push through one of the walls and risk destroying the scanner. I pivoted to face another doorway.

We moved forward, blanked, and "opened our eyes" again. This time we were in a tunnel. Tara hadn't used the word very loosely at all. Instead of what I had imagined—a long, straight corridor stretching to infinity—the tunnel had curved, irregular walls and a curved ceiling. The tunnel was roughly circular, but with a flat yellow floor patterned by small rectangular tiles. The path the tunnel took through the ground was curved also; the view ahead was obscured by a turn to the left. In some ways, it wasn't all that much of a change from the *Redshift.*

I swiveled the view around 360 degrees. The door leading to the spiral staircase was lettered "5.70 W." Shortly after the view pointed down the tunnel to the right of the direction we had entered from, Tara said, "Forward."

Forward it was. What we could see of the tunnel was unoccupied. No direct lights were overhead; rather, the entire tunnel ceiling glowed softly with a pale yellow tint.

I navigated twists and turns in the tunnel as we proceeded, drifting perilously close to the walls often enough to make me tense. Not long after, we came to an intersection marked by "5.50 W."

"Just a perimeter tunnel," she said. "Straight ahead."

I followed her instructions. The interference on the screen was gradually worsening. We traveled another several minutes, seeing occasional closed doors leading off the tunnel, but seeing no people at all, and then a figure suddenly appeared around a curve ahead. He wore a flowing white robe, edged with simple black piping along the hem and sleeves.

Rather than try to keep moving along the tunnel and run blind while he passed us, I waited for him to reach us. Damage to the scanner was unlikely even if he ran into it on one of its sub-millisecond journeys into layer zero, since his body was soft, but he might feel the scanner brush against him and realize something unusual was going on, and he could alert whomever there was to alert.

So I sat there, continually readjusting our position, drifting first one direction and then another, but trying to stay centered in the tunnel. I managed to say "Know him?" as he approached.

About the same moment that Tara said, "Stranger," I had to switch off the scanner. For a second or so, I tried to repeat the cycle of course corrections that had kept us centered, and then I turned the scanner back on. A clear view stretched ahead now; the man was behind us. I resumed our journey toward the Tower of Worship. This sure was a lot of trouble to go to church.

Along the way, occasional closed doors in the side of the tunnel bore gradually decreasing numbers. We passed a few other people, a couple of whom Tara knew. The noise in the picture increased still more before we reached a larger intersection labeled "5.00." Besides the main tunnel, and a right-angle cross tunnel, a third tunnel turned the intersection into a circular, six-outlet chamber.

"Turn right," Tara said. "Wall screen."

I turned the view to the right and saw what she had led us to: a large map accompanied by a long roster of names in tiny print. The list seemed to include thousands of names.

I moved us closer to the map. It looked rather like a bull's-eye, superimposed on a cross, seen through a distorting fluid. Primary east-west and north-south tunnels met at the center of the map. Wavering rings, also presumably centered on the Tower of Worship, made additional connections, and all along almost every section of main tunnel were short offshoots, almost as though the network was some bizarre root structure and it was spreading tendrils.

At the intersection of the primary eastern tunnel and one of the large circles, a large predictable note told us, "You are here."

It was all I could do to read that large print. I couldn't read individual names on the list, even when I got still closer and the list loomed large on the viewer. We were drifting too much as I tried to keep the ship in sync with the planet. I pulled back and tried to give Wade enough information so he could review the recording I had been making.

"Recording this in memory," I said. "Still frame in reverse. Enlarge to read."

Wade understood quickly. "Where are the controls to review and enlarge?"

I felt in front of Daniel for the right sections of the console. "Playback. Magnification. Will come up on left screen."

While they looked for Marj Lendelson's address, I concentrated on hovering near a wall so no one walked into the scanner from behind me. A group of robed figures was approaching from the direction of the Tower of Worship.

"All right. You've got it," Wade said a moment later, probably talking to Daniel. "Now let's blow it up. All right. Larger. The L's are down there. Good. Lower."

Wade was silent for what seemed like a long time. The group neared the intersection.

Finally Wade said, "I don't understand. I don't see her name on the list. Tara, I thought you told me you saw your name on the list the day you got here."

"I did. They update all the wall displays as soon as a ship arrives. And, as soon as the newcomers have picked where they want to live, the display is updated with their locations. If she came here, she should be on the list."

"But she *had* to come here," Wade said, his voice rising. "The transmitter's here."

"Maybe they found it," I said. I maneuvered back into location. "Maybe expelled."

Wade was saying something angry and challenging when I caught a glimpse of a face I thought I recognized. I sucked in my breath, and I leaned forward instantly, and pointlessly. A round-faced old woman at the back of the group was turning into one of the intersecting tunnels. She wore a hood, and I had seen half of her face for only an instant, but I had to know if I was imagining things.

I moved the ship to follow her. I realized my heart was pounding. My face was hot and tingling.

Wade said, "What the hell are you doing, Jason?"

I didn't reply. I just kept moving the ship along the tunnel after the robed figures. Six or seven people were in the group, all walking rapidly. Now all I could see were their backs. Four of the group wore hoods.

"Jason, what's going on?" Wade's voice was growing more insistent and angry.

"Just a *minute,*" I said.

The figures ahead rounded a curve in the tunnel. I reached the turn and was navigating the ship around it when Wade's voice sounded louder. He must have gotten out of his chair and moved to stand next to me. "Stop us where we are. Right now."

"I will in a minute."

The group had stopped in a widened section of the tunnel. They formed a ring, facing inward. Looking this way were two of the faces of the ones who wore hoods. I started moving the ship to the left so I could see the other two faces. I had just seen another glimpse of the face when a hand smashed into my ear, knocking me to one side, and tearing the command goggles off my face.

"Try another stunt like that, Jason, and you're finished," Wade said.

"Right, sure," I said, looking up at the big screen just in time to see a black-and-white view of what I had seen a second earlier, and then we drifted out of the tunnel. The screen went black.

"Are you listening to me?" Wade demanded.

"Is there a choice?" I got my hands back on the controls and jogged the ship first one direction and then another, but either the scanner had been knocked out, or I missed the tunnel. I took my hands off the controls.

"What got into you just now?" Wade was taking this lapse in following orders quite seriously.

I glanced at Tara. She seemed puzzled and worried. She cocked her head.

I turned toward Wade. "I'm all right now. I just thought I saw someone I knew. From my childhood."

== 11 ==
Expedition to Xanahalla

Wade and Tara spoke at the same time again. Wade said, "You saw a friend you had as a kid and you almost got killed for that?"

Tara said, "Was it a friend?"

I said to Wade, "Relax. It's not going to happen again." To Tara, more softly, I said, "No. It wasn't."

Actually the face I had glimpsed probably wasn't one I had seen before. The odds were overwhelmingly against this woman being a former Redwall overseer. I had seen such a brief view, that my imagination had to be filling in most of the details. Maybe my subconscious had been stealing back to that time, refreshing even more memories than I had realized. I shivered.

"Get us back on the surface, Jason." Wade had apparently given up on getting more of an answer from me.

I took over the controls again and slowly began to relax. As we rose, I checked the status of the scanner. No good. By then it must have been a permanent speck on one of the tunnel walls on Xanahalla. After I estimated that we had risen far enough to be safely out of the planet, I switched on another scanner.

This time the view screen brightened and we could see an aerial view of the cauliflower forest. I picked the command goggles off the floor and put them on the console. They seemed undamaged.

"All right," Wade said. "I guess we'd better get on with it."

"You mean just forget about Marj?" Daniel asked.

"There's nothing we can do now, unless we make a house-to-house search, and that would take forever. Once she hears the treasury has been removed, she'll know it's time for her to leave. And she'll know how to find me."

Wade turned to me. "Move away from the console. Daniel and I have things to discuss for a few minutes."

Tara and I took seats where we had been earlier. Wade and Daniel moved to a corner and began to talk quietly. The guards watched me closely.

"It wasn't a friend?" Tara whispered. Between her eyebrows were those tiny wrinkles of concern.

I whispered back, "If she was who I thought she was, she was certainly no friend, but I must have been mistaken. I only caught a glimpse."

"Who did you *think* she was?"

"Neddi Pulmerto. An overseer on Redwall. Not just a sentry, but an owner-operator. Neddi's a power broker, always matching one need with another in any way that gets her more power and more wealth. And more pleasure."

"You reacted pretty strongly to seeing her."

I hesitated. "Some 'business people' don't involve themselves with day-to-day operations. They just, for instance, buy a wine shop, let someone else run it, and occasionally stop by for an inspection. If Redwall had been a wine shop, on Neddi's visits she would have broken open a vintage flask and sampled until she was drunk. I would have preferred a visit from an unknown customer who might well turn out to be a psychopathic slasher. But it couldn't have been her down there. I can't imagine an incident horrifying enough to make someone like her repent."

Wade and Daniel finished their conference and came over to stand near us. Wade said, "We're going down there shortly after their night starts. We should easily be able to do everything necessary before morning."

I said wearily, "Isn't it about time you just gave all this up? You can't translate to normal space anywhere near the Tower of Worship. So you'll have to walk in. All it will take is one person perceptive enough to tell a robe from a black suit, and you're finished."

"You underestimate us," Wade said. "Just because we hoped for the easiest possibility doesn't mean that's all we were prepared for. We have an ample supply of robes that will easily conceal hand weapons in shoulder holsters. You know, those large sleeves are terrific for our purpose. Besides all that, we also have a former resident who knows how to find her way around and who can help the team pass for residents."

Tara shook her head and said, "I wouldn't help you navigate to the bathroom."

"And you, Tara, underestimate the value of pain and other forms of coercion." Wade turned toward me. "And we will have a *Redshift* officer along to guarantee no tricks when the team's ready to get back aboard."

"Anyone I know?" I asked.

"You, Jason. I have this hunch that you'll be more effectively kept under control with the threat of harm to Tara. And vice versa. If either one of you tries to get away, we'll kill the other one immediately. If somehow you both manage to get away, we'll kill a dozen of the crew. But we shouldn't dwell on these negative thoughts. Just behave and everyone will be fine."

My last glimpse of the *Redshift'* s bridge before leaving for Xanahalla showed Bella and Razzi, Razzi looking unharmed but thoroughly irritated. She sat before the navigation console, a black-suit guard on either side of her. Her motions were abrupt, jerky, as though every action she took was a forceful reminder of the situation. She snapped the viewer magnification higher and then slapped her hand on the console control that would move the jump corridor slightly closer to the planet's surface.

I wouldn't have been surprised if she had been swearing out loud with each action, but the only noise coming from her direction was the occasional slap, snap, or thud.

"You be careful, Jason," she called as Wade led us out of the room.

"You, too. You could hurt yourself like that."

Daniel pushed me through the doorway. He could get himself hurt, too, but I was too busy trying to figure out the potential snags in Wade's plan.

In the corridor on level seven, one of Wade's team had already laid out robes and jumpsuits. Two of the team had stayed in the bridge, and apparently the four others besides Wade and Daniel were all who remained. Tara and I waited, under guard, as the team members stripped off shirts that had sleeves long enough to show underneath the robes. The one female team member, the woman with closely cropped blond hair, briefly turned her back to us as she changed.

Underneath their robes, they all wore two weapons, one in each of two shoulder holsters. One weapon was a needler with a choice of needles built into the handgrip: probably ranging from knock-out to killing. The second weapon was a bulky laser pistol, built to handle far more than mere flesh and bones. Wade and Daniel hung hyper-layer transmitters from their belts.

When Wade's team was ready, Tara and I were given robes. With easy grace, Tara pulled her arms inside her bathrobe until it hung around her like a cape. She donned the formal Xanahalla robe, dropping her bathrobe in a clump at her feet and then poking her arms through the enormous sleeves. Wade gave her a pair of shoes.

I removed my ripped uniform shirt, my arm stinging as the material slid over the cut. My pen fell out of the shirt pocket, so I stuck it in my back pants pocket. I started to don the robe when Wade said from behind me, "Jason, I had no idea you liked to play so rough."

Tara moved over a step when she realized Wade was looking at my back.

There was no way I was going to talk to Wade about the mass of scars nearly covering my back, or Redwall. I said, "You play your way and I'll play mine." I got the robe over my head and covering my back, but not before I heard a stifled gasp from Tara.

I didn't meet her eyes. I didn't want pity if that's what she felt. I looked back at Wade, virtually daring him to say more.

Surprisingly he dropped the subject.

All but three of the team members proceeded to don jumpsuits, making sure Tara and I were under guard the whole time.

Night was approaching on Xanahalla. It was time to move.

Wade called the bridge from a nearby comm panel. Razzi was holding the ship in position, and focusing the jump coordinates, so when we translated to layer zero, we'd have only a short fall to the ground. With beacons guiding the ship, we could have translated over and still been on the same level surface. Without beacons, we could easily wind up knee deep in the ground if we didn't allow a margin for drift. The *Redshift* mapped into about half solar-system dimensions in layer zero, so focusing our jump-point on the same place the scanners went was critical.

The first of Wade's team, a thick-chested, burly man with bushy eyebrows, twisted his helmet into place. On a signal from the bridge, Wade gestured with his upturned thumb, and the man pressed his *translate* switch. He disappeared and a second later the *pop* from air rushing in to occupy his former volume reached my ears.

Another signal from the bridge indicated the first voyager was safely out of the way, and a second jumpsuited figure disappeared.

When Tara and I were left with only Wade, the blonde, and one other black-suit, Wade handed me a jumpsuit. As I struggled to get the robe to fit inside the jumpsuit, I noticed that the chest control had been locked on *remote,* as it would be in the case where we had to transport an injured person. Wade controlled my jump; there was no way I could use the suit on my own.

Wade at least gave me the courtesy of warning me when he was going to push the switch. I didn't blink at exactly the right moment to cut off the flash of light that came simultaneously with the jump to layer zero. In the instant that my eyes started to adjust, I felt weightless. My field of view grew dim, and then I could see the ground a half-meter below me.

I dropped easily onto the yellow, vegetation-cushioned surface of Xanahalla.

Daniel was already out of his suit, no doubt having already signalled the watchers on the bridge that he was safe. I moved away from the arrival point and removed my jumpsuit. Not twenty meters away towered one of the enormous reddish-brown cauliflower trees. Cut into the trunk wall was a door. The yellow tendrils beneath my feet gave so easily I was sure I would leave a permanent trail of footprints in the crushed vegetation, but as I walked the tendrils sprang easily and firmly back into shape. The sky was a deepening mauve where the sun's disk had almost dropped below the horizon. Far overhead, the rings glistened brightly in a dark-blue sky.

I had once seen an entertainment recording of *The Wizard of Oz.* The beginning of the recording had seemed to malfunction; the view was flat. When the main character arrived at a fantastic destination, the screen suddenly bloomed into the standard full three dimensions. When I plopped into layer zero, I felt what I imagined a viewer of that recording would have felt.

Around me were more shades of green than I had probably seen in the last year. The sweet aroma in the air reminded me of the one time I had been in a greenhouse. A soft breeze gently cooled me.

As I stood there in my robe, feeling foolishly dressed, Tara popped into the air and dropped a short distance to the ground. She came close to falling over, but was able to maintain her balance. She moved aside and removed her helmet, and shook her hair free. In the dimming light, her eyes looked sad.

Soon came another *pop,* and a sagging jumpsuit flopped to the ground. Daniel pulled it from the arrival area and withdrew a small briefcase.

Three more *pops* brought Wade and the remaining two black-suits to the planet's surface. Moments later, everyone stood in a circle, all wearing robes.

"So," Wade said. "Everyone made it all right. Good." His mouth moved in unison with his words' arrival. It took me a short while to readjust to speech and sight once again being in sync. I snapped my fingers lightly, marveling at the feeling of knowing clearly which direction the sound had come from.

"One last thing before we go," he said. "The collars."

At first I thought maybe Wade meant to activate them, but he didn't. I had been wondering how he expected us to pass for normal while wearing them. Obviously, now that he was in an environment where normal weapons were more useful, the collars were not as critical as before. Daniel approached Tara and me one at a time, pushed the right switches on his wrist unit, and our collars snapped free. Two black-suits collected the pressure suits, the collars and controllers, and deposited them under a spreading, emerald-green shrub taller than I was.

The pile of gear was obviously meant for the return trip to the ship, but I wondered how many people would actually make that trip.

"Don't forget what I said earlier," Wade said, directing his comment at Tara and me.

"Something about staying with the tour guide and not getting lost, if I recall correctly," I said.

Wade looked hard at me for a moment before he said, "Close enough. Let's go."

At the base of the giant cauliflower tree, Wade opened the door and gestured for Tara to lead the way. I went next, followed by Wade and then the rest of the team. If a month ago someone had asked me what I thought I'd be doing today, descending a spiral staircase in the center of a tree, accompanied by an armed team dressed in robes and bent on stealing Xanahalla's collection plate probably wouldn't have been my first guess.

Faint echoes of our footfalls came so rapidly that at first I felt a little claustrophobic, but I told myself it was just the environment. The staircase was actually roomier than the stairwells on the *Redshift*. Being able to tell the source of sounds made me feel a little like someone who took off an eye patch that he'd worn for a long time.

The interior walls were blue, so they felt claustrophobic, too. Blue normally meant an object was approaching fast, so the walls seemed to be collapsing inward, ready to squeeze us into pulp.

Unharmed, we completed two circles and reached the floor below. The door before us, labeled "tunnel," certainly led to the main tunnel, but I noticed another door set in the side of the stairwell column. "What's that for?" I asked Tara.

"Just maintenance. Equipment storage, I assume."

I tried the door but it wouldn't slide. It wouldn't even pivot on hinges.

Wade pushed me away from the maintenance door and toward Tara. "Let's go. There isn't any mess to clean up, yet."

I had been more interested in whether it would be useful for a temporary hiding place. I had to believe Wade couldn't plan for every eventuality—or that somehow I would find a way to upset the plan. The alternative was that Tara and I were living the last few hours of our lives.

Tara slid open the door to the tunnel. We filed into the empty yellow-floored corridor and followed Tara as she turned to the right. Some of the echoes of our footfalls were long delayed, so the tunnel felt more comfortable than the stairwell had. I walked by Tara's side, and Wade's group came along behind, two by two.

Tara had been right about people retiring for the evening. We encountered no one for the first fifteen minutes of rapid walking.

The walk gave me a chance to wonder what was in Daniel's briefcase. Whatever it was, they considered it valuable enough to risk appearing slightly unusual. I glanced back and realized that the blonde must be carrying the briefcase under her robe. Her left arm was tucked inside her robe, and, as the robe swished along, the outline of the case occasionally showed.

Infrequent doors broke the tunnels walls. Some were labeled with people's names, probably indicating tunnels leading directly to cottages. Other doors were labeled with numbers and letters that, from Tara's earlier description, made them seem to be short side tunnels leading to clusters of cottages. Once in a while we passed a door that bore no designation. When I asked Tara about the blank doors, she told me they, too, led to maintenance equipment storage, or so she had been told. I irritated Wade twice by trying the doors. One door was locked; the other door opened to reveal nothing but a motionless yellow-orange autoscrubber silently charging its batteries.

Near an intersection ahead, we almost had to pass a solitary walker, but he turned into the side tunnel just as I rounded a curve. We slowed down to give him plenty of space before we passed through the intersection. It turned out we gave him more space than necessary. There was no sign of him at all. Down the side tunnel I could see a door. The door was too far away to see whatever legend it bore.

Against one wall of the intersection chamber, there was a wall screen with the list of residents. Marj Lendelson's name was still missing.

As we neared the Tower of Worship, Tara proved more and more valuable as a guide. Three- and four-tunnel intersections made navigation progressively more difficult, particularly with the tunnel twists and turns that also grew more pronounced. I felt as if I were in the enormous burrow of a drug-crazed monster rabbit.

Finally our tunnel dead-ended into the side of a straight tunnel. On the outside wall of the tunnel were numerous other tunnels, the space between them hardly wider than the tunnel mouths themselves. Along the inside of the perimeter were doors, spaced to match up with each tunnel.

"This is it," Tara said softly. "The Tower of Worship." She stopped at the edge of the tunnels and said to Wade, "You still have time to change your plans. They'll know if something happens in there. We'll never get away."

"Then you don't really have anything to feel bad about. If we're caught, all you'd have to do is explain. But they're not going to catch us. Let's move."

Tara led the way to the door. I wondered, not for the first time, if my real purpose here was to be a decoy. I was also amazed that we hadn't met one insomniac.

When Tara got close enough to the door to let the elevator know we wanted to use it, a voice came from the adjacent elevator ten meters down the hall. "No waiting at this station," the smoothly modulated voice said.

We crowded into the elevator. The elevator itself was the most mundane article I had seen here so far. It was fancy, but could easily have been transported directly from some office complex built centuries ago. Mirrors covered everything except the control panel. The voice said, "Please step to the rear and make room for me to close the door."

The control panel was simplicity itself. A lighted touch panel, adorned with the outline of a seven-pointed star, indicated we were at the main tunnel level, the higher of the two underground levels. Above us were about a dozen discrete floors, beginning with the main floor of the Tower. Above those floor indicators was a bar graph that indicated we could travel almost all the way to the top of the Tower. Below us was a maintenance level, with the inscription, *Authorized Personnel Only.* No doubt it was key- or password-protected.

Tara was about to touch the indicator for the main level when Wade grabbed her hand.

"No. Let's get a look from one of the upper floors before we try it." He touched *three.*

The elevator said, "Going up to the third floor," and began to rise at a leisurely pace. Wade touched the indicator again for a second and the elevator tripled its acceleration.

On the third floor, everyone but Tara was facing the wrong direction when the elevator said, "The interior door is about to open." The opposite side of the elevator opened wide and I finally began to appreciate how immense the Tower of Worship must be. In the distance, I could see the far wall, lined with several tiny rectangular elevator doors. The wall was so far away the air itself blurred fine details. A large hole in the center of the floor was cut away, surrounded by a protective railing. The railing gleamed like polished gold even in the artificial lighting. Over that hole was a similar hole cut in the ceiling. During the day the place must have been even more spectacular. If the *Redshift* had contained a room this large, you could probably have seen a sizable fraction of a minute into the past.

The elevator said nothing after the door opened, probably because it was programmed to be quiet inside the Tower of Worship.

On Wade's command we filed out of the elevator and stayed near the door. I kept thinking about day versus night and then I realized that the dark sections I could see between the distant elevator doors must be windows. I turned to the black, shiny wall next to our elevator. When I cupped my hands to shield the interior light, I could see the stars, partially blotted out by the rings.

I backed away from the window thinking that anyone out there in the dark could easily see me backlit by the interior of the Tower, but to the residents I probably looked more natural than I felt in this robe.

In the four corners of the room were doorways, presumably for the stairwells Tara had mentioned, going all the way to the top of the Tower.

This floor seemed to be totally unoccupied and still. Except for the soft shuffling of the team members, the place was as quiet as a Confederation parliament meeting right before the holidays.

Wade gestured for us to move toward the center of the floor. With so many awe-filled expressions, we probably looked more like a genuine group of newcomers on a sight-seeing visit than a team of pirates.

The floor was broken into sections. At repeated intervals around the perimeter were large sections of pews, all facing toward the center. On either side of them were wide aisles with decorative designs set into the floor. Next to the aisles, an assortment of long, thin green benches were laid out irregularly in what at first looked to be a random arrangement, but I was sure would appear deliberate and symmetrical if one looked down on the whole floor from above.

Above us was a high green ceiling supporting the fourth floor. Through the round opening in the center, we could see the guard rails on the fourth and fifth floors. They must have used strong construction materials, because the ceiling above was supported only at the walls. I saw no beams or support columns at all.

The floor was covered with a thin transparent layer that protected the decorative designs beneath our feet. Rich metallic reds and blues were interspersed with shiny sections of what appeared to be gold and silver, edged with the sheen of platinum.

Nearer the center opening, Wade motioned everyone to stop. He and Daniel continued cautiously to the railing. When they were apparently satisfied that no one else was around, Wade summoned us.

Even though we were only on the third floor, I was impressed by the height. Below us was the second floor with its corresponding central opening. Through that large cutaway we could see a large, polished silver disk set into the floor. It must have been ten meters across and a meter high. It bore a large, gold, stylized "X." The vault.

I looked up. I thought I caught a flicker of motion near the railing on the fifth floor, but when I looked directly at the location, nothing was there. I looked farther up.

It seems funny that looking *up* should activate acrophobia, but it did. The world shifted, and I felt I was perched on the edge of a giant hole with four flat, sloping green sides that met in a distant point. Craning my neck to see the view somehow added to the uneasiness because I wasn't in a natural, secured position.

The sides of the tower, above the level of the highest floor, appeared to be striped. Twenty vertical elevator shafts, five rising against each wall, reached almost to the apex. Faint, horizontal lines must have been walkways connecting the stairways Tara had spoken about. As I looked upward, the entire volume of the Tower of Worship seemed to turn slowly. I was almost surprised to see no clouds inside. Instead of clouds, geometrical shapes were suspended, all shiny and smooth. A cube hung near the railing about five floors up.

By peering down over the railing, Wade had apparently satisfied himself that the main floor really was deserted. I still had trouble accepting the fact that such a large structure was actually empty of its rightful inhabitants. I was disappointed, too. If Wade had been surprised by a huge congregational meeting, he wouldn't have his team start shooting. At least I didn't think so.

We returned to the elevator and started down to the ground floor. Tara turned toward Wade and said, "Why don't you give up? You're never going to get the contents of the treasury out unless you use enough explosives to vaporize what's inside. And if you start prying loose gemstones, you'll be caught long before you've stolen enough to make this all worthwhile."

"He might have a way to get the contents out," I said, voicing a suspicion that had been growing. "That briefcase might contain the components of a thruster."

She obviously didn't know what a thruster was, but Wade said, "Very good, Jason."

Tara looked at me questioningly and I said, "You set up a thruster to focus on a certain volume. When you trigger it, it generates a strong warp field. If you do it right, you can translate whatever's inside the focus from one layer of space to another. For instance, from layer zero to layer ten."

"Oh," she said, and in her expression I could see all the implications click into place. She even went past the obvious results of the vault contents winding up near the *Redshift* and moved on to the next implication. "What happens to whatever *isn't* inside the focus?"

"Damage," I said. "Lots of damage. A shock wave forms on the boundary between what goes and what stays. It will be a little like using an enormous explosive that destroys whatever's outside of the vault instead of whatever's inside."

"How bad—" Her voice broke and she started again. "How bad would it be? Could it do structural damage to the Tower?"

I spread my hands to indicate I couldn't tell. I was afraid it could. She was probably already more angry than she had ever been before, just thinking about her friends' treasury vanishing. If the resulting shock was strong enough to raze a structure this large and this beautiful, I didn't look forward to seeing her face when she saw the damage.

While the elevator was still falling, Tara suddenly sagged, as if she was going into a faint. I moved toward her to support her, and Wade moved closer. We were starting to slow to a stop when Tara's knee swept violently upward and caught Wade directly where she had obviously intended.

Wade screamed, loudly, painfully. Even before my grin and wince reached my face, there were four needlers trained on Tara. I moved carefully toward her, to indicate that nothing would happen to her unless they dealt with me, too.

Wade dropped to the floor, writhing in pain. I think that if Tara had tried to kick him then she probably would have been shot, but she stood stiffly, exactly where she was.

"Good form," I said softly to Tara. "I'd give it a hundred percent."

She flashed an angry, frustrated look at me. At the same moment, Daniel trained his needler on me.

"You're a little late," I said to him.

Wade was still squirming on the floor when the elevator doors opened. It was not an auspicious entrance to the main floor of the Tower of Worship, but it did feel good to get out of the elevator. With that many people trying to avoid touching Wade, we had been cramped for the last few seconds.

Wade could finally talk, as evidenced by his quiet swearing. Despite the pain, he was obviously acutely aware of where he was. Finally he staggered to his feet. He approached Tara, bringing his face within centimeters of hers. He said, "I'll deal with you later." His voice was hoarse and vicious.

I tried to relax the muscles that had tensed as I readied myself to interfere. As I did, Wade's team members slowly moved outward from the epicenter, each totally watchful, each with a drawn weapon. Earlier I had hoped for an opportunity to snatch a weapon and do enough damage to eliminate the threat of retaliation, but that possibility was nonexistent now. Everyone was as alert as a pilot whose instrument panel had just gone dark.

The ceiling over this floor was taller than on the third floor, but the area was just as deserted. We moved quietly past rows of empty green pews and approached the gleaming raised disk in the center of the Tower of Worship. Wade took the lead now. He reached the disk and gestured for the blonde to come forward. She lowered the briefcase to the floor and then carried it outside her robe. Such a small case for so much potential for destruction.

As the blonde approached the vault cover, I moved slowly forward, thinking that if I could somehow damage the thruster then none of the pending destruction would have to happen, and, therefore, maybe Wade wouldn't have as much need to eliminate witnesses.

Before I got much nearer, though, Daniel grinned at me and motioned for me to back away from the area.

With no choice, I sat down in a pew. Daniel backed toward the center of activity, splitting his attention between keeping track of me and scanning the perimeter of the room. Tara continued to move toward the center of the room. I was able to stay seated for only a couple of seconds before I stood up, only to have Daniel motion me back again.

The blonde had opened her briefcase. She withdrew four shiny black cubes, each about as wide as her outstretched fingers. As Wade and Daniel watched, and as the rest of the team scanned the perimeter for new arrivals, she began to place the cubes at equidistant points around the cylindrical vault cover. As each cube was deposited, she made an adjustment on the cube's face.

As she started to place the third cube into position, one of the black-suits glanced up suddenly and immediately began to lift his arm. He opened his mouth to say something, but, even as he yelled a warning to the others, a small silvery sphere thrown from somewhere above plummeted to an impact near the center of the vault.

Wade and Daniel had just started reacting to the threat when the sphere exploded, instantly creating a huge round cloud of red smoke that swept over Tara and the entire crew. I sat where I was. After the initial dense cloud dissipated slightly, I could see the team members keeling over, apparently unconscious or dead even before they hit the floor.

=== 12 ===
Jason's Run

The cloud of red smoke rapidly grew larger and more transparent until there was nothing but a faint red tinge to the air in the center of the Tower of Worship. The sound of running feet on the level above seemed as out of place in a religious temple as the red cloud itself.

At the back of my mind was shock that the Xanahallans would have been this prepared for a surprise visit, but foremost in my thoughts was Tara's condition. I approached the remnants of the cloud, unsure if the effects were still potent. The gas could conceivably be poison rather than a knockout. When I saw Wade's chest expand slowly, I felt as relieved as I had when I'd escaped from Redwall.

I stood motionless for at least another second. So many hours had passed since I'd had a choice, it seemed hard to believe I really had one now. I could sit quietly and wait for the people upstairs to reach me, then explain which of us were good guys and which of us were bad guys. And hope that they believed me. Or I could get away from here and put myself in a position where I had more leverage in case they were inclined to be suspicious of an armed team secretly entering their temple.

In the end, I really had no more choice than I'd had during the time I'd spent with a collar around my neck. I moved.

I started toward the group of sprawled figures in the center of the Tower, thinking at first that if I could carry Tara away then it wouldn't matter too much what else happened. But the footsteps upstairs had already become inaudible. That would mean the residents were at the elevator or stairs, ready to descend. Even if there were time for a detour like that, carrying Tara could make me more easy to catch. And that would defeat the whole purpose of moving.

I started moving again toward Tara, but checked the motion. Damn. There was too little time to get her and find an adequate hiding place.

A needler had slid toward me after it dropped from the hand of the black-suit who had been guarding me. I scooped it off the floor and veered away from the red-hued air, moving quickly toward the wall. I glanced upward furtively, to see if another silver sphere was on its way down, but apparently I had been still enough that when whoever had thrown the first sphere peeked over the rim, he had seen only Wade's gang and Tara.

On my way, I debated whether to try the stairs or an elevator, and picked the elevator. Not only would it take me longer to reach the stairs in the corner, they might lead me straight to a group of descending residents. If an elevator opened quickly, it would probably be one that was standing idle and empty. I hated leaving Tara there, but that was the only alternative I could imagine that would leave me free to do something about this turnabout.

I reached the edge of the main floor before anyone arrived. As soon as I approached an elevator, a nearby door slid open. With that many elevators, I would have been surprised not to find at least one resting on this level. I scrambled inside and indicated that I wanted the fourth floor. As the elevator spoke, I said "Be quiet!" under my breath, but there was no stopping it. At least this wasn't the *Redshift.* There, the sound would have remained as proof that someone had been escaping.

The door stayed open. I scanned the panel and found the control for closing the door and activated it. At a leisurely pace, the doors began to slide together. I stared at Tara's still form.

The doors had not quite met when through the gap I saw an elevator door on the far side of the room begin to open.

There was no way to tell if they had seen me leaving. But since my current freedom depended on not being noticed, I did the only thing I could think of. Rather than have the indicator outside change from *one* to *two,* I halted the elevator.

Emergency building codes required public elevators in Confederation office buildings to have escape hatches, but I had no idea whether the people on Xanahalla cared for governmental regulations. It would be just like them to totally separate church and state.

Above me was a lighted grillwork concealing the true ceiling of the elevator. I hoped the residents had merely purchased the elevators from a company who built them for the mass market. I searched to find the mechanism to swing the lights out of the way. I found it. To one side was a set of three spring-loaded catches that I released one at a time.

One end of the hinged, apricot-colored light-panel swung down halfway to the floor. Revealed in a corner of the ceiling was a rectangular panel with a knob on one edge. After putting the needler in a robe pocket, I slid the panel aside and jumped high enough to grip the edges of the roof. I pulled myself into the opening.

The elevator shaft rose at a slight angle, pointed toward the peak of the Tower. At intervals, red lights shone dimly, probably designating the floors above. Beyond them, at more widely spaced intervals, were faint blue lights. Far, far above in the distance was a single weak white light. That would be the top of the shaft, I assumed.

Wondering which would arouse more suspicion—a rising elevator or a stalled one—I considered dropping back to the elevator floor and letting the elevator proceed on its journey. A compromise seemed best. I would wait for ten minutes and then release the hold. Maybe by then, the defenders would have decided they had found all of the team members and would be carrying them to someplace they could lock up the team while they asked questions. Or maybe someplace where they would be locked up until the authorities arrived. If I could find where they went, I could use the needler to get them free.

I surveyed the top of the elevator while I thought and waited. A sturdy, taut cable vanished upward into the dark column, gleaming faintly in spots near the lights. Angled struts connecting the cable to the corners of the elevator box provided enough of a handhold that I would feel relatively safe if I had to ride the elevator on the outside while it was traveling.

On the inside-door-side of the elevator were two sets of large wheels to keep the elevator from scraping the side of the shaft as it traveled up and down in its tilted path. Between the elevator and the wall, bordered by vertical wheel-tracks, was a space that looked to be wide enough for a person to hang onto while an elevator passed by. Horizontal struts set into the side of the shaft at about one-meter intervals formed a large shadowy ladder.

In the gap below I could see the red light on the ground floor of the Tower. Below that light was another red light. That must have been at the tunnel level where we had come in. And below that light was still another, probably the maintenance level.

I was puzzled when I looked at the opposite side of the elevator. On the side facing away from the interior door, facing away from the inward tilt in the shaft, was another set of wheels. But these didn't engage in wheel-tracks; they just stuck out into the gap between the elevator and the side of the shaft, not quite reaching the side of the shaft. I decided the elevator must have been purchased as a standard item and normally the wheels engaged in tracks on both sides of the elevator. Here, the unusual tilt to the shaft made one set of wheels unnecessary.

I had stalled the elevator long enough. I made sure I would be able to pull the grill into place from on top, and then lowered myself through the access hatch and landed lightly on the floor. I released the hold, scrambled back up through the hatch, pulled the grill into place, and slid the hatch closed while the elevator resumed its upward journey.

As I crouched in the sudden darkness, I could feel the cool air slowly flow past me and the rising elevator. A faint whine came from far above, and the wheels made a gritty sound as they compressed small pieces of dirt into the wheel-tracks.

With the advantage of hindsight, I wished I had pressed the indicator for the tunnel level. Maybe if I could have climbed down the struts from there to the maintenance level, I would have been able to move about with a smaller threat of being discovered. Also, I supposed Tara and the others would be taken out of the Tower of Worship to be questioned.

The elevator roof carried me past the red lights and vertical hairline cracks indicating the second and third floors, and began to slow as we neared the fourth floor.

Soon after the car stopped on the fourth floor, I heard the doors open. In the quarter-minute they stood open, I heard no indication of anyone stepping into the elevator, and I felt no small sudden drop as though a passenger's weight had been deposited.

As soon as the doors closed, the elevator began to drop. Since it had been resting on the main floor, it seemed logical to me that it was programmed to stay there when idle. Sure enough, it stopped on the main floor and kept its doors closed. I wondered if anyone had noticed the display change.

Someone must have, because a moment later the door opened and I could hear voices besides the elevator's.

"It only stopped on four," someone said.

"You three get up there," another voice, a calm voice, said. "We'll watch out down here."

I had been trying to decide whether to stay atop the car or try my luck on the struts now that I was close to the maintenance level. The next voice convinced me to move.

He said, "If you find any others, don't take any chances. Kill them if you have to. We've got most of them."

Even as I was registering surprise at what seemed a fairly severe approach, I was moving lightly to the side of the car. Maybe these voices represented security guards employed by the colony—guards who formed their own opinions about how best to protect the residents.

I stepped onto a strut just above my foot, and gripped the strut about two meters above. I hoped the elevator would clear my body where the strut even with my waist prevented me from flattening myself against the wall. The alternative was to leave myself open to being found on top of the elevator. And being found by someone who would be inclined simply to shoot me or push me over the edge.

Before the elevator door closed entirely I realized how difficult it was going to be to keep hanging onto the struts for a long time. I needed to get lower quickly, in case my fingers gave out. The five-degree slant in the elevator shaft wasn't all that far from vertical.

The elevator began to rise, and I expelled as much air as I could. I felt my robe flutter in the breeze. I wished the robe were thinner or I had discarded it. If I had misjudged the clearance, two separate halves of my body might soon be falling down the elevator shaft. At least I was in the right place for praying.

The top of the elevator brushed my buttocks on its journey. I didn't resume breathing until the bottom of the elevator had cleared my head.

I looked down. In my haste I had made an oversight. The struts didn't continue down in a perfect ladder because the doors to each floor were on the same wall of the shaft. The rectangle surrounding the door stuck out from the wall of the shaft so it would fit against the elevator when it was in place.

I needed to get below the door opening quickly. The elevator's return would probably prevent me from moving downward, and, if it returned while I was still navigating the doorway, the results would be fatal.

With one hand I gripped the strut at my waist. Carefully I lowered myself until my foot scraped the top of the doorway enclosure. The shelf extended far enough out that it made a more convenient ledge to stand on than the struts. It also made navigating down the elevator shaft much more difficult.

The whine of the rising elevator stopped and the shaft became quiet except for the sound of my breathing. With one hand gripping the strut where I had been standing, I reached down to feel the ledge I was perched on. I leaned out from the wall far enough to see the hairline crack of light where the doors met. The bottom edge of the enclosure surrounding the door looked like it might be far enough below that I'd have to let go of the top and drop.

Despite being only one floor above the maintenance level, the idea of falling into that dark shaft bothered me a lot. The fall might not kill me, but I had no idea what lay at the bottom. There might well be emergency shock absorbers to give a falling elevator a chance at survival, and I didn't have a clue to how they might be shaped. I just felt certain that landing on a surface cluttered with hard machinery of various sizes was a risk I wasn't yet prepared to take. Besides my own safety, there was Tara's to consider.

I reached to one side to get a feel for the possibility of using a wheel-track to maneuver past the doorway. It seemed wide enough for my body plus a little more so I could provide pressure from side to side. Its inner surfaces felt clean but not shiny smooth, and there didn't seem to be any lubricant.

I gripped the strut as tightly as I could, and then twisted into position, wedged between the sides of the wheel-tracks. My cut arm scraped the lip of the track, but I ignored the discomfort. My knees pressed against the other side. Without breathing, I let go of the strut and used my arms to force my back against the side of the wheel-track. The side was narrow enough that only about two-thirds of my back was in contact.

Above me, the whine of the elevator resumed.

I forced away thoughts of what those wheels would do to my body if I were still in the track when they caught up with me. I concentrated on reducing the pressure my hands and knees were exerting on the surface in front of me, and lowering myself with a series of short, semi-controlled, heart-stopping drops.

This work was significantly harder than maneuvering down the struts, and significantly more nerve-wracking. I wriggled farther down, thinking all the time about a backup plan in the event the elevator reached me. Jumping seemed to be the only alternative. Twice I craned my neck to see how far I had come; the second time I was almost even with the bottom of the first floor door frame.

The elevator came lower, close enough to blot out all light above, like a giant hammer coming down on an insect. I prepared to jump. Sweating hard, I heard the elevator whine drop in pitch, as though it was slowing down. I held my position. Seconds later, the large lower wheel came to a full stop, less than a meter over my head.

There was no time for feeling thankful. The elevator could possibly resume its downward journey in seconds. I moved down another half-meter so I could reach a strut, and then levered myself around the wheel-track and back into an upright position on the shaft wall. My knees hurt, but for the moment I felt better.

Thinking I was momentarily secure, I looked down to see if I could make out the bottom of the elevator shaft. I couldn't.

In a series of maneuvers from one strut to the next one down, I reached the top of the maintenance-level door outline. The elevator door above had closed again as it was parked on the main floor. I heard no more voices, and the elevator remained stationary.

I debated trying to force open the door to the maintenance level, but decided that with a search potentially still on it would be wiser to hide a little longer. If I could rest my arms and legs at the bottom of the elevator shaft, then I could come back to this door when I might be less likely to find a group of searchers nearby. I needed to locate Tara as soon as possible, but the odds of meeting searchers were still high.

No sounds were audible through the closed maintenance-level door, so again I swung myself into the wheel-track.

Beneath the maintenance-level door, I swung back onto the struts and continued down. Since I was lower now, I felt less nervous about the potential of a fall, but there was still no sign of the bottom of the shaft. I was tired enough that I was almost ready to drop anyway.

I traversed only three more struts before I finally realized that something was wrong.

I should have been near the bottom of the shaft by this time, but the sound wasn't right. The shaft above me was filled with minute *creaks* and *snaps* and assorted sounds that came from a long hollow structure subjected to shifting stress and strain as it vibrated and settled, expanding and contracting with tiny temperature variations. Below me there should have been a dead zone, an area generating less sound, absorbing some of it, reflecting some of it to yield soft echoes. Instead the shaft below sounded much like the shaft above.

I peered down and tried to make sense of the dim image. After a long moment, I decided that what I saw still didn't make much sense. There seemed to be a surface slanting down and out of sight.

I tightened my grip on the strut near my waist, and I leaned out from the shaft wall, as far as I dared. What I saw made my scalp itch. It also made me extremely grateful I hadn't risked jumping to the bottom of the shaft. Because it would have been a long fall.

Whether or not it made sense, not far below my current position, the elevator shaft bent slightly. From my vantage point, I could see a series of blue and red lights that looked like mirror images of the ones above.

Unless this was some optical trick, the elevator shaft extended as far into the planet as the Tower of Worship projected into the sky.

I pulled my body tight against the shaft wall. The elevator shaft held no offer of a temporary resting place. The wheel-track on this side of the wall ended not far beneath my feet, and a different set of wheel-tracks began on the other side of the shaft. If the elevator dropped past the turning point, the other set of wheels would be pressing on the outside of the shaft. And if I kept trying to descend the shaft, fairly soon I would have to be clinging to the underside of a five-percent slope rather than to the topside.

I had to make the most of my strength immediately, so I began maneuvering upward. As long as the elevator stayed where it was, the only choices I had were forcing the maintenance-level door open, or clinging to the side of the shaft for as long as I could hold on, until my fingers and legs finally ran out of strength and my body plummeted down the shaft.

As I climbed, I wondered about the underground section of the elevator shaft. What was down there? I wondered whether this shaft was unusual, and the only one to go below the maintenance level. But the odds of my finding the one shaft seemed small enough that they suggested the likelihood that every elevator shaft extended into the ground, together forming an enormous inverted pyramid whose shape would be the same as the exposed portion of the Tower of Worship.

My hand reached the lower lip of the door enclosure.

I pulled my chin even with the vertical line between the two doors. I leaned from side to side, but I couldn't see anything between the doors except a diffused glow.

With one hand I tried to slide one of the doors away from the closed position. It refused to move.

I maneuvered into the wheel-track and moved high enough to get a grip on the top of the door frame. Standing on the edge of the door frame, hanging onto the wheel-track with one hand, hoping the elevator above wouldn't be commanded to descend, I tried to pull the door open. My fingers slid over the surface of the door.

I expelled a deep breath and considered my options once more. Climbing up the wheel-track had been significantly harder than descending.

I tried the door again, with similar results. I swept my hand over the door's surface, feeling for a spot with more friction, wondering if the door on the other side was the one that controlled whether this one opened, and I felt something. A small hole in the door, high up.

Maintaining my balance, I carefully reached into my pants pocket and retrieved my pen. I located the hole again and the pen fit. I pulled. Nothing.

I briefly considered the options again, weighing conservation of strength for an upward climb against needing to get out of here. And I wondered who might be beyond the door if I were able to get it open.

I pulled again, using the wheel-track as an anchor. I pulled just as hard as I could.

Nothing.

I took a deep breath and thought. I swept my hand over the door's surface again, stretching to cover as much as I could. This time I felt a lever high up near the corner. It jutted out far enough into the elevator shaft that surely it was meant to be engaged by the presence of the elevator. I pushed it. I pulled it and heard a soft mechanical *snick*.

Trying to simultaneously keep the lever engaged and apply pressure to open the door, I yanked on my pen again.

The door opened several millimeters, and a column of light streamed into the elevator shaft.

I maintained my pressure. No more progress. I relaxed the pressure little by little, and the gap remained open. I jerked the pen toward me, and the door began to slide slowly open.

One of the security people could have shot me dead right then and my only thought probably would have been: *I did it! I got it open.* But no one was on the other side to squeeze a trigger.

I wedged my foot between the doors and then grabbed the edge of the door with the hand I had used to pull on the pen. A moment later I stood in a deserted hallway and the elevator doors snapped together like huge jaws of a frustrated carnivore.

I replaced the pen in my pants pocket, and I drew the needler from my robe pocket, listening attentively for indications that anyone was approaching. I heard none. I put my hand in my pocket, but I didn't release the needler.

The elevator indicators on this level—obviously "maintenance level" wasn't exactly the right term—were more complete than the indicators above. Here, there was an additional set of numbers: negative numbers representing the lower half of the Tower. The numbers confirmed that the tower was as deep as it was tall. Someone really knew how to keep a secret.

I felt decidedly uneasy, but the mood shift wasn't due solely to finding out that the situation wasn't as straightforward as it had seemed. The atmosphere on this level felt less innocent than the floors above.

Where the upstairs and the main tunnel level had been colored with light and dark greens and yellows, this level was darker, with charcoal and gray. The clear mirrors above corresponded to smoked mirrors here. My reflected image seemed to have the red tinge of the nerve-bomb cloud upstairs. I had to find Tara fast.

I moved cautiously around the elevator column and found a tunnel leading away from the Tower of Worship. The tunnel, too, was a darker shade than the tunnel above. I wondered if the tunnels on this layer ran parallel to the ones on the main level.

A tunnel with, by definition, only two ways to escape felt risky, so I turned toward the stairs that should be at the corner of the Tower. The area was still empty of people.

I traveled from the elevator column to the corner, stopping and listening several times, wondering if I had somehow been located and was unknowingly being followed, but I encountered no one.

The stairs were as Tara had described them, except they didn't lead up. And I assumed the main level stairs didn't lead down. The top and bottom halves of the Tower of Worship were seemingly connected only by the elevators. Elevators that indicated only the top existed.

Working with the theory that anyone wanting to go down very far would take the elevator, I walked down several flights of stairs, past a sign saying *Level –2,* before I stopped to rest and think.

There were too many things I didn't know. I wondered if Tara had known all along about the way things were here, and kept silent for whatever unknown reasons she might have had. Or whether she'd had no idea this lower section existed. Either way, this whole business raised more questions than I'd found answers to so far.

I kept listening for the sound of footsteps above me or below me, but the stairwell was silent. I took stock and examined the needler. The gun was a standard Uzette ninety-six-shooter set for tranquilizers. The needler would help me deal with a group if I had to, but ultimately I would run out of needles, even if I was willing to switch over to lethal needles. I twisted the load cylinder in the gun butt and watched the display cycle from "Trank 35" to "Heavy Trank 36" to "Untrank 3" to "Kill 21" and back to "Trank 35." One needle had been fired so I had ninety-two chances if I left the needler on single action.

I couldn't contact the ship without one of the transmitters that Wade and Daniel had carried. I probably couldn't get back to the jumpsuits without getting trapped in a tunnel, and I'd probably take forever if I had to find my way on the surface.

And even if I were confident that I could get back to the suits, it didn't seem a safe idea at all to leave without finding Tara. The security team's willingness to kill me on sight, and the existence of this underground half of the Tower of Worship both made me concerned that questioning of the prisoners once they awoke might not be gentle. Particularly if they viewed Tara as a traitor because they had found her with the team.

My arms and legs felt better already. I continued down the stairwell, placing my feet carefully and being quiet.

At the sign saying *Level -3*, I slid the stairwell door open just enough to see through the crack. This floor possessed a gloomy atmosphere, too. I couldn't see toward the center of the level, but the interior walls running parallel to the elevator banks were decorated with vertical stripes, alternating dark red and brown. The floor was a mosaic of large squares of dark red, black, charcoal, and light brown. The lines and squares seemed to vibrate. The overall effect gave the impression that their interior designer had been given a short time limit. And asked to work cheap.

Hearing nothing, I slid the door all the way open. It slowly slid itself closed as I arbitrarily picked the right-hand path. Ahead, opposite each elevator door, were corridors leading inward. I reached the first corridor and began following it. The striped color scheme continued here. The walls on both sides of me were broken by a single closed door on each, and ahead was an indication of more symmetry. The corridor continued toward the center of the floor, where a railing suggested this floor had a circular opening in it just like the ones upstairs. The ceiling, also cut at the same point, was decorated with thin red and black lines radiating from the center.

A sound came from behind me, and I forced myself to move calmly as I looked around for the source. In my robe I might actually pass for someone who belonged here if I didn't panic. Even before I had turned completely, though, I knew the source of the sound. One of the elevators was moving.

I went back to the hallway parallel to the wall. The elevator two doors away was descending. I moved partway back into the corridor leading to the center of the Tower. As I watched, the indicator changed from *-1* to *-2* to *-3*. It seemed to pause at *-3* in an unnerving demonstration of subjective time-dilation, and then it moved on. The indicator finally stopped at *-10*. I assumed the indicators in the upper part of the Tower were saying the elevator was on the "maintenance" level.

I wondered what kind of "maintenance" went on down here. And I recalled the favorite expression of the first crew chief I had reported to when I started working in maintenance: if it ain't broke, don't fix it.

More and more curious, and more and more apprehensive, I walked softly toward the center of the Tower. One intersection stood between me and the center. The cross corridor had curved walls, and seemed to be a circle around the middle of the Tower of Worship. No one was in sight. I slowed as I approached the railing around the hole cut in the floor, not wanting to be seen by anyone on a floor above or below. The inner wall circled the railing, about a meter away, so a round walkway reached around the entire circumference.

I reached the railing and looked over the edge. The view brought to mind an inverted image of the upper portion of the Tower of Worship, as though I had fallen through some extraordinary distorting mirror on my way down here. The seven floors below me all had matching cutaways so the bottom of this half of the Tower was in sight. Dark elevator shafts reached deep into the planet's surface, almost meeting at the lowermost tip of the inverted pyramid. The tip itself was invisible in the shadowy circle directly below me. The railings ringing the floors below reflected dark reds and browns from the nearby walls.

On the ceiling two floors above me was another distorted mirror image. Instead of an exact duplicate of the gold "X" on a silver background, this "X" had a blood-red tint and the silver background seemed darker. I retreated from the railing.

On the way back toward the elevators, I drew my needler and tried one of the doors along the hall. The door slid open silently and smoothly to reveal an unoccupied room. Overhead lights came on automatically. The disturbing feel to this lower half of the Tower of Worship had partially prepared me for the contents of the room, but I was still chilled by what I found there.

In the center of the room lay a bed equipped with manacles. Nearby was a reclining chair, similarly equipped. Standing in the corner were two tripods and an assortment of recording equipment. Along one wall was what at first glance seemed to be simply an untidy workbench. But the tools and implements were not ones typically used for repairing a kitchen appliance or making a set of shelves.

I backed through the door, sure I'd already spent too much time recuperating and investigating. I had to find Tara.

I'd seen enough that I almost dialed my needler to *kill* right then, possibility of ricochet or not.

Moving back toward the elevator bank, I was grateful I hadn't run into anyone yet, because until this moment I might have been inclined to give whoever it was the benefit of the doubt. After all, we were the intruders here. It was only fair that they try to protect their rights and their privacy. But the room with the bed and manacles was a far stronger invasion of rights and privacy than I was willing to know of and do nothing about.

I turned the corner and returned to the stairwell. Besides not wanting to have the indicators showing an elevator in motion, I didn't know how to select floors down here since the control panel was missing some critical information. The elevator a few minutes before had gone to level minus-ten so I headed down the stairs, going even deeper, thinking there was such a thing as too much religious freedom.

13

Downbelow Xanahalla

I took the stairs downward one at a time, moving carefully. I saw no obvious indications of surveillance cameras mounted in corners, but that wasn't any guarantee against their presence. Certainly whoever controlled Xanahalla had mounted a few scanners somewhere on the upstairs levels, and I hadn't noticed them. And equally certainly, whoever had set up this place wouldn't be inhibited by the concept of violating people's rights to privacy, but I hoped they assumed such precautions were unnecessary below the public area.

I reached level minus-ten without seeing or hearing anyone. Most of the residents must have routinely used the elevators. The absence of people, coupled with the pristine condition of the stairwell, gave me the feeling I was the first person to travel this route since this place was constructed. I wondered if the construction crew who worked on the lower half of the Tower had been members of whatever group moved freely down here. And, if not, how their silence had been guaranteed.

I slid the door to level minus-ten open just far enough to peer through the crack. I saw nothing except two diverging hallways. Cautious because the moving elevator had convinced me someone was on this level, I closed the door and took the stairs down one more level.

The view was much different at level minus-eleven. At first I thought the area on the other side of the stairwell door was completely dark, but when I opened the door farther I could see all the way across to the far corner of the inverted pyramid. A walkway clung to each wall, forming a large square that connected the four corner stairwells and the elevator doors lining each wall. I saw no one, so I slid the door open just far enough to get through and stood to one side as the door closed softly behind me.

Above me was the floor of level minus-ten, with the circular cutout in the center. I could see the guard rail on the far side of the lip, but nothing else. A circular column of light beamed down through the cutout, as though originating at the top of this underground section and collimated by the ten circular openings in the intervening floors. Dust motes twinkled in the shaft of light.

The colors of the walls were quite dark, and little light filtered from the central column to the solid surfaces and the walkway, so the scene seemed to be in black and white. I'd been away from the *Redshift* for only a few hours and already I had been spoiled by seeing inanimate objects in color.

Extending downward into the planet was an image confirming what I had seen from level minus-three: a dimly lit mirror image of the top of the Tower of Worship. The walls formed downward-pointing triangles whose deep tips met in a dark circle far below me. Walkways marked each level in a series of telescoping squares vanishing into the depths. Even though I was prepared for the sight, I was still amazed at just how deep it really looked.

The enormous cavity was still except for ambience of small creaks and faint echoes of the tiny sounds my shoes made on the walkway. The soft, almost imperceptible, rumbling gave me the impression that someone had recorded a full auditorium of people talking and laughing and bumping into one another and spilling drinks, and then played the recording with the sound level set just below my threshold of hearing.

I had started to move quietly back to the stairwell door when I heard the scream. It wasn't quite like screams I had heard at Redwall, not sudden, shrill full-throated outcries of fear and pain. I could hear the pain in it, but it was almost a mixture of a sigh and someone beginning to cry, as though this hoarse cry was far from the first time this particular person had screamed. The voice sounded deep enough to possibly be male, but pain intense enough to cause a scream like that had probably long ago stripped away the barriers between the sexes.

The sound had come from above. Its echoes faded into the ambient noise as I looked through the cutaway in the ceiling, wishing for a clue as to who had screamed. And why. While I stood there, back to the wall of the Tower of Worship, something moved on the floor above.

A naked body fell through the cutout in the floor of level minus-ten. From this distance, I wasn't sure whether the body was male or female, but I could tell that the trunk and limbs were distinctly red-tinged.

As I stood transfixed, the body fell the equivalent of another five levels, still lit by the column of light from above. And the body seemed to be growing smaller. Smaller not because it was moving farther away, but because something was happening to it. The flesh was being vaporized. The body fell another second or two and there was nothing left but a skeleton.

Even the bones never reached the bottom of the pyramid. They fell no more than two-thirds of the way down before they had even less substance than a cup of water dropped from the same height.

More dust motes twinkled in the vertical shaft of light.

Anger swept through me, carried on a tide of adrenaline. If that had been Tara, this entire evil place would dissolve to its component atoms before I was through with it. And I'd hear more screams before I was finished.

I started back toward the stairwell door but then paused as I became a bit more rational. I'd wait another minute or two in case anyone above looked down. As I stood there in the semi-darkness, I slowly raised the needler and twisted the dial to "Kill."

I began to move again, stiffly, as though coming out of a trance, and then my muscles loosened. Halfway up the stairs to level minus-ten, I set the needler back to "Trank."

I slid open the stairwell door and stepped into an empty intersection. At the first turn toward the center of the Tower, I hesitated, and then moved into another empty hallway. The view toward the center was blocked by what looked to be a wall about twice my height. I moved quietly toward the end of the corridor, seeing no one, but hearing voices somewhere ahead.

The wall ahead was circular, surrounding the center of this floor of the Tower. I reached it and found a circular corridor running around the wall's perimeter. I turned and followed the wall. The voices grew louder as I moved, apparently originating inside the circular wall. Ahead and on my left was an opening in the wall.

I slowed as I neared the doorway. The voices were audible, but I couldn't make out what they were saying. I was about to peer around the corner when I saw a shiny silver canister on a table just inside the enclosed area. Reflected on it was the distorted image of three robed figures standing between the doorway and the center of the Tower.

I waited and watched. The voices sounded more like chanting than conversation. The figures' heads bobbed in unison. The images weren't totally clear, but the figures all seemed to be facing away from the doorway.

A better opportunity might not present itself, so I leaned around the corner and squeezed three almost-silent shots, one needle into each of three hooded robed backs. *Pffft. Pffft. Pffft.*

One of the three had enough resistance to start to move an arm toward the itching spot on his back. The other two immediately folded over.

With my needler still ready, I scanned the rest of the area and saw no one else in a position to cause trouble. From here I could see the cutout in the floor above, but no one was in sight up there.

I moved fast. There was no way to tell how soon anyone else would arrive here or when the three were due wherever they were going next. I checked one of the three's pulse and found it slow enough to convince me the needle had been effective.

The circular area between the wall and the center hole in the floor was ringed with the kind of wheeled tables normally used in hospitals to move an unconscious patient from one location to another. At each station along the wall were nozzles and connections for tubes and wires. One of the tables was occupied.

I should have first concealed the three robed bodies in case anyone was on the floor above, but I couldn't wait. The body strapped onto the table was female, and I was horribly afraid it was Tara. Even from a distance I could see welts on the skin, and the discoloration of bruises.

I moved closer, a metallic taste thick in my mouth. I reached the table. The woman's hair was gone and her face was so disfigured that at first I couldn't tell if she was Tara or not, and then her eyes opened.

I was never so glad to avoid seeing someone I was half expecting. The woman wasn't Tara. The eyes weren't hers.

Even as I felt the incredible relief that she wasn't Tara, I looked into those eyes and felt intense pain. The woman's expression was that of an animal pinned in a trap so powerful and cruel that it had nearly severed a limb.

The woman's mouth opened slightly, revealing missing teeth. Before she said anything, I said, "I'm not here to hurt you."

She blinked away a tear, and tried to talk. The sound was all but inaudible. I leaned closer.

Her voice was almost impossible to make out, but this time I understood her. She said, agonizingly slowly, "Kill me. Please. Now."

I looked her full in the face and this time I recognized her. She was what was left of Marj Lendelson. No remnant was left of the confidence and poise she had displayed aboard the *Redshift*. Surprisingly, I felt no hate for her for the disaster that she had contributed to; I merely felt pain and pity.

"That's really what you want?" I said.

She nodded and blinked.

I nodded back. "All right. I think I understand."

As I twisted the dial to "Kill," Marj Lendelson began to cry. She didn't have much energy, because she sobbed only three times slowly, but tears came from her eyes.

I put the muzzle next to her arm and she looked into my eyes. She nodded once more to urge me on, and she clenched her jaw. I squeezed the trigger once. *Pffft.* Marj didn't even flinch.

Squeezing the trigger was like activating a time machine. For one suspended instant, the gratitude in Marj's eyes took me back to Redwall where I had killed Rissa's attacker. Coupling the act of killing someone with the pride that gave me in those two circumstances drove uncomfortable messages into the intellectual part of my brain, but I could no more have refused Marj Lendelson's request than I could have stayed out of that fight on Redwall.

A few seconds later, I closed Marj's lifeless eyes and then wiped my own stinging eyes.

I expelled a deep, shuddering breath, and willed myself to concentrate on what to do next.

Information. That was what I needed. I went back to the three unconscious robed figures on the floor. They were two men and a woman with an orange necklace. I picked one of the men, lifted him onto a nearby wheeled table, and strapped him down securely. Satisfied that he wouldn't be able to struggle free, I looked around and found one more strap which I fastened so I could apply leverage against his throat.

Still concerned about being seen from above, I put the other two bodies on the tables so they'd look like normal victims except for being clothed. I twisted the needler dial to "Untrank," and shot my trussed prisoner in the arm.

I waited impatiently for the needle's contents to revive the man. He looked to be about forty, the hair at his temples starting to gray slightly. There was a small cleft in his chin, and his pronounced cheekbones gave his cheeks a hollowed appearance. He didn't look like a monster any more than most of the Redwall patrons had.

Almost a minute passed before his facial muscles began to twitch. I tightened the strap over his throat until his breathing became labored. He frowned, as though experiencing a bad dream, and a moment later his eyes opened. He squinted against the light and probable pain, apparently assessing his condition before he started to talk. The strap was meant to ensure that he didn't yell.

"Who are you?" he said finally. His voice was raspy because of the strap across his throat.

"You might call me a seeker after knowledge. I need some information from you."

The man said something very rude to me, not at all what I would have expected from a person of deep religious conviction.

I tightened the strap and said, "You're probably still a little confused from the aftereffects of the needle in your arm. You don't tell me what to do; I tell you what to do. See how it works now?"

"What do you want?" His voice was no more than a whisper.

"I want to know what goes on here and why. And I want to know where the prisoners are. But I guess I need to qualify that last statement. I want to know about the prisoners you acquired just a few hours ago, from upstairs on the main floor."

"Ask someone else."

"I think you still don't understand." I looked around to see what intimidation tools were readily available. A moment later I stood by the table, holding the ends of a pair of wires with saw-tooth clips. The wires were connected to one of the outlets on the wall. I touched the clips together briefly, where the man could see them, and sparks flashed at the junction.

I fastened one clip to his earlobe, not really very concerned that the teeth on the clip drew blood. I dangled the other clip in the air carelessly. "You people have gotten spoiled, having all your patients brought to you down here. You probably aren't even aware that some people still go to the trouble of making house calls. I can guarantee you, though, that you're not going to like my bedside manner."

The man's widened eyes tracked the swinging clip.

"Let's try this again," I said. "Where are the new prisoners?"

He said nothing. I let the clip dangle closer to his body. He remained silent except for the sound of his labored breathing.

"I don't want to do this," I said. "But I will."

He was still silent, so I brought the dangling clip past his eyes and let it graze the top of his ear. His head jerked away, temporarily pushing his neck harder against the strap.

He was so stubborn that I had to let the clip touch him a couple more times. I was careful not to touch him anywhere likely to cause too much current to flow through his heart or brain.

I was choosing another target for the clip when he finally blurted out, "They—they're up on two."

"You mean level minus-two, or level two in the top half?"

"Minus."

I couldn't afford to be lied to, so I lied to him. "Come on. I just came from there and there's no sign of them." I let the clip swing some more.

"I swear they're there. In holding cells. No more than half an hour ago."

"Are they unharmed?"

"I think so. Most of them. Move that farther away."

"I'll consider the request. Were you torturing Marj Lendelson because she led us here?"

"She what?" He twisted his neck under the strap.

"So that's news to you?"

"Yes."

"Then why?"

"We were running low. It could have been anybody."

"Why?" I said, letting the clip brush him lightly.

He shuddered. "You—you wouldn't understand."

"Try me. I'm a very understanding guy."

"They die for us. The pain sets us free."

"You mean that in some physical sense, or are you talking about, for lack of a better description, religious beliefs?"

"Satan creates a constant level of pain in the universe. If—if someone else experiences it, then there's less left for us."

Exploring that subject was bound to take more time than I could afford, and would undoubtedly make me even angrier, so I switched to another topic. "No one gets here without a substantial donation. I suppose in the process you get the victims to sign over whatever wealth they have left?"

He said nothing, so I dangled the clip a little lower. He nodded, his gaze never leaving the clip.

I thought back to the glimpse of a face I had thought I recognized from years ago, and I thought about the similarities between Redwall and Xanahalla. "Who runs this place? Is it Neddi Pulmerto?"

His eyes widened so much that I wouldn't have believed a denial. He nodded.

I felt cold and angry. I wanted to connect the second clip to his body and just walk away. I didn't, though. I'd already spent too much of my life doing what I didn't want to do, and not doing what I did want to do, to change the pattern now.

No, that wasn't precisely true. The pattern had changed when I finally accumulated enough determination or desperation. And punishing this miserable bastard wouldn't make me feel better. But if Neddi Pulmerto were here on the table, that might be another story altogether.

I could still see the terrifyingly blank expression on Kerri Gangorra's face after Neddi Pulmerto and a couple of male friends let her loose from a private party that had lasted two days. Kerri had seemed to be so far gone that she was past pain and suffering. Five days later she killed herself by drinking a whole container of cleaning solvent. By that time, Neddi had been off-planet, on her way to some other adventure, no doubt every bit as cruel and, for her, usual.

"Satan doesn't create pain," I said finally. "People like Neddi Pulmerto and you create pain. Or maybe people like Neddi feed on pain. I can just imagine how this place came to be. She probably found a group of crazies like you who maybe at one time were on the receiving end of discrimination. And then she found a way to let you get revenge, and a way for her to get more wealth. And if it wasn't that, she probably would have created a situation that would result in a group like you."

There was no use questioning this sorry, despicable man any longer. Either he knew far more than I suspected, which seemed doubtful to me, or he was simply a cracked person in the right place at the right time for Neddi to manipulate. And she was good at that. Still feeling sickened, but paying little attention to my prisoner, I removed the clip from his ear and hung the wires back on the wall. I dialed the needler control back to "Trank" and fired another needle into his arm. As his body relaxed, I loosened the strap over his neck.

I searched his robe pockets and found nothing but a small seven-pointed star. I was going to leave it behind, but when I searched the other two bodies, I found they also possessed nothing but a similar seven-pointed star, and I remembered the decoration in the elevator. I put all three stars in my own pocket.

I left the four bodies on their respective tables and made my way back to the stairwell. I tried to be quiet as I climbed, but I took the stairs faster than I had on the way down. If they had hurt Tara, I couldn't imagine any revenge that would even begin to compensate for the pain. I almost stopped in midstride as that thought hit home and I realized how important her safety had become to me.

I continued up the stairs, my needler poised. Here I was, trying to locate and protect a woman who, for all I really knew, could have been a former downstairs resident here, sent out to recruit still more wealth and victims. But I couldn't accept the idea that Tara knew all there was to know about this place. She had to be an innocent dupe, encouraged to recruit, but ignorant of the full extent of the interpretation these people gave to the word "sacrifice."

I reached the door marked *Level −2*. Beyond it was another junction of two empty corridors. Right now I was grateful that Xanahalla seemed to have a low population density. Probably it was a natural result of some of the residents killing other residents.

The decor here was less depressing than the lower floors had been, as though the designers had deliberately employed a spectrum of shades starting with somber tones near ground level and deepening into oppressive colors along the way to successively lower levels. Where the upstairs levels had been open and airy, the downstairs levels were more like office buildings designed by agoraphobic manic-depressives. The black and white and brown textured pattern on the walls reminded me of dead leaves, leaves dry enough to crumble between your fingers.

I put my needler in my pocket and walked quickly and purposefully, as though I had every right to be here. And, as far as I was concerned, I did. Just before the first corridor leading into the center, I halted. No one was visible, so I resumed my search, faking nonchalance.

This level seemed to be laid out in a rectangular grid. The first cross-corridor was straight, unlike the circular corridor a level farther down.

I continued toward the center, unsure of where to look for Tara, wondering if I'd been lied to after all. Closer to the center, I began to think I had been told the truth.

Near the end of the corridor was a wide hallway circling the center. The interior wall blocked access to the central column, so the setup wasn't the same as where I'd found Marj Lendelson. It was similar, though. This corridor was also occupied by three Xanahalla residents.

The initial similarity ended at that point. This time they saw me as soon as I turned the last corner.

I kept walking, feigning tranquility. Only one of the three had seen me. She was facing me, seated. Her two companions also sat, one facing the opposite direction, the other facing the two doors in the nearby wall. All three were armed with snub-nosed paralyzers, and the woman facing me was already raising hers when I shot her.

I wasn't fast enough. Her gun sizzled and the beam caught my leg before my needle put her out. My whole left leg went instantly numb, and I lost my balance.

On my way down, I fired two quick needles, one at each of the two conscious guards. One of the needles must have missed, because I heard the sizzle of another gun as I hit the floor and I fired several more needles.

Just as I managed to roll into the concealment around the corner, I realized I hadn't heard any more sizzling sounds. In fact the only sounds I'd heard were those of bodies crumpling onto the floor. I waved a few fingers around the corner and heard no firing. After a suitable delay, I peeked around the corner and pulled back fast just in case.

All three guards were slumped on the floor.

I tried to get to my feet, but my numb leg convinced me that crawling would be easier. I crept around the corner and moved toward the guards, my needler ready to deal with any tricks.

The paralyzers seemed to be surprisingly humane weapons for such a slimy crowd to be using, until I thought about what these people were likely to do with any victims once they recovered. A quick death with a laser or poison needle would deprive them of some quality time spent engaged in playing doctor.

I reached the first guard and checked her pulse. She couldn't have been faking. I pulled the paralyzer away from her outstretched fingers. The other two guards, both males, were similarly sleepy. Besides more seven-pointed stars, one of the guards had in his pocket a small silver sphere that looked a lot like the one that had been used to knock out Wade's team upstairs.

Only after I had the sphere and their weapons in my robe pockets did I turn toward the outer wall of this circular corridor and see the three windowed doors. Faces showed in all three windows. And in the window on the right, I saw Tara.

She looked tired and worried, but she smiled when she saw me look her way. I hadn't felt so good in a long, long time.

I used one of the chairs to hoist myself up so I was standing upright, although a little wobbly. Wade and a couple others of his team were in the same room with Tara. The center room contained still more members of the team. The last room contained a couple of people I hadn't seen before.

I dragged the chair with me as I approached the door to Tara's prison. I wished the numbness in my leg would wear off, but it would probably take several more minutes. With my needler poised, I pulled on the lock and slid open the door.

Two of Wade's team tensed as though considering the possibility of taking the needler away from me, and I said quickly, "Don't anyone move. I'm taking Tara, and I'll leave you a weapon so you can protect yourselves."

Tara said, "Am I ever glad to see you. How did you get out?"

"I'm glad to see you, too. But I wasn't in a cell." I looked at her for a long moment, supremely thankful that she appeared unhurt. My gaze was on her so long that the two decided to rush me anyway.

My leg was still numb, but that didn't affect my right arm. I shot two needles, and two bodies collapsed before they reached me. In a way they succeeded, though, because Wade used the opportunity to whip his arm around Tara's neck and cry out, "Stop right there, Jason! I'll break her neck." As though to demonstrate his sincerity and readiness, he put his other hand against the side of Tara's forehead, ready to apply leverage.

= 14 =

All the Traps of Xanahalla

"If you do anything to her, you'll lose all your bargaining power and you'll regret it for the rest of your short life-span. I personally give you my guarantee." I kept my needler aimed in the direction of Tara and Wade, considering how accurate my aim was, whether I could shoot faster than Wade could act, and how lucky I felt. So far this had not been a very lucky day.

"Toss the needler over here, Jason. I give you my word that I won't kill either of you if you just give me the needler."

"I think there's a lot you don't understand. You'd better listen to me for a minute."

"Give me the needler *now* or I'll break her neck." Wade's voice stayed loud, tense.

"Listen to me or you're a dead man. Tara comes out with me now or she dies. Right here and now. I'd rather kill her myself than leave her here alive. I can explain that, and you'd better listen."

Tara's eyes went wide. "Jason, what are you talking about?" Her voice was ragged from the pressure Wade exerted on her throat.

"Talk fast," Wade said. He looked unmistakably and understandably suspicious.

"All right. Some of what I have to say is going to sound unbelievable to you, but I can prove it. I assume you woke up here and you don't know where you are?"

"Right," Tara said. Wade nodded.

"And you're assuming that sometime soon there will be authorities here to rescue you or take you away to an institution, as appropriate."

"Of course," Wade said.

"Well, you're wrong. If it's up to the locals, you'll never leave here alive."

"Oh, don't exaggerate, Jason," Tara said. "I realize that what Wade was trying to do was terrible, but nothing happened. Their treasury is safe. No damage was done to the Tower. They aren't *that* vindictive."

"I don't exaggerate, and that's not the issue. My guess is that no one who comes downstairs involuntarily ever gets to leave. They're tortured until they're killed."

"What?" Wade and Tara said almost together. And then Tara said, "And what do you mean 'downstairs'?"

I was thrilled to hear her ask that question.

"Where do you think you are? I mean that underneath the Tower of Worship there's a mirror image. An inverted pyramid sunk into the planet the same distance. That's where we are right now. We are three levels *below* the main floor of the Tower, and terrible things go on down here."

That was obviously a lot for Tara to accept. "Are you sure you're all right?" she asked. She no longer looked as happy to see me.

I guessed that with Wade's history of lying he would more easily believe that other people could be in the wholesale business of hurting people. Unfortunately, he also seemed to distrust me and my story.

I told them quickly most of what I had seen down here. "I don't know that we've got much time," I said. "But I've got to convince you. Will you at least believe there might be something to what I say if I prove to you we really are downstairs?"

Tara shrugged as best she could in Wade's hold. Wade said, "No tricks, or I'll do it."

"Follow me. We don't have time for any tricks."

I left my chair behind and leaned on the wall, dragging my numb leg. I moved slowly, trying simultaneously to make sure none of the other residents surprised us, and that Wade didn't have an opportunity to escape. I didn't want to have to worry about Wade *and* the residents. Wade and Tara followed me, both taking short steps. Faces watched us through the windows in the other two cell doors.

We followed the circular corridor until a hall lead toward the center. As we neared the center, we could see the guard rail around the opening, and the opening above us, but we weren't close enough to see downward, so we could still have been upstairs for all I could prove.

I held up my hand and the three of us stopped. I whispered, "The more time you spend near the rail, the higher the risk that someone above or below will see us, so don't spend any more time than it takes to convince you. I'll put my needler on the floor when you get closer, so you can look without worrying about being shot."

Wade forced Tara along with him and they approached the center. Wade watched me carefully as I put down the needler, and he continued to glance frequently in my direction.

They got close enough to see over the edge. They both looked down and I heard Tara's intake of breath. In silence, they both looked up at the large red-tinted "X."

I picked up the needler as they started toward me. Tara's face was white. No one said anything until we were back at the open cell door.

"What's it going to be?" I asked. "I want Tara alive, but I won't leave her here for those butchers. They'll be convinced she's a traitor, and nothing she can say will convince them otherwise."

Wade was silent as Tara and I held each other's gaze.

"All right," Wade said. "There is an underground. But that doesn't prove the rest of what you said."

My voice hardened with the frustration and anger. "We're running out of time. Listen to me very closely, and pray that you can control your reactions. If you hurt Tara, I'll leave you here alive, a prisoner for them to mutilate. You understand my warning? Listen and don't react?"

Wade nodded.

"I found Marj Lendelson down here. She had been hurt very badly. Not twenty minutes ago, at her request, to put her out of her misery, I killed her."

Wade said instantly, "You're lying. She's safe here somewhere. She's just not in the register yet. You can't get away with that, Jason. There's—"

Tara must have accepted everything I'd said by that point, because she sagged slightly against Wade's grip and her gaze fell to the floor.

"One last time. I killed Marj Lendelson. I saw her here. She has—she had a triangular birthmark just above her navel."

I could see Wade finally believed me. He leaned back against the wall, and his grip came loose from Tara. For a moment, his eyes weren't focused on me.

Tara grabbed the opportunity to get away. She moved a meter from him, leaving him alone in my line of fire. Tara rubbed her neck where Wade had been applying pressure.

"It's all true, isn't it?" Wade said softly, to no one in particular.

"Yes, it is. Every bit of it." I was looking at Tara, sure that if she had any remaining doubts they would evaporate when she realized that now

I had absolutely no motivation to lie. I could have simply shot Wade if I'd wanted to.

Wade seemed to pull out of his stupor. He looked at me. "So, you're going to just leave me here for them?"

"I hate to admit how tempting that idea is. But no one deserves to die the way they intend for you to. Not even you."

"What then?"

"In there," I gestured toward the room they had been held captive in. "Move back to the far wall."

"Why?"

"Because I said so." Maybe I dragged this confrontation out longer than I needed to, but having our positions reversed, and having Tara safe, made me giddy.

Wade backed into the room, stepping over the two paralyzed bodies. I waited until he was all the way against the far wall. I withdrew one of my confiscated weapons from my pocket and dropped it just inside the door. "I'm leaving you a paralyzer. Don't waste your time trying to fire through walls or windows, but it should give you an edge when people come back for you. Once we get back to the ship and summon help, I'll tell the authorities where to find you."

Wade nodded glumly. Maybe he would have fought more under other circumstances, but I got the feeling that he really was numbed by Marj Lendelson's death.

I slid the door closed and locked.

Tara helped me move to the next door. My leg was beginning to tingle, so I should soon be able to move faster. "Thanks," I said.

"Thank *you,*" Tara said, her face close to mine.

I felt better than I had in years. Somehow the idea that my future might be measured in minutes fled from my mind for that instant.

At the door containing Daniel and the burly guy with bushy eyebrows, I gestured for them to move back to the far wall. When they had, I opened the door slightly and said, "You think you're the bad guys, but you haven't seen anything yet. This should help you out when they come for you." I tossed down another paralyzer and slammed the door shut.

At the third window were two faces I didn't recognize, a man and a woman slightly older than me. Tara wasn't sure she recognized them either, so we decided to take no chances in case these were downstairs residents placed here for some contingency plan. I gave them the third paralyzer, but left them locked up. Only after seeing them did I realize there was no sign of the blonde woman on Wade's team. I supposed that meant she was being questioned somewhere.

I dumped the three unconscious downstairs residents in a nearby room so whoever arrived next wouldn't immediately know how bad the situation had been. Maybe they would think the three guards had been summoned elsewhere.

"Back to the ship?" Tara said.

"Right. Let's hope we can do it without getting caught." Not totally in jest, I added, "If we can't, what do you think about a suicide pact?"

"Only if the one other choice is to be tortured to death and there's absolutely no way out."

Tara and I left the others trapped in their holding cells, and we started for upstairs and freedom from religious persecution.

"So you never had the slightest clue about the bottom half of the Tower?" I asked once we reached the comparative safety of the stairwell.

Tara shook her head. "Only the kind of thing that makes sense afterward. Like occasionally being surprised by faces that seemed unfamiliar even though I had seen most of the people here. My friend who I had thought was here and who wasn't here when I arrived. I suppose she was one of their victims. Just like Marj Lendelson."

We climbed a few more steps in silence before she turned to me and whispered, "Why? Why do they do it?" Her eyes shone and her voice was gravelly.

I whispered back. "I don't know. Power? I think you can always find people willing to take advantage of other people. You can dress it up in politics or religion or sex, but I've met too many people who get enormous pleasure from having that power. Mix that instinct with a set of rules designed to let you convince yourself you're actually doing something that makes sense and is beneficial to at least some small group, and everyone else had better watch out."

"Sounds sick to me."

"That's what I said."

We reached the door to level minus-one. I looked at the stairs continuing up to the "maintenance" level, and I hesitated.

"What's on this level?" Tara asked. Her cheeks had regained their color, and her eyes were more animated.

"I don't know." I slid the door open just enough to see through. There wasn't much to look at, because immediately on the other side was a darkened cubicle that appeared to be an airlock.

"Maybe they don't want light from the stairwell getting in," Tara said just as the thought occurred to me.

"Let's take a quick look."

With the stairwell door closed behind us, the only thing keeping the cubicle from being totally dark was a set of dim ceiling panels emitting no more light than a dozen malnourished fireflies. I stood there a moment, listening to Tara's quiet breathing, letting my eyes adjust.

Warily, we opened the inside door, and stepped through into a dim hallway that ran parallel to the bank of elevators. The hall was empty and quiet. At intervals were doors leading inward.

I whispered, "Let's just peek and then go back up."

"Right."

We peeked. On level minus-one was what appeared to be their war room. Maybe the downstairs residents didn't see it that way. Maybe they called it their mission-operations room or their monitoring-and-control area. Whatever they called it didn't matter. A weed is a weed is a weed.

Suspended in the air over the semi-dark array of chairs and control panels were enormous holograms showing what must have been live scenes of upstairs locations. The circular opening in the floor was surrounded by a light filter field that barely permitted us to see the disk with the large "X" on the ceiling above. Inside the column was easily visible a scaled-down image of the top half of the Tower of Worship. Tiny robed figures walked on the main floor and several of the higher floors.

Surrounding the Tower of Worship was the square image of what seemed to be the tunnel level, and spreading out from it was a diminutive replication of the interconnected tunnel tendrils, along with stairways leading upward, presumably to individual cottages. The network of tunnel images also showed tiny people traveling along them.

At regular intervals along almost every section of tunnel, and at every cottage tunnel location, were indications of "maintenance" stairways leading downward. And below every section of tunnel image was a blue line indicating to me that a second set of tunnels ran beneath the public tunnels. That would explain how victims were moved from their cottages or other public areas to the downstairs section of the Tower of Worship without anyone else realizing what was happening. For all the public knew, the victim could have just said, "Good-bye. I'm going home."

But instead, that person might unknowingly and unwillingly be on a one-way trip to a painful downstairs visit. I leaned toward Tara and said, "I've heard of organized religion before, but this is ridiculous."

Tara put her lips near my ear and breathed, "They probably saw us as soon as we reached the tunnel, and they just waited for us to show what we were up to. And they'll see us if we leave by the tunnels."

"I agree."

As I watched the activity in the room, hoping for an inspiration, a new hologram grew from a point near one of the tunnel-to-surface stairways. It moved as it enlarged, until it hung unobstructed below the other displays. The view was evidently from inside one of the cottages on the surface.

The room in the hologram was sparsely furnished but attractively decorated with walls of pale green and blue. Showing in one corner of the view was a wooden storage chest topped with an upholstered seat. In the center of the room was a good-looking, tall blonde woman taking off an orange robe, apparently getting ready for the shower that became visible when the view of the room shifted a moment later.

I turned to Tara and said, "Maybe it's just me, but even when these people aren't actively kidnapping and killing, they still don't quite fit into my image of nice folks."

"I don't think it's just you." The anger in Tara's voice was stronger now. "Maybe we should get to the surface so we won't be seen in the tunnels."

"That *might* work. But we have another possibility."

"What?"

"I don't actually see more than five people. I might be able to shoot them all before anyone realized what was happening. They're all seated, so we won't have to worry about the noise of bodies falling onto the floor. I'd use this, but they're not close enough together." I showed her the silver ball I had confiscated earlier.

"Sounds risky to me."

"We're at the point where we have to take a few risks. You have a better idea?"

"Yeah. Let's find a safe spot and shoot one of them. When the others come to investigate, we'll throw the ball."

I looked at Tara. "You're a more devious person than I first thought. Let's clarify this 'we.' Who shoots and who throws and who watches for anyone we might have missed?"

"You've done well so far with the gun. I can throw accurately, and you can spot and shoot if we've missed anyone."

"This sounds crazy, you know that?"

"What third choice do we have that offers higher odds?"

I thought for a second or two. "Let's do it."

The nearest downstairs resident was halfway toward the center of the area, so we quietly entered the room and stood in the shadow of a nearby instrument rack. No audible sign of surprise came. The woman in the hologram stepped into the shower.

I whispered in Tara's ear. "It's funny how seeing someone get clean can make you feel dirty."

"You'd better concentrate on which direction we need to run as soon as we're finished. Assuming we can run."

"I think my leg's fine. We need to go that way." I pointed toward the wall on our left. "That tunnel ends up at the spaceport, and I assume the hologram is oriented to match the real world."

"So you have been thinking ahead."

I kept my silence. I think ahead, but sometimes I was convinced I spent too much time thinking about the past. Maybe that came from living on a ship where everything a person sees is in the past.

"Who are you going to shoot?" Tara asked.

I peeked around the corner to make sure the nearest person still faced away from us. He was. I gestured. "How about if we separate? If I shoot him from about over there"—I gestured again—"then if you miss anyone when you throw, I'll be able to get a better angle." I handed her the silver ball.

Tara nodded.

I was about to move toward the place I had gestured to, but I hesitated. "I'm sorry about what's happened to some of your friends."

Soft light bounced off Tara's eyes. "I am, too. But I'm glad you're here."

I moved away silently, staying in the slightly darker fringe near the side of the room. An adrenaline high was keeping me alert, and I felt a stronger sense of accomplishment than I had recently, a sense that I was really contributing in a way I hadn't before. And I felt a powerful sense of pride in having pleased Tara. The feeling was so strong that it made me conscious of it, wondering how she could have that effect on me, or whether I was doing it myself.

In the hologram, the woman finished washing her hair and began to scrub her body. Whoever was controlling the display rotated the view by about thirty degrees and caused a second hologram to join the first. The new view was from a point on the opposite side, so the two 180-degree views gave the entire war room complete visibility. I couldn't have asked for a more efficient distraction.

As I watched these people watching the woman, I suddenly wondered if my habit of holding myself apart from others—looking but not touching—was really any different.

I reached a bank of equipment racks far enough from my victim that I wouldn't be engulfed by the cloud of smoke, but close enough that I thought I could hit him. I rested my arm against the cabinet for steadiness, and took careful aim. He moved slightly in his chair, and then was still.

I squeezed the trigger.

The robed figure perked up and glanced to his left, as though he had heard a puzzling noise. He glanced to his right as I shifted my aim and fired a second needle.

The robed figure twitched and then his head tilted forward so his chin rested on his chest. I breathed a deep sigh no louder than the needler's *pffft*.

From the shadows I watched the remaining downstairs residents. I had counted six others by now. I wondered if Neddi Pulmerto was among them.

No one seemed to notice the fate of the resident nearest me. I considered shooting another resident, but I held back. One unconscious person might imply a health problem; two would obviously be the work of some outside agency.

Several minutes passed, and I began to worry more about Tara or me being surprised by someone new entering this level.

When my eyes seemed fully adjusted to the dim illumination, I thought I could see one more person than I had originally counted.

The woman in the hologram finished her shower and turned on the blower to dry. Apparently I had shot the hologram controller, because when the woman finished with the blower she walked off-stage without the view following her.

A moment later came a "Hey!" from one of the conscious residents. When my victim remained silent, the yeller came to investigate. As he approached, he said something angry that I couldn't make out. He shook my victim's shoulder.

To my non-surprise, the victim didn't wake up. Two more of the downstairs crew came to investigate. They couldn't rouse the sleeper either. As the remaining residents came to investigate, I realized that one of them carried what looked like a physician's toolbox.

The one with the toolbox put it on a nearby console and was opening it when I realized we couldn't wait much longer. Two stragglers were still too far away from the victim to be affected by the gas bomb. As the one with the toolbox brought something out of the box and moved toward the victim, I aimed for the farthest resident and squeezed the trigger twice.

Tara's timing couldn't have been better. Just as the person with the medical device reached the victim, Tara's sphere arced out of the dim perimeter of the room and exploded in the midst of the small group. Even as that was happening, and as my second victim was falling to the floor, I had the last resident in my sight.

I squeezed off one shot and then another, but I was too late; he dropped into a crouch and began to run in a zig-zag away from the expanding cloud. I still had seen no sign of anyone else, so I took after him on the run. Everyone near the cloud had fallen to the floor.

My leg wasn't as controllable as I had thought. I ran my thigh into the low edge of a console and then straightened and resumed the chase. As I ran I wondered for an instant how many shots I had used, and for just a millisecond a scene flashed through my brain. In a parody of an old-time entertainment feature, the tough law enforcer finally cornered the last of an enormous gang after a lengthy shoot-out, and he said something like, "I know what you're asking yourself; did he shoot ninety-five times or did he shoot ninety-six times?"

As quickly as the thought had come, it was gone. I cut across an open area toward the runner. I sped through the darkened room, following the sounds of my intended victim. The next instant, though, the sounds stopped.

I suddenly realized I was not near any convenient cover, and I wondered if, despite his running away, maybe this guy was armed. Just as I dodged left toward the safety of a pair of consoles, the *sizzle* sound of a paralyzer reached my ears.

I stumbled in my haste, but I reached the cover I needed. I knelt behind the consoles and realized the beam had missed me entirely. And then I realized I was in a bad position. I was hiding behind one of two low, connected consoles surrounded by an open area. If my intended victim had time, he could circle around me until he could get a clear shot. And Tara was unarmed.

I peeked around the edge of the console. Just after I snapped my head back, there came another *sizzle.*

I had spent less than five seconds trying to figure a way out when Tara's voice sounded clearly in the semi-dark room. "Back off, Jason. Here comes another one."

An instant later, I realized what she meant. A silvery object came flying in a high arc toward my opponent.

He suddenly began running. Hearing his footfalls, I reached around the corner and shot him in the back. He pitched forward onto the floor.

While this was happening, the object Tara had thrown bounced on the floor and skittered away under a console. She had thrown the seven-pointed star.

Only then did I consciously put it all together. Tara had tricked our victim into thinking that if we had one knockout bomb we could have a second, and that if he didn't get away then, he wouldn't have another chance. I had unconsciously done the right thing because I knew we didn't have a second bomb.

I looked in Tara's direction and saw her step from the shadows. She shot one fist up high. I couldn't see her face from here, but I could easily imagine her grin.

We started for each other and met near an unattended console.

"You do good work," I said. "That was brilliant."

"Thanks. But let's get out of here."

"One thing first." I led her to something I had seen from the corner of my eye as I ran.

"Help me get this out of the rack," I said. "I saw one of these on Redwall. It's their disrupter. Without it running, the people on the ship can see what's going on if they get worried about why we're not back yet."

I pointed to a rack-mounted blue chassis decorated with a circular symbol showing a slanted line drawn through the image of a leg stepping through an opening. Tara followed my lead and unsnapped the catches on her side. Together we slid the unit out horizontally. The top was sealed.

I said, "This box probably holds only a few cubic centimeters of vital components, but it'll be quicker to dump the whole thing. I don't want them to be able to repair it quickly."

We snapped the power connectors off the back, unhooked the unit from the rack slides, and carried it toward the center of the room. We lifted it onto the guard rail where it disrupted the light filter field. Pinpoints of white light danced like electrical sparks in a narrow line all around the box. We pushed the box gently over the edge, and it tumbled silently into the chasm.

I never heard the disrupter hit bottom. I was curious about whether the disintegrator field down there was always on, and what effect it would have on aluminum and assorted metals and composites, but we were running before the unit could have even reached the level immediately below us. I probably could have made up for years of childhood unhappiness by destroying the rest of the equipment in the room, but we had no time.

On our way out of the control room, I saw that our latest victim had been a woman, and I retrieved the paralyzer she had dropped. The woman wasn't Neddi Pulmerto. I was puzzled about not having seen her here or with the prisoners, but I couldn't spend time now worrying about where she was. I turned to Tara. "You know how to use this, right?"

"Right." Tara accepted the weapon and curled her fingers around the grip, and we started for the edge of the room.

The stairwell lights made me squint for a moment when we started upward. At the "maintenance" level, I peered through the gap at the edge of the door, and suddenly pushed the door all the way closed.

"What's the matter?" Tara whispered.

"There's someone out there, going to an elevator." I pried the door open barely wider than a hair.

"So we wait a minute, right? What then?"

"We could try the elevator." I reminded her that the seven-pointed stars might be keys. "But that hologram down there made it seem that a set of tunnels are on this level, running below the tunnels you're familiar with. And the lower tunnels probably aren't monitored. For all we know, that person is going down to the control room right now. So he'll see the mess we left and he'll be watching the monitors."

"Fine by me. Let's see if the tunnels are here."

A moment later, I pulled the door wide open. "Let's go."

Tara and I moved quietly and quickly down the hall and then turned away from the center of the Tower of Worship, heading toward the spaceport. Two more turns brought us to the start of the tunnel leading in the direction we wanted to go.

This tunnel was unlike the one we had come in on one level above. Where the winding public tunnel had rounded ceilings and a yellow floor, this tunnel was perfectly rectangular and looked like it had been cut with a laser. Far ahead, the walls met in a point. Maybe a hundred meters down the tunnel, a stairway in the center of the tunnel led into the ceiling. On each side of the tunnel were tracks for a levitational, rapid-transit vehicle. And on the left track stood one of the vehicles, motionless, ready for us to use.

We stepped into the car, and took seats. Some of the seats were equipped with manacles on the arm rests. We picked two that weren't. Near Tara's chair was the simplest control panel I could remember seeing. It had only one lever, free to move either toward or away from the Tower of Worship. Tara pushed it away, and we began to move. She pushed it all the way to the limit, and we moved fast. A soft whine grew in pitch as the wind rushed past us.

Stairways with distance markers like the ones upstairs flashed past. We were about two-thirds of the way to where we needed to get out when the vehicle on the other side of the tunnel sped by us, apparently going as fast as we were, but moving toward the Tower of Worship. I glimpsed four robed figures.

"Uh-oh," I said. The other car was slowing to a stop.

"I see them," Tara said. "I've got this thing pushed as hard as it will go."

In the distance the other vehicle stopped and reversed direction, coming toward us now. The other vehicle would probably be no faster than ours, but we still didn't have much of a margin. Guessing whether we could reach our jumpsuits without getting caught was no easier than correctly predicting a one-vote-margin election.

The distance markers were slowly growing closer to the point where we had come underground. The other vehicle had matched our speed, but didn't seem to be gaining.

"Our stop is coming up," Tara said, pointing at one of the stairway numbers as we sped past it.

I nodded, looking back at the vehicle keeping pace with us. A moment later, I asked, "Are you ready to run?"

"As ready as I get. This is our stop. Hang on."

Tara swung the lever all the way to the Tower of Worship end of its slot, and we nearly slid out of the chairs as the vehicle decelerated. It was still moving when we jumped off and ran for the stairway leading upward. My leg buckled as I hit the stairs, but I recovered and followed Tara up.

The other car was already slowing to a stop. I had my needler ready in one hand and had my other hand in my pocket, reaching for one of the seven-pointed stars I was sure was a key of some kind. Fortunately we didn't need it; the door ahead slid aside as soon as Tara applied pressure to it. We raced through the doorway and found ourselves where we had been before, at the bottom of the spiral staircase. Another nearby door led to the public tunnel.

"Go on up there!" I said. "Get any two suits except the ones you and I came in. They say 'remote' on the chest. Put the others near the door up there. Get into a suit and set it for layer *one*. *Not* ten. And see if you can find one of the collar controllers."

Tara was on her way up the circular staircase as I slid the door almost closed behind us and pointed my needler into the gap. I said, "When you're in your suit and you have mine nearby, find some cover. Signal to me when I come out and then get out of sight."

"Right, but hurry." Tara sped almost noiselessly up the stairs.

I fired three needles into the gap and caught the first pursuer. The second one tumbled over him and I shot a needle into his back. The others scrambled for cover.

I took a quick peek through the gap, and saw a robed figure aiming a weapon at me. I ducked back and heard a *crackle* as though a high-power laser had just melted a pocket in the other side of the door. I waited until I heard another *crackle,* and I moved behind the wall instead of the door. Left-handed, I shot a few needles toward the laser holder.

The laser's next shot burned a hole through the door and sent a spray of material exploding from the edge of a stairstep. He must have had his gun plugged to a belt-pack to get that much power. When this guy went hunting, he probably used heat-seeking missiles.

I moved my needler to the gap, ready to take another shot to convince him to stay back. Hot metal splattered against my knuckles as the gunner's beam caught the door just beside my hand.

I hoped Tara was making good time; holding these guys off was turning out to be harder than I had anticipated.

I twisted the control to rapid fire and let the muzzle of the needler show through the gap for an instant before I jerked it away. The gunner returned fire immediately. He obviously was a devoted subscriber to the theory that it's better to give than to receive.

I don't like that in an opponent.

I let the needler show again. As he returned fire, I dropped to my knees, poked the muzzle through the bottom of the gap, and sprayed.

My finger must have been a little sluggish in releasing the trigger; the remaining count had dropped to twenty-two.

I set the needler back to single-action and waited, listening.

The silence lasted a long moment, and then I heard a footfall on the stairs. I waited another second, and unleashed another trio of needles.

This time I waited longer. I needed to convince the remaining one or two people that the next silence from me didn't necessarily mean I was leaving.

I heard another sound, feinted with the needler, and fired again from higher up.

The returning laser fire made both edges of the door melt and glow. On impulse, I pulled the door shut. Moving as quietly as I could, I ran up the stairs, hoping that a few seconds would be enough to let the metal cool and weld the door shut.

I reached the door at the top of the stairs and raced out into the daylight.

There was no sign of Tara.

Something Wicked This Way Jumps

In a panic, I looked around for Tara. All I saw was a collection of jumpsuits spread on the ground. The daylight somehow made the rust-tinted rings above seem closer.

Before my heart had time to completely seize up, I saw a waving arm back to my left. "I'm all set!" Tara yelled. The rest of her body was concealed by a small cauliflower tree.

I pointed my needler at the suits on the ground and hosed them, hoping to make them leak enough to be unusable, and I ran toward Tara, shedding my robe as I ran. As soon as I reached her, I handed her the needler and threw my robe under a nearby bush.

Tara was suited except for her helmet. I moved behind the concealment she had selected and said, "Keep watch and shoot if you see anyone coming this way."

With her left hand she held the paralyzer. In her right, she gripped the gun. Fortunately the jumpsuit gloves were thin enough to admit her finger to the trigger guard.

I pulled on the other jumpsuit, and the idea of a diagnostic safety check—drilled into my brain ever since I started working on the *Redshift*—never occurred to me at all.

I set my chest controls for layer one, and checked hers. All correct. I said, "Punch this button as soon as you've got your helmet on. I'll catch up shortly."

"Why can't we go together?"

"Impossible. I'll explain later."

Her eyes widened as she looked past me. "Oh-oh. They're out."

"Give me that." I grabbed the needler and handed her helmet to her.

She dropped the paralyzer as she accepted her helmet. "But I don't—" she was saying even as her helmet clicked into place. I pressed her departure control and she vanished in mid-sentence.

The followers might not have seen us before that point, but the loud *pop* caused by Tara's body departing was sure to tell them where I was. I clicked the needler control to rapid fire and sprayed needles toward the cauliflower tree until the magazine emptied.

I snapped on my helmet and began to run, zig-zagging as I went. Layer one was about eleven times smaller than layer zero, so if Tara and I were a meter apart when we jumped from here, we'd wind up superimposed. And dead.

Ahead and to my right, a clump of the upper growth of a small cauliflower tree burst into flames. I ducked lower and ran to my left.

I swerved and dodged as I ran. I was almost as far as I needed to be when my suited foot caught a root protruding from the ground.

I pitched forward, and another laser hit ignited shrubbery in front of me as I pushed the switch on my chest. The world went black and gravity vanished.

I tumbled in the darkness, thankful to be intact. I wondered how familiar the shooter back there in layer zero was with the concepts of hyperspace and jumpsuits. For all I knew, he could have thought he just shot a balloon and popped it.

As my eyes adjusted to the dimmer light, I could see the control images on the inside of my helmet. I turned on my shoulder lights and radio.

"Tara, can you hear me?"

No reply.

I told myself the reason for that was probably as simple as Tara's not knowing how to turn on her radio. But I worried. I saw nothing of her jumpsuit reflected back from my shoulder lights. I couldn't see the beams, but a glow around the rims of the lights told me they were indeed on.

I told my jumpsuit jets to stop my tumbling. I felt several pushes against my chest, and a moment later the blood pressure in my head seemed to diminish. Still no sign of Tara.

With the jets I twisted to my left and there she was.

I jetted slowly toward her.

"Are you all right?" I said when I was able to touch my helmet to hers. I couldn't see her face without pointing my shoulder lights directly into her eyes.

"Now I am." The conduction path made her voice tinny. "How do you turn on the radio? And are you all right?"

"I'm fine now." I told her how to use her eyes to command jumpsuit functions. We both switched our suit radios to local communications.

Tara's shoulder lights turned on, and her voice began coming through my helmet speakers.

"I can hear you fine," I said.

"Much better. Now where are we?"

"We're adrift in layer one. We still need to get back to the same layer the *Redshift* is in. Are you ready to jump again?"

"Tell me what's going on first. Why did we have to jump separately? And I thought the speed of light was slower here in hyperspace, but I'm not noticing any communication lag."

"It is slower, but only by about a factor of five and a half. Each layer out from zero it drops that same ratio. Corresponding distances drop at twice that rate, so the speed-of-light travel time drops by a factor of two for each level. Clear?"

"Enough for now, I suppose. So if we were a meter apart now and we jumped back to layer zero, we'd be eleven meters apart. And if we jump to layer two we'll be one eleventh of a meter apart, so—so we'd kill each other—we'd overlap."

"Right. Each time we jump another layer toward ten, we'll have to separate. Our lifebelts will keep our internal activities going at the proper speed." I considered telling her that if we jumped to layer ten right now, we'd also jump directly into the *Redshift,* assuming it was anywhere close to Xanahalla. The volume of a small solar system in layer zero would all map into the volume of the *Redshift* in layer ten. A ship-controlled jump from layer ten to layer zero could be focused, but, unassisted, we would materialize at points corresponding to our centers of gravity.

"All right," she said. "I'm ready. I think."

"One more thing. Were you able to get one of the collar controllers?"

"It's on my wrist."

"You're beautiful."

"Tell me that when you can see me."

Maybe I will, I thought. Aloud, I said, "We'd better get ready for the next jump. Set your controls for layer two."

When Tara and I were both ready, I gently pushed against her suit. I let our separation increase to about twenty meters before I said, "See you in the next layer. Go when I reach zero. Three—two—one—zero."

This time the translation was less disconcerting. Despite the brief flash of light, going from zero-gee in black vacuum to zero-gee in black vacuum was comfortable. Tara winked out of existence and an instant later she was there again, hardly more than a meter away. I couldn't tell who had been first to reach layer two.

"That was easy," Tara said. "Are the rest of the jumps going to be like that?"

"Pretty much. But we have to be careful before the last."

We set up for a jump to layer three and separated again. With a series of jumps and separations, we reached layer nine. Since the speed of light here was between fifty and sixty meters per second, an almost imperceptible delay told me we were getting close to what had been normal for me for years. My shoulder lights swung past Tara, and the lamps seemed to be aimed slightly behind where I knew them to be.

"All right," I said. "This time has to be different. We could be sitting right on top of the ship right now, and there's no way I can tell for sure. It's a sphere with a diameter slightly over fifty meters, so that means it overlaps this space with a sphere with a diameter of about eleven times that. About half a kilometer. We've got to get at least a couple of kilometers from here to be safe, and I can't accurately gauge our speed, so we'll have to underestimate it."

We linked arms and both gave our jets a long blast. The force felt as strong as in a quickly accelerating land vehicle, and we let the jets blast for over ten seconds, so I pegged our velocity at least ninety percent of the speed of light here, which meant we were probably moving about fifty meters per second.

"We'd better coast for at least a couple of minutes," I said. "If our clocks are slowed down significantly, we'll go a lot farther than we need to, but that's still better than translating directly into the ship."

"We separate again once we're far enough away?"

"Right. But this time we don't go simultaneously. I'll go first and then translate directly back to this layer. If you don't see me, you'll know we didn't go far enough."

"And I'll—I'll know that you're dead."

"Well, yes."

"Jason, let's go at the same time. I don't know that if you're dead—"

"Sorry. Decision's been made. If I don't pop right back, use your jets for a burn three times as long and coast for five times as long before you translate to layer ten. The ship's got enough gravity that you'll fall toward it." I told her how to open the airlock.

We had traveled what I estimated to be a safe distance when I gave

Tara directions to separate to a distance of about twenty meters. We hung there in the blackness, our shoulder lights directed at each other.

"You understand?" I asked. "You don't translate to ten until you see me come back."

"Yes, sir, Mr. First Officer, sir."

"Tara."

"I understand."

"Tara, I—I think a lot of you."

She had started to reply when I pushed my switch.

I found myself in blackness, complete except for the glow of light reflecting from my jumpsuit arms near the shoulder lights. I breathed a sigh of relief that my calculations had been conservative enough. I was just about to set the controls for a jump back to layer nine when Tara materialized in front of me.

"Fancy meeting you here," she said innocently.

"I thought I told you to stay in layer nine until you were sure it was safe to come through," I said.

"Punish me later. I wanted to be with you. And we're both still alive, right?"

We hung together in the starless night of layer ten. As my body slowly turned, my shoulder lights swept past Tara's jumpsuited body. I couldn't see her face inside the helmet. "That's not the point."

"Well, what is?"

"Two points, actually. We're on a mission. If we fail, other people die. We can't afford two leaders, and I've had a lot more practice in this environment than you've had."

"I understand what you're saying, but that all sounds like one point to me."

"The other point is that—that when you popped into this layer all I could think about was what would have happened to you if the ship was here."

"Jason, I'm sorry. I'm not very good at following orders unless I understand them and agree with them, but I'll make an effort."

"All right. If I have time, I'll explain everything I tell you to do. But I've got to know that you'll do it anyway if I don't have time, or else you stay outside for a while when we get back to the ship." I didn't point out that following orders only when one agreed and understood didn't really amount to following orders. I was extremely glad she was there and I was having difficulty facing that fact.

"Agreed. I guess I lost sight of the goal for a little while, too."

I started to say, "Too?" but Tara had another question. "Are you sure the ship is even still here? I can't feel that I'm being pulled any particular direction."

"You wouldn't feel that. We're falling toward the ship, wherever it is, just as though we were in a falling elevator. In a falling elevator, you feel certain you're going toward the ground, but you don't really know that. You just feel as though you're in zero gee, like now." I flipped on my jumpsuit's mass detector.

"The ship's over our heads," I said a moment later. "We're falling toward it roughly headfirst."

"How far away?"

"Probably a few minutes at our current acceleration. Plenty of time to reverse our attitude. Even if we don't, we'll probably hit lightly enough not to do any damage. We can't fall any faster than escape velocity, and that's less than nine meters per second."

"That sounds fast to me."

"Put another way, it's no faster than you'd be falling in normal gravity, from a height of less than four meters. And that's absolute tops, assuming you fell from infinity. We probably won't reach even half that speed. Come on. Let's flip over so we'll land on our feet."

"Fine by me. I've got *two* of them. And if I break one, I'll get by."

"We'll be fine." Actually there was one danger here, but we couldn't do anything about it, so there was no point in worrying Tara. If the ship began to change position and we happened to be close to the warp point, we'd be compressed into a lump of closely spaced subatomic particles.

I linked arms with Tara and let my jets do the attitude correction for both of us. We turned so slowly that I couldn't perceive the change, and, when the mass detector indicated the ship was in the darkness "below" our feet, the jets gave one short blast to stop the tumble.

As we fell, I unhooked one light from my shoulder and pointed the beam downward. I saw nothing except our booted feet.

"You're sure the ship's down there?" Tara said.

"That's what the mass detector says."

"And it can't be wrong."

"It's unlikely. We're back in layer ten, remember. It's going to take the light a while to get back—"

"There it is—the ship!"

Sure enough. Below us was a violet-tinged spot of light bouncing off the hull of the *Redshift*.

"We're coming toward it awfully fast," Tara said.

"Not as fast as it seems. Since we're approaching the ship, the travel time for light is constantly decreasing, so we're seeing maybe ten seconds of image compressed into six or eight seconds. So the distance appears to be closing faster than it really is—like looking at your approaching reflection in a mirror."

"If you say so." Tara sounded unconvinced.

"We'll slow down soon, anyway." I let another few seconds pass, and used the jets to brake and correct the slight tilt induced because the braking jets weren't lined up with our combined center of gravity. The violet tinge below us faded, and the reflected light looked to be a neutral gray.

We hovered a half-meter off the surface of the ship until I finally cut the remaining power. We landed as gently as a falling hair.

"This way," I said, pointing my light in the direction I had seen an airlock. I could have maneuvered us closer with jets, but walking was simpler.

As we walked, Tara said, "I always thought hyperspace ships would have insignia on the outside of the hull."

"I guess they figured it was cheaper just to *tell* people they were there."

I knelt at the airlock cover and punched in my access code, hoping Wade's compatriots hadn't thought to change them. They had no reason to, if they were expecting Wade to call them with a transmitter, but if it were me, and I was covering every contingency I could imagine, I'd have changed the codes.

The alternative to going in through the airlock was much riskier. I could do some careful calculations, jump to exactly the right height, and, as I fell, translate to layer nine. After measuring exactly the right delay, I could translate back to layer ten, appearing in midair in level seven of the *Redshift*. Of course the slightest miscalculation would mean that I might appear with my lifeless body dangling from the ceiling, my head embedded in the bulkhead. Or materialize with my feet rooted into the deck below.

The airlock refused to open.

I tried the series again, hoping that my distracting thoughts had made me garble the sequence. This time the airlock door swung silently ajar and light began spilling out around the edges. I pulled the door the rest of the way up, revealing what seemed more reminiscent of an enormous empty refrigerator than the gateway to home.

"Is the light on all the time?" Tara asked, as though she were reading my mind. I could virtually hear the grin in her voice and I wondered how two people could be thinking such inane thoughts when there were far more important things to be worrying about. Defense mechanisms?

"You want to close the door and then open it real fast? In this environment, you can actually find out." Even as I spoke, I was lifting her over the airlock opening and lowering her toward the floor. In another bizarre image I couldn't force away, I saw myself in the old-time tradition of carrying Tara over the threshold. Except that the *Redshift* wasn't our home.

"Is your radio still on?" Tara said an instant later. "Are you listening?"

"Yeah. Sure. Did you say something?"

"I asked where we go from here."

As I edged over the lip of the airlock and dropped to the floor next to Tara, I was wondering the same thing. "I think a two-pronged approach is best. I'll go to the bridge, and you'll free the prisoners at the swimming pool. Only two of Wade's gang are aboard, and they should both still be on the bridge."

The overhead airlock door sealed, and atmosphere was admitted to the chamber. After the pressure built up to normal, I indicated to Tara that it was safe to take off her helmet.

"Are you sure?" she asked. "Last time you did this, you passed out."

"All right. Keep your helmet on."

I started to remove my helmet but Tara stopped me. "If there is trouble like that still, it's better that you be the one to stay awake."

I protested mildly, but she was right, and I let her convince me. What was left to do could call for knowledge of the ship. And for killing. Tara twisted her helmet off and took several deep breaths. She grinned and shook her hair loose from the jumpsuit's collar.

I took my helmet off and began shedding my jumpsuit, remembering only then that I was without a shirt. Tara wiggled out of her jumpsuit, letting her robe unfold back to her feet as she did.

"I expect you'll need this," she said, unstrapping the collar controller from her wrist. She handed it to me, looking into my eyes as I took it.

I nodded, returning her gaze. I strapped the unit on my wrist and examined it briefly. Apparently, pressing the two *unlock* buttons simultaneously would release the collars. Pressing any other button could be instantly disastrous.

"Jason?"

I looked back up.

"Don't do anything—sacrificial, will you?"

I was silent for a moment. "They're my friends. They would do whatever it took if they were in my position. But I don't expect to have to do anything like that."

Tara's eyebrows fell a millimeter and her lips pursed. "I understand that. I guess I'm just saying they're not your only friends. Don't take *too* many chances, all right?"

"We've already taken a few risks together."

"You know what I mean."

I nodded. As I turned to release the inner airlock door, Tara twisted my chin and kissed me full on the lips.

Surprised, I looked at her and said, "Thanks. I needed that." I couldn't say such a silly line without grinning.

"So did I."

I returned her kiss, with less humor and more feeling.

Seconds later, I slowly pulled open the airlock door. No one was in sight. We turned right and tiptoed quickly down the hallway toward the nearest stairwell.

"We're at the south pole," I told Tara. "You think you can find the swimming pool?"

"Easy. And I'll go on to the dining hall once I've let the passengers out?"

We reached the stairwell and started down, the spectrum of lights changing hues as we descended. "Right. But be damn sure the passengers don't use the comm panels or anything else that might warn those two on the bridge. If I'm successful, there will be a ship-wide announcement. Tell the crew the situation. They can use their own judgment on what to do or not to do."

"You got it."

At the fifth level, Tara told me her intended path to the swimming pool.

"Exactly right. Good luck."

Tara touched my arm. "You're telling *me* to have good luck?" And then she was gone.

I descended another flight of stairs and walked onto level four of the *Redshift.* It felt good to be back. I felt as soiled in a matter of hours in Xanahalla as I had in years on Redwall. I would probably never see a legitimate church again without thinking back to Xanahalla or wondering if the church had a basement.

The ship was quiet. I encountered no one as I neared the bridge. At an emergency locker, I entered my code and withdrew three disablers. I put one in each of my back pockets and held the third ready to use.

I reached the door to the bridge. The longer I delayed, the more likely a passenger was to do something that would alert the bridge, so I pressed the two *unlock* switches on my wrist controller, and slid the door aside.

A fraction of a second later, I saw Bella and Razzi, both sitting at the main console. Razzi still wore her running suit. Flanking the two women were the two black-suits left behind as guards. None of them had had time to see me or to start to react.

I turned my head and said, as though to someone behind me, "Sure, they're still here, Wade. You don't have to be so damn pushy—"

As I finished talking, I launched myself awkwardly into the room, as if I had been shoved. I let myself bounce off a nearby console, directly for Bella and Razzi, whose images were just now reacting to my arrival. I could see their collars hanging loosely from their necks.

The two guards wasted at least two to three seconds by pushing useless switches on their wrist units. Just as they drew their knives and began to close in, I slid two disablers toward Bella and Razzi. As the disablers skidded nearer my friends, I clutched my own disabler and started for the closer guard.

The guard I picked must have been tired, or worried by the change in plans, because he froze. As I moved closer, he began to retreat. I feinted and then slashed my disabler past his face, not touching him, but letting him know this environment gave me a strong advantage.

He made a tentative swing, and then another. I made a feint, and kicked hard at his kneecap. I connected.

The blow was solid, so I risked a quick glance toward the other guard. He was already cornered by Razzi. Bella was standing by in case either of us needed help.

As I looked back at my opponent, he threw his knife away. It skittered into a corner. He just sat there, grimacing from the pain, holding his knee with both hands.

I retrieved his knife and moved closer to the man Razzi held at bay. As I approached from one side, Bella approached from the other. The remaining fighter looked at the array of disablers and a knife he was now up against. He probably couldn't help missing the expression on Razzi's face, either. She looked as angry as if someone had been watching *her* in the shower and she'd found out about it.

The man dropped his knife on the floor and kicked it toward Razzi. Silently she retrieved it.

Bella surveyed the two black-suits and then she grinned. "Jason, I'm mighty glad to see you, even if you are out of uniform. What took you so long?"

"What's it to you? You don't pay me by the hour." I grinned back.

"Remind me to review your salary. Is everything else under control, or are there more of this motley crew left to deal with?"

It seems that no two events are ever truly simultaneous aboard the *Redshift,* but, in my frame of reference, at the same time I said, "It's all under control," someone else said, "Yes and no."

Bella and Razzi and I whirled to face the doorway. Standing there, holding Tara by the neck, was a jumpsuited figure taller than she was. In the person's hand, pointed at Tara's midriff, was a high-power laser pistol connected to a belt pack.

The face showing through the jumpsuit visor was Neddi Pulmerto's.

Beyond Neddi and Tara, in the hallway, was another armed and jumpsuited figure. While Tara and I had been on our way back here, Neddi must have been busy, too.

"Listen closely," Neddi Pulmerto said. She seemed to have aged very little since I had last seen her clearly. The helmet obscured most of her hair, but the little that showed was still a deep red. Her skin on her round face seemed almost as smooth as Tara's, but Neddi had tiny laugh lines spreading out from the corners of her eyes, and several minute vertical creases to either side of her mouth. Her eyes could have been the eyes of a charismatic revolutionary leader, feared and respected by all.

She continued, her voice emanating from a speaker on her collar. "If I see anyone start to move toward me, I'll cut this woman in two, and then point the gun at whoever moved. There's enough juice in here that the beam will probably reach everyone else still in the room, not to mention do a lot of damage to the controls."

"But you don't want us all dead, do you?" I said. "You'd prefer us alive, for—religious ceremonies, wouldn't you?"

Neddi focused her gaze on me. "Do I know you?"

"Not that I know of. Unless you've traveled on the *Redshift* as a *paying* passenger. I seem to have misplaced my uniform shirt, and I'm the first officer." If Neddi didn't recognize me, that was lucky for me. After the damage I did to Redwall when I left, she might have been willing to destroy the rest of the ship just to make sure she had me.

"What ceremonies are you talking about, Jason?" Bella asked.

I spoke without turning away from Neddi. "Xanahalla's a sick place.

A significant fraction of the arrivals are tortured and killed. Apparently most of the rest of the residents know nothing about what goes on. And the third group, no doubt represented by our visitors here, conduct the 'ceremonies.' "

"That's enough," Neddi said. "We need a pilot."

"What for?" Bella asked. "And what makes you think you'll get one?"

"I want to drop off my companion back on Xanahalla. And I don't doubt that I'll get a pilot. How many people do you think I would need to kill in front of you before someone is willing to do the job?" Neddi tightened her grip on Tara's neck, and Tara winced.

"I'm a pilot," I said suddenly, not wanting any deaths, and sure that Tara's would be the first if the killing started. Unfortunately, I didn't want to pilot, because the certain outcome of letting Neddi's companion off on Xanahalla was the arrival of more of Neddi's friends.

Bella obviously wasn't keen on the plan, either. "You won't give her any help, Jason."

Even Tara thought my offer was a bad idea. "Let her kill me. Blowing up the ship would be better than letting her loose."

I said, "I don't want any of us ending up dead. Where do you want your friend put down?"

"Halfway between the spaceport and the Tower. His suit has one jump left, so it had better be accurate," Neddi said as Bella said, "Absolutely not. Get away from the controls, Jason."

"There's too much noise in here," Neddi said. "Use the paralyzer."

Tara's body sagged against Neddi, and an instant later I heard the sizzling sound of the paralyzer. I was lucky Neddi had told me ahead of time her friend was only paralyzing Tara; I don't think I would have been able to stay motionless otherwise.

Neddi's companion stepped into the doorway and with his foot pushed Tara's body out of the way. He held a bulky paralyzer in his gloved hands. I could see the gun-metal-blue tint in the muzzle, so the gun had been specially built for this environment. The weapon was so large it could barely be called portable.

"Now the two women and those two," Neddi said. "But give them a chance to sit down first."

The man with the enormous paralyzer moved toward Bella. Without the threat of Neddi's laser, he might not have had any advantage over an unarmed opponent.

"I'm overwhelmed by your thoughtfulness," Bella said bitterly. She and Razzi and the two black-suits were careful to make no sudden moves as they took seats. Bella looked at me and said, "You're going to have a lot to answer for, Jason."

Razzi said, "Be careful," just before she slumped in her chair. The sound of *sizzles* reached my ears.

Bella might be right, but, for the first time, I had an idea that might work, thanks to something Neddi had said.

"Where's your origination point for controlled jumps?" Neddi asked. Her companion kept his paralyzer aimed at me as Neddi moved to a position where I would be between her and the view-screen.

I told her.

She sat down and gestured for me to take the controls. "Turn on the viewer and let's go."

The chair was cold against my exposed lower back. I looked up at the view-screen. The focus for jumping and viewing had drifted well off the surface of the planet. At first I saw only a starry sky. Then I turned the ship until we could see Xanahalla straight out in front of us.

"What's in it for me if I could drop off your friend inside the Tower, directly over the main floor?" Despite the paralysis, I knew Bella and Razzi and Tara could hear me. I hoped Bella didn't burst a blood vessel.

"You can't. There's a disrupter in the Tower."

"Not anymore."

"And just how would you know that?"

"I destroyed it." I should have shared the honor with Tara, but there was no need to focus Neddi's anger on her.

"Do that and I'll let you die painlessly. There are lots of other alternatives."

I paused to make her think I was considering the offer. "How do I know I can trust you?"

"What choice do you have?"

After a moment I shrugged. "All right. Here we go."

As Xanahalla grew in the view-screen, Neddi told her companion to go to the proper location in the hallway and be ready to jump.

I looked around the bridge. Neddi sat behind me, her laser ready. Bella and Razzi slumped in their chairs as though they had just attended a week-long training class.

Neddi said, "Don't even think about trying anything."

"I wouldn't dream of it." This was a time for doing, not for trying.

Neddi was silent for a moment as the view on the screen expanded. Then she said softly, "Your back." Even as I heard her words I realized she might be connecting the scars on my back with another chapter of her past. "Turn around."

I turned my head only partway toward her and said, "You want your friend deposited or not?"

"I *do* know you," she said, the astonishment plain in her voice. "You're Jason Kraft. You're the son of a bitch who cost me millions. You've grown quite a bit, but I still should have recognized you. Oh, Jason, you've been a bad boy."

It was too late to pretend she was wrong. "Does that mean you take back you offer?"

As I talked, I heard Neddi rise from her chair. I tensed, but when I glanced at her, she was apparently regaining control. She was sitting down.

"I don't know about that, Jason. I'm not sure I can let you off so easily after all." Neddi always had been frank. "You caused me a pile of trouble. For a long time after you left, the other kids kept coming up with ideas about getting out of there. I lost probably a dozen of them to failed escape attempts. And that whole process cost me a lot of time. I like to set things in motion, watch them run on automatic. You interfered, and you interfered more than necessary just to get away." She fell silent, no doubt considering my fate.

It sounded to me as if Neddi viewed her projects the way some parents saw their children. Her maternal instincts were satisfied by breathing life into offspring like Redwall and Xanahalla. Offspring that would be better off stillborn.

She said at last, "Jason, you should know as well as anyone about the levels of pain. If anything goes wrong now, I can guarantee you'll feel a lot more pain before I let you go. Do it right, and you'll get only what you've got coming for Redwall."

"Nothing will go wrong." I sincerely hoped that was true.

The Tower of Worship showed below us, gleaming brightly in the sunlight, looking like a spike in a pit waiting for someone to fall through the camouflage. As the view came closer, I reinstated the course-matching motion I had established earlier. From this distance, the Tower of Worship appeared stationary.

I took several deep breaths, trying to breathe slowly enough that Neddi wouldn't notice. I was going to need all of my energy supply available in just a few minutes.

We came closer to our destination. I was going more slowly than necessary, busily trying to figure out angles and speeds.

"When we're in there and ready for the jump, your friend is going to have to act fast," I said. "I can't keep the ship synchronized with such an exact point for very long. You want me to give the order to go?"

"No. I'll do it from here."

If Neddi could handle the comm panel near her chair, she was more familiar with the bridge than I had guessed.

"All right. But be as quick as you can." Maybe this would still work anyway.

We came closer to the side of the Tower of Worship. I adjusted the focus as far in as I could and still have the Tower showing clearly.

"When we go through the wall, I'll have to shut down the view-screen for a minute so we don't lose the sensors. You understand?"

"Yes."

I deliberately did not put on a set of command goggles. Either I got this right, the way I planned, or I didn't. And either way, I would need to move fast.

I made final calculations using the ship's computer to draw vectors on the view-screen image. Mentally, I made corrections to what the computer told me. "Is your friend on the mark?"

Neddi snapped on the comm line to the jumping off point and asked him. A moment later she said, "Yes. He's ready."

"All right then. Here we go."

The side of the Tower of Worship came closer, rising at the same time. We seemed to be no more than a meter away when I adjusted the focus even tighter and then stopped the scanner. A half-second later I had initiated the attitude correction I hoped was right, and started a countdown timer.

We flew blind, with me hoping desperately we were on the right course.

The display screen seconds counted down. They neared zero. I felt my body push sideways in the chair.

I took a deep breath and snapped the viewer back on.

At the bottom of the view-screen was a black-and-white view of a large circular plate with the familiar stylized "X" centered in it. The rest of the view was out of focus.

Neddi cried, "Go!" into the comm unit.

Only seconds later, the view-screen contained the image of a jump-suited figure, his feet no more than a meter from the circular plate.

I knew everything had worked exactly right when, instead of falling feet-first to the plate, the jumpsuited figure began to rise, accelerating as he went.

I estimated the time when Neddi would see the same view of her companion moving the wrong direction. If I waited too long, she'd shoot me in the back. If I moved too early, she wouldn't be distracted by the view.

Time to move. I scrambled out of my chair and ran for the open doorway. Neddi would at that very moment be figuring out that I had positioned us upside down in the *bottom* half of the Tower of Worship, and her friend was falling head-first into the disintegrator.

I reached the speed of sound even before I got to the doorway. At first I thought I had wasted some time by diving through the doorway, but Neddi's laser scarred the wall across from the doorway, at about chest height. She *had* been leading my image with the gun, so the environment wasn't totally alien to her.

I picked myself up and ran. If I could get to the dining hall and let loose the rest of the crew, Neddi would never be able to stop all of us. And being killed instantly with a laser would almost be a blessing compared to Neddi's techniques.

I zig-zagged as I ran. I heard nothing from behind me, and looking back would tell me only what had happened several seconds ago. The downward-curving corridor ahead contracted and shifted up into violet. I kept running so fast I couldn't hear my own footfalls, and I hoped Neddi's jumpsuit would keep her from following as fast as I moved.

A high horizontal section of the wall ahead glowed briefly. I didn't have as much of a lead as I had wanted. The good news was that the dip in the corridor made me a smaller target for Neddi. The bad news was that what showed the best was my head. I tried to crouch and still run as fast as I could.

Ahead was the door to the dining hall. If I could pull the peg loose so the crew was free before Neddi shot me, she wouldn't be able to overcome all of us.

I reached the door and stopped abruptly. The sonic boom shook my head. I pulled out the peg.

And then I saw that the door was welded shut; probably with Neddi's laser. I pounded on the door, partly in frustration, partly to let the people inside know they should try the door again. Maybe the laser seal wasn't as strong as it looked. I could have tried a knife on it, but that would have taken too much time.

I ran. Another laser hit brightened the ceiling over my head. Neddi was no doubt trying to run and shoot at the same time. I turned at the intersection, grateful for at least a few-second reprieve.

I had to get away from Neddi. But she could always see where I had been in the last few seconds. I could whip open a door while she was out of sight, hide in the room beyond, and be blithely blasted out of existence because she had watched my seconds-old image betray me.

I neared a stairwell. I thought about the extra area on the levels above, and then I thought about the limitation on running speed up there. And then another idea occurred to me. I slid open the door, another sonic boom hitting me as I slowed. Neddi's beam sent doorframe material splattering onto my bare arm. I went down the stairs, deliberately slowing as I went. I talked as I descended, hoping Neddi would hear the words and be angry enough that she might not be thinking as clearly as she could.

"Neddi Pulmerto, you stupid old woman. I'm Jason Kraft. I beat you on Redwall, and I'll beat you here."

I slid open the door to level three. The increased gravity reminded me how tired I was. I turned into the corridor and began to run, slightly more slowly than I had upstairs. I neither zigged nor zagged, remaining directly in the center of the corridor. Ahead of me and behind me, the corridor apparently stretched straight into infinity.

Now I dared to look back. My timing had to be accurate here.

There was no sign of Neddi.

And then she burst out of the stairwell door and looked both directions. She appeared confused for just an instant, probably because she saw two images of me, one approaching, one receding. She must have adjusted quickly because she raised her laser.

What I was seeing was all several seconds in the past of course, but so was her squeezing of the trigger. I fell flat on the deck for about a second, praying I had anticipated her reactions correctly. A second later, I was up on my feet again, running straight down the center of the corridor. Far ahead was an image of Neddi's back as she followed me, her gun arm raised.

She hadn't fired twice in rapid succession, so I risked another three or four seconds before I swung open a stairwell door and stepped into momentary safety. I hoped what I had done would work, but I didn't dare wait in the stairwell to find out. I raced up the stairs.

I looked back at the stairwell door. No sign of Neddi.

I ran to the dining hall. The door was still closed. I retrieved a kitchen knife from the supply room across the hall and used the blade on the crude laser seal, pounding on the crust and watching for signs of Neddi.

Some of the flowed metal had formed a thin icing. The knife bit through it.

I bent the knife blade trying to use it as a lever, but it was strong enough to move the door a centimeter. Instants later, the door slid open and I saw the crew.

"A through M, get to the bridge and guard it against whatever shows up. N through Z, free the passengers locked in the swimming pool. Bensode, come with me."

Bensode still wore his collar. As soon as he reached me, I said, "A laser-armed enemy was last seen on three. I need your help."

Bensode accepted my statement with no wasteful requests for explanations.

I explained what I hoped had happened, why I hadn't seen Neddi in the last minute, but cautioned Bensode that she was devious.

We descended the stairs to level three and took positions on either side of the doorway. No sound came from the corridor beyond.

I risked a quick glance.

Neddi's body lay no more than ten meters away from the stairwell door. Her laser pistol was still connected by an umbilical cord to the power pack on her waist, but the gun wasn't in her outstretched hands. Far in the distance there was still visible an image of Neddi falling to the floor, and even farther away, I saw myself exit the corridor via the stairwell doorway.

Bensode acted as backup while I went out to verify what had happened. I hugged the side of the corridor until I neared Neddi. Then I kept my head down and reached for the laser pistol.

I disconnected the gun from its power cable.

Neddi Pulmerto wasn't faking. She really was dead. The charred, puckered hole in the back of her jumpsuit confirmed what had happened; with her high-power laser, she'd shot herself in the back.

There wasn't much flow of blood; the laser had coagulated blood as it had seared into her back. Her blackened skin showed through the hole in the suit, indicating that her lifebelt was still functioning, even if it wasn't doing her much good.

While she was shooting at me, I had fortunately been able to get her so angry and distracted that she didn't stop to think about light circling the ship on level three. The laser bursts, that had missed me while I kept mainly in the center of the corridor, had circled around behind her. By now, unless she had been able to fire perfectly level at exactly the right height, the residual laser fire would have been spent on the walls, floor, or ceiling.

I stood there, my knees suddenly weak. I looked down at a person who had cut me so deep at a time that seemed far more recent than it really was, and memories came at me so fast I lost touch with the present. I saw Rissa's gratitude and the worried realization in her attacker's eyes all there right before my own eyes, as if light from those days was also still circling the deck of the *Redshift*.

When, some unknown time later, conscious thought began to resurface, I decided that, all things considered, the only epitaph for Neddi Pulmerto that fit was: what goes around, comes around.

I finally looked back toward Bensode, who was holding his uniform shirt bull-fighter style in the center of the corridor at the right height to detect any remaining laser fire. A few seconds later, after allowing time for light to completely circle this level, he put his intact shirt back on. He said, looking worried, "There's nothing left to worry about, Mr. Kraft."

"How can you say that?" I asked, forcing myself out of the spell. "If we can't believe in the infallibility of our religious leaders, who *can* we trust?"

"Mr. Kraft, I think you should come up here and take a look at this."

Bensode's call came while I was on the bridge with Bella and Razzi. We'd had time to send a complete trouble report over the net, together with position information on Xanahalla. While we waited for help to arrive, we had been monitoring to make sure the remaining downstairs residents stayed downstairs and didn't get access to escape vehicles. A few jumpsuits filled with water and translated into the middle of vital equipment made the apparatus useless. I suppose they were our equivalent of water balloons. Generally the entire process was sober and deliberate, but I derived a substantial amount of satisfaction when we launched the suits.

I found Bensode on level six. He and two crew members had a large shroud fastened over a bumpy section of a wall. When I reached them, Bensode said, "Here's a friend of yours that you're no doubt curious about. I guess he managed to get loose and tried getting back here in a blind jump."

Bensode pulled up one edge of the sheet and I saw the jumpsuit leg. He pulled the sheet higher, and I saw the rest. The rest that was visible, anyway. The jumpsuited figure was embedded in the wall. About a third of the body showed: one leg, one arm, a slice of torso, and a profile of the helmet.

I bent over and craned my neck to look through the small section of visor that stuck out from the wall. The man's features were pasty white, not because he was dead, which he certainly was, but because his lifebelt was buried in the wall and was no longer functioning.

A metallic taste formed on the tip of my tongue. We were lucky his arrival hadn't killed anyone.

"I suppose you know what this means, Bensode?" I said at last.

"Sir?"

"It means Wade Midsel doesn't have much chance for an open-casket funeral."

The *Redshift* participated in rescue operations. Our passengers, once they were let out of the pool and given a change of diet, seemed to acquire an adventurous spirit as they helped us assimilate upstairs residents getting ready for the voyage home.

I'd slept for a solid shift and then immersed myself in the daily operations, forcing myself to think of nothing except the job. Or trying to. Despite being in an environment full of relative values, my lack of successes was absolute.

"Jason, I need your opinion on something up here. Can you get free?" Razzi's call took me from the bridge to a storeroom on level six.

When I opened the door, though, instead of Razzi, I found Tara sitting on a supply crate. I said nothing, feeling even guiltier for having ignored her recently. She was nervously gnawing on a fingernail, but she glanced up quickly when she saw me arrive, and she once again looked calm and unruffled.

Tara's black hair shone like polished obsidian. She wore a red blouse. The color, associated mostly with objects receding from view, made me suddenly and acutely aware that my inaction was forcing her away.

"You're looking good," Tara said. The way she looked at me made me feel she could read my every thought.

"So are you."

There was another silence, which Tara broke. "You're afraid, aren't you? You don't want to ask for something and risk the possibility that you'll be turned down."

"No. Maybe. I—"

"Jason, Jason. I still see you better than you do. We've shared some risks together already. Some life-and-death risks. Take another risk."

I couldn't speak.

Tara stood up and approached me. "I see you clearly, Jason. And I like what I see. Is the problem that you don't like what you see?"

"No," I said huskily. "That's not it at all. I like what I see. Very much. It's just that I—I don't know—I suppose I've spent enough of my life unhappy that sometimes it seems that's all I'll ever be. I don't want to let anyone down."

Tara sucked in her breath. "Let anyone down? I don't think I've heard you say anything that silly before. Jason, I've seen what you do for people you barely know, and what you do for people you like and trust. You wouldn't be letting anyone down."

I looked into Tara's blue eyes and I felt even more light-headed than the low gravity could account for. I swallowed. Maybe I couldn't do everything right, but, compared to Wade Midsel and Xanahalla, I certainly wasn't all that bad an influence. And if I wouldn't risk getting closer to someone as extraordinary as Tara, I knew with certainty that I'd never let anyone get close again. Ever.

Finally I said, "You're right once again, you know that? Compared to what we've both been through, what's one more risk?"

Her swift, energetic smile took me back to Rissa's gratitude, but this time *I* felt grateful, too. Tara had fallen into my shell, or I had escaped.

Tara wrapped her arms around me. I'd had no idea she was so strong.

END

PHENOMENA ABOARD THE
REDSHIFT

Liability Disclaimer

The owners and operators of the Far Star Line, to which the *Redshift* belongs, encourage passengers to attend a complimentary orientation session before their first hyperspace voyage. By failing to attend such a session, passengers waive all rights to accident and injury claims while aboard the ship.

A Short Guide to Relativistic Phenomena

Aboard the *Redshift* light travels at ten meters per second. Sound travels at approximately six and two-thirds meters per second. All other results stem from these values. For passengers new to relativity, these effects have all been verified in normal space, and are all attributable to Einstein's Special Theory of Relativity, Einstein's General Theory of Relativity, or Newtonian mechanics; the only significant difference is that on board the *Redshift* they happen at easily observable speeds.

Contraction: Objects moving past you at speeds that are a significant fraction of the speed of light appear to contract in their direction of motion. (You, of course, appear contracted in your direction of motion, when observed by someone not moving along with you. The fact that you feel normal is one of the things that relativity is all about; your point of view affects your observations.)

Doppler Shift: Objects moving away from you rapidly have their colors shifted toward the red (lower) end of the spectrum. Objects moving toward you have their colors shifted toward the violet (upper) end of the spectrum. The shifts can be great enough to move the light outside the visible spectrum. This works for sounds as well, with slightly different equations, resulting in higher pitches during approach and lower pitches during departure.

Gravitational Red Shift: When light moves out of a gravitational field, it loses energy, so the colors shift down toward red. When light falls into a gravitational field, it gains energy, so its colors shift up toward violet. The shifts can be great enough to move the light outside the visible spectrum. If in a high-gravity-gradient location a single-frequency light over your head appears bluish, the same light held below your head will appear reddish.

Light Bending: In hyperspace layer ten, light travels slowly. Just as in normal space, however, light is still affected by gravity, so it falls noticeably. When light bends, you can be fooled into thinking curved surfaces are flat, convex surfaces are concave, and numerous other permutations. You have to learn to treat a flashlight the way you might use a water hose on Earth.

Mass Increase: As an object nears the speed of light its mass increases (as measured by a non-moving observer), therefore it takes more and more energy to keep accelerating it, and it can come close, but never attain the speed of light. The combined effect of apparent increased mass and apparent diminishing velocity increase is to conserve energy.

Reference Frame: All activity and measurements on matter in your own inertial frame seem normal (although, to observers in other reference frames, measurements may disagree).

Simultaneity: No two observers moving independently of one another will agree on the simultaneity of two events separated in space. All observers will agree on cause and effect; none will observe an effect before the cause, but they will disagree on the events' separation in spacetime.

Sonic Booms: Sonic booms are not a relativistic effect, but are heard by motionless observers when a supersonic object passes by, and all the sound created along its past journey arrives nearly simultaneously just after the object does. Aboard the *Redshift,* a jogger can create sonic booms for the people she passes.

Speed of Light: Light always travels at the same rate as measured in the local frame (the rate of time progression may vary, so an outside observer thinks the speed has changed).

Time Dilation: People moving past you at speeds that are a significant fraction of the speed of light appear to be experiencing time at a slower rate than you do. According to general relativity (as opposed to special relativity) those people in motion see you as an unaccelerated observer, apparently speeded up (consistent with the so-called Twin Paradox). Also, gravitational fields slow down time in proportion to the strength of the gravity. This means that on the lower levels of the ship time progresses more slowly than on the passenger level. If you wish to have a shorter trip, and don't mind the higher gravity, the *Redshift* has a small number of staterooms available. Conversely, if you don't mind having a longer (subjective time) trip, we have a few low-gravity staterooms up on level seven. We urge all passengers to arrange their schedules according to the ship's master clock.

INVENTING THE *REDSHIFT*

I know what you're saying. You're saying, "You can't fool me. He just made up all that stuff. There isn't really a Xanahalla, is there, Virginia?"

Maybe. Maybe not. But I didn't invite you here to talk about Xanahalla. Or the weather. Let's talk about the *Redshift*.

There will be readers (you know who you are) who take issue with the assumptions I made in this novel. I can hear one of you now, saying, "But, but, but—what about gas molecules?"

Yes, I realize that gas molecules typically move faster than the speed of sound. But if you slow them down enough to be consistent with the environment in this novel, they won't be in gaseous form any longer. More about this later.

Okay. I'll take another question. You in the back. Yes, you with your arm waving.

"But, but, but—what about electrons in orbit around atoms?"

Right. That's another potential problem area. I realize that orbiting electrons move at a significant fraction of the speed of light. Slow them down and you've got even more problems. I'll get to that, too.

Okay. I'm sorry. No more questions for the moment.

The point of all this is, I had to make a few convenient assumptions not central to the primary thrust of the novel; otherwise the basic idea is not nearly so interesting. I know that's heresy; perhaps to some readers it makes this book more of a fantasy rather than the hardest science-fiction novel I've written so far. So sue me. I thought the idea deserved treatment anyway.

I'm not saying I don't want to hear about where I went wrong; in fact, I hope this novel generates some arguments. I do hope also, though, that the liberties I took don't interfere with your willing suspension of disbelief. The remainder of this section traces the developmental history of the *Redshift*.

Maybe I can make all this clear. On the other hand . . .

Suppose you saw a jogger run past you fast enough that her body was contracted in her direction of travel. (If this concept makes no sense to you and sounds painful, you'll probably be better off at this point if you find an introduction to the theory of relativity. This part, I'm not making up. Honest.)

All right. You're imagining a significant change to our environment, so we can easily encounter relativistic effects at low speeds.

A jogger in this altered environment would find that as she runs fast, stationary observers she passes appear contracted in her direction of travel. Stationary clocks would be speeded up. Of course, those clocks wouldn't actually be fast; her internal clock would be slowed. Just like the traveling twin in the so-called twin paradox, she is moving through time more slowly than her sister who sits in a chair by the pool taking in the chlorine. If she runs fast enough, she can slow her internal clock to the point that she experiences only one second for every minute that her motionless sister ages. Looking at it another way, by running she slows her own aging process, so jogging really is good for her health. This is known as the run-for-your-life school of motivation.

The idea of relativistic effects happening at low speeds is the initial idea that led to *Redshift Rendezvous*. The balance of this section shows the evolution of the idea, the ripples it generated, the dead ends it led to, the expedient assumptions required, and the weak areas I haven't yet come to terms with. This information might be of interest to writers wanting to develop an environment from a single assumption, or to readers wanting to find the holes or think of even more implications. Or to trivia buffs.

I had several goals when I began *Redshift Rendezvous*. The idea stimulated my sense of wonder, and I hoped it would do the same for readers. The *Redshift* seemed a good vehicle for teaching about relativity, pun intended. And I was curious about how life in an environment like this would affect people. After all, if a story doesn't depend on people, it isn't fiction, and may as well be a dull article. Like this one.

An explanation like this runs the risk of lessening the enjoyment of the work for some people, just as knowing how Hollywood special effects are generated sometimes makes the viewer more conscious of technique than story, but I felt it would be of interest to a portion of the audience. And besides, it can't hurt *me*.

The idea of relativistic effects happening at speeds at which people could move without assistance led to two possibilities: either people must somehow move very fast (which sounded painful and really hard to justify), or the speed of light has to drop significantly. I chose to lower the speed of light. As my very first totally arbitrary decision, I picked ten meters per second as the speed, a little slower than current human running-speed records. To justify the speed of light being lowered, I presumed the existence of multiple layers of space, hyperspace, in which the speed of light decreases as one moves farther from layer zero, our familiar region of space-time. (Table One shows the dimensions of the *Redshift*.)

So that it would be useful to go into these other layers, I also assumed that distances between corresponding points in these higher layers would shrink by an even greater factor, so the light-speed distance between two corresponding points drops by a factor of two for each level farther from level zero. Hence, light-speed travel in layer ten is equivalent to 1024 times as fast as light-speed travel in our layer zero, even though ships move at not quite ten meters per second. High-speed communications occur with the help of hardened equipment placed in layer fifteen. (I've assumed that layers higher than ten are progressively more hostile to human life because of molecular instabilities.) Table Two shows the relative dimensions and speeds in each layer of hyperspace. To give you a practical idea of these dimensions, if you took every hyperspace passenger from one ship and lined them up head-to-toe, you'd have very little repeat business.

These assumptions about quantum layers of the universe are unjustified fabrication on my part, but at the same time they are probably going to be hard to unequivocally disprove for a few years (at least for someone with *my* education and inclination). Slow light in alternate hyperspace layers is the foundation for all the resulting ideas. Where I was unhampered by worrying about contradicting known facts or values, I've picked values that make the relativistic effects pronounced, in the same way that authors sometimes exaggerate trends or traits to look at a society skewed in one direction or another, e.g. what would a society be like where everyone had blue hair?

The hyperspace craft, the *Redshift,* resides in layer ten so it can cut travel time between widely spaced points. In layer ten, I've attempted to keep the rules of physics as we currently know them unchanged. The only alteration is to make the speed of light ten meters per second instead of 3×10^8 meters per second. I hope you'll agree this is a lot more interesting than, for instance, 3×10^7.

As long as I assumed people in this future know enough to warp space so they can translate between hyperspace layers, I assumed they also know enough to warp space to simulate a mass large enough to create a comfortable gravitational field. As long as curved space causes gravity, why not eliminate the mass? For the *Redshift* itself, I picked a spherical shape like a miniature planet, with spherical levels for floors. That way, gravity pulls the inhabitants toward the center of the ship, unlike one conventional approach that uses spin to create centrifugal force in the opposite direction, (which wouldn't work for a sphere anyway). Figure One shows the configuration of the *Redshift*.

Immediately, the ten-meters-per-second velocity of light leads to an environment in which a runner sees the surroundings undergo relativistic contraction. Also, the clocks in the motionless frame of reference appear to run fast. By the way, for those readers who think the motionless clocks should be going slowly when observed by the runner, bear in mind that this environment is not the special relativity environment in which two *unaccelerated* observers pass one another. Since a gravitational field is present, and the runner is accelerated while running around the circumference of the ship, we are dealing with general relativity.

About the time I reached this stage of idea development I ran across a reference to *Mr. Tompkins in Wonderland* by George Gamow (reprinted in *Mr. Tompkins in Paperback*). I was immediately incensed to find that someone else had used the idea of a slow speed of light to make relativity more understandable (and had done so more than forty years ago). I felt much better when I located *Mr. Tompkins in Wonderland* and found it to be a short work of non-fiction which doesn't touch on a lot more than I've already described. And the good part is just starting.

Okay. We're at the point where contraction and time dilation are justified. So is Doppler shift of light. The runner sees objects ahead of him shifted higher into the spectrum. He always measures light as having the same velocity, so the fact that the distance between him and approaching objects is decreasing shows up as increased energy in the light, hence higher frequency. Objects in his wake are similarly red shifted down the spectrum.

As I was growing more comfortable with the effects that stem from the original assumption, I remembered that light is deflected by warped space (large masses). In this environment, with light moving so slowly, that effect is enormously magnified.

On the Earth's surface, as in any gravitational field, light falls at the same rate as mass does. We don't think much about it because light speed is so high that the fall rate is negligible. Take two vertical face-to-face mirrors and shine a light perpendicular to one of the surfaces. At the same time, throw a ball directly perpendicular to one of two face-to-face walls. The ball will bounce back and forth, falling under the accelerating force of the Earth's gravity. So will the light. The ball and the light, although traveling at much different horizontal speeds, will reach bottom at the same time.

Aboard the *Redshift,* the same is true. The only real difference is that since the light is traveling slowly, it falls in about the same arc that a fast-moving object would move. Hence, light from a flashlight takes about the same path that water from a pressure hose would take.

Bending light is certain to cause more optical illusions than I have even thought of yet. I'll probably be thinking of them just as this book goes to press. At exactly the right distance from the central warped space, the speed of light matches orbital velocity, so the curved path that light takes when traveling around the circumference of the *Redshift* tricks the eye into thinking the light moves in a straight path on a level corridor.

Downstairs, inside that same radius, gravity makes light fall fast enough to cause different optical illusions. On level two, if you aim a flashlight at a wall ten meters away, the light falls about half that distance on the way there. You have to point the flashlight higher than the spot you want to illuminate. Since light moves slower than orbital velocity, it falls to the floor. Light from the floor out of direct (straight) line of sight curves around the body of the ship, so the observer can see much more of the floor than would otherwise be visible. This means that the light reaching one's eyes horizontally comes from the floor, and in turn this means that there is generated the illusion that the inner levels are bowls rather than the spheres they actually are.

I was busily drawing paths that light would take on the seven levels of the ship when I realized that with light dropping so fast, gravitational red shift would probably be easily observable. In fact, it's a major factor, especially on the lower levels. As light rises through a gravitational field, it loses energy, and hence lowers its frequency. The converse is true also. Looked at another way, if you place a single-frequency light source at an arbitrary height above the floor, the color perceived by individuals is a function of how tall each person is—or at least how far above or below the light source his eyes are.

Light travels from the source either up or down to eye level, turning redder if the eyes are higher, turning bluer if the eyes are lower. Reflected light has the same characteristics, so if one light-path takes photons to the ceiling and back to the eyes, the light loses energy on the way up, gains the same amount on the way back down to the original level of the source, and loses the balance on the rest of the journey. That means a room illuminated with a single-frequency light source would appear to be one color, and that color would change if the observer crouched or stood on a chair. This could lead to really atrocious color schemes.

Okay. We've got bending light and gravitational red shift. The next ripple is—why is the light bending? Because of gravity, of course. But that's not the precise answer. Warped space, which gives us gravitation, makes light bend because time slows down in gravitational fields. I promise I'm not making this up.

In our part of the universe, the lower east side, the speed of light in vacuum is constant. But, as verified during eclipses, light from distant stars does indeed bend around the sun on its way to Earth. It curves either because one side of the wavefront is going slower than the other —not acceptable because the speed of light is constant—or because time is slowed on one side of the wavefront. If time is slowed, light is still moving at the constant speed of light; it's only an observer outside the field who thinks the speed has apparently decreased.

So gravitational fields slow down time. It's true here, and it's true on the *Redshift*. But when you plug $c = 10$ into the gravitational time-dilation equation, there's a huge influence generated by the pseudo-mass at the core of the *Redshift*. Therefore, the closer one gets to the center of the ship, the more slowly time progresses. Each level is its own time zone, as though, for instance, time progresses more slowly in Denver than in New York. But I'm getting into another theory entirely. Back to time zones. Not only does the rate of time passage depend on what level you're on, no matter where you are on the *Redshift*, time progresses more slowly at your feet than at your head (assuming you're standing). One side benefit of this is that you don't have to cut your toenails as often as your fingernails.

It would seem at first that if your heart is pumping a constant supply of blood through your body, and time is going more slowly at your feet, that eventually there will be a gruesome explosion. Instead, there's a phenomenon analogous to water flowing through a pipe that varies in diameter along its length. In the narrow portion of the pipe, the flow increases, just as in the lower part of the body the *subjective* flow rate increases.

By the way, the slowing down of time in a gravitational field provides an alternate rationale for gravitational red shift. Light originating deep in the gravitational field seems to have a lower frequency when measured by an observer who is outside the gravitational field and whose clock is therefore not slowed down.

If light is going slowly enough for gravitational red shift to occur with the moderate gravity on board, the next conclusion is that some of the interior of the *Redshift* constitutes a black hole. This is one concept that I haven't thoroughly explored, however. The primary obstacle is that currently there is a fair amount of disagreement as to what is actually true just inside and just outside the event horizon.

Let's look at some of the fringe areas this environment requires. For instance, if the speed of light is ten meters per second, what's the speed of sound? In fact, since at room temperature on Earth, air molecules move at several hundred meters per pound, why doesn't the air on the *Redshift* freeze out?

As we start dealing with molecules and atoms, we start to enter the land between rigidly worked out implications and handwaving. I think that even if the idea development stopped here, the *Redshift* environment still makes an interesting thought experiment, and I liked the idea enough that I would have been willing to do even more handwaving if required, but there's an obvious attraction to having everything rationalized.

Let's look at molecules in air for a moment. Oh, humor me; *pretend* you can see them. On Earth, not only do they move faster than they are allowed to in the *Redshift* environment, but we've got problems with atoms as well. Atomic orbital electrons move around their nuclei at a big fraction of our normal speed of light. I've assumed (handwaved) that in the *Redshift* environment atomic particles are moving at almost the new speed of light, and hence are heavily mass shifted. This means electrons move more slowly in their orbits, (at larger radii) and it means chemical reactions will slow down. For convenience, I've assumed that however physical constants change from one layer to another, they will allow the weak and strong nuclear forces, and electromagnetic force, to maintain values appropriate to keep matter intact and inert.

This also means that most molecules move at almost the speed of light and are heavier than normal. This extra mass-shift-caused mass coupled with the slower motion results in the same total kinetic energy as the molecule would have here. And since the combined molecular kinetic energy determines temperature, the air doesn't turn into a freeze-dried mist.

The speed of sound depends on the average molecular speed in air, since sound is transmitted by those same molecules bumping into one another. On Earth, for oxygen, the speed of sound is about two-thirds of the average molecular speed. On the *Redshift,* if we assume the average molecule speed is nearly ten meters per second, that makes the speed of sound about six and two-thirds meters per second. Therefore, a person can run faster than the speed of sound and create sonic booms for people along the way. Here, anyone annoyed by joggers will be even more provoked. Plug this new speed of sound into normal Doppler equations for pitch changes, and you find that walking away from someone as you listen lowers the voice pitch you hear.

One side effect common to light and sound is increased directionality. Since in the *Redshift* environment the frequency is normal but the velocity is reduced, the wavelength must be shortened, which implies less spreading of the wave front. Hence, talking to someone without facing him increases the risk of not being heard. Determining the direction that a sound came from must be done based on relative loudness of the sound at each ear, because the delay time that gives us stereo hearing is magnified to the point of uselessness here.

Lifebelts are one of the weakest elements in the environment, but vital, since a human being whose synapses are slowed to ten meters per second won't live (at least it certainly wouldn't be a comfortable and productive life). If the environment were unavoidably deadly to people, it would be deadly dull to the reader.

Lifebelts generate a field within which the speed of light is the familiar rate in this universe. To eliminate some of the magical quality of the lifebelts, I assume the speed of light in our universe is still an absolute maximum, so lifebelts are not capable of making light go even faster than we currently believe, but rather compensating for a characteristic in hyperspace layers other than layer zero.

Reflected light is another weak area. I assume that any person or equipment protected by a lifebelt field will reflect light normally. However, any unprotected surface consists of molecules whose electrons move so slowly in their orbits that they don't resonate at the frequencies required to absorb and then reradiate selected bands of reflected energy. Here I've taken the unjustified approach that, depending on the surface, light either bounces off those surfaces diffused but unaltered, or it is totally absorbed. Hence, unprotected surfaces can be seen in shades of gray.

The final weak link is the gravitational time-dilation equation I used. The main problem is disagreement among the several sources I've found; the most common formula I've seen says that time slows down infinitely at one-half the event-horizon radius, yet the texts say it should slow down infinitely at the event horizon itself. I've therefore chosen the form of the equation that allows the most interesting environment. I hope you can treat this as a first-cut hypothesis, rather than dogma. I wrote a novel; I don't intend to devote my life to black-hole theory. Not even a few years.

Table One shows the dimensions of the *Redshift*, with the actual values used in and generated by the equations. I arbitrarily chose the central pseudo-mass and the dimensions of the levels to maximize the phenomena inherent in the idea. If I had made the ship much larger, then the gravity changes from level to level would be small, and hence so would the other changes, like time zone differences. Table Three shows the equations used.

The research for the *Redshift* was not without dead ends. One reader who saw an early draft raised the possibility that with the gravity differential of over four gees downstairs to less than one-fifth gee upstairs, all the air might fall to the bottom level. I worried at first, considering the possibility that level one might not be habitable, or that the levels would require pressure doors and independent ventilation systems.

Finally after some time spent looking at air pressure as a function of height, I realized that common sense could have saved me some trouble. (This is another universal law.) Air pressure in an open system such as the Earth's atmosphere merely amounts to the weight of the air above that point. In the *Redshift*, even if the four-gee gravity extended twenty meters from the floor of level one, that would still result in a column of air the equivalent of only eighty meters high in one gee. You will feel a pressure difference by rising eighty meters from the Earth's surface, but it's not an effect large enough to worry about.

Docking is an easier concept. If our normal environment were a *Flatland* plane and the *Redshift* took the form of a bull's-eye, then the dock would be a second bull's-eye. Moving cargo and passengers from dock to ship could be accomplished by moving in the plane, through doors cut in the circles that represent the levels of the ship and the dock.

If, however, we weren't confined to the plane, one could merely pick up the ship bull's-eye and move it in the third dimension so it was directly over the dock bull's-eye. Traveling from dock to ship would then be accomplished simply by translating from the plane of the dock to another plane a small vertical distance away in the third dimension.

The *Redshift* docks in much the same way. It superimposes itself over a spherical dock in layer zero, allowing the people and cargo to be translated from layer zero to layer ten, never having to pass through a door. The only complication is the difference in relative distances between equivalent points in alternate hyperspace layers.

I had an enjoyable time inventing the *Redshift*. It turned out to be more work than I had expected, but it also turned into an even more interesting environment than I thought it might. I've exposed some of the weaknesses of the environmental construction partly to say that I at least thought about them, and to provide a few starting points for those readers who enjoy either discovering loopholes or inventing patches for them.

I attempted to include most of the prominent relativistic effects, but the novel doesn't feature *every* possible effect. There are bound to be implications that haven't yet occurred to me. Discovering all the ramifications immediately would be a little like having someone involved in the early days of television anticipating *The Gong Show,* or an actor becoming president. If, for instance, the environment were expanded to encompass black-hole theory, one possibility to think about is the idea of black-hole wastebaskets. I imagine something that looks and acts a little like a black version of an electrostatic insect-zapper. If we can warp space to provide gravity for the ship, we can make tiny warps strong enough to trap any free material that comes within, say, a centimeter. One obstacle to overcome is to make sure the warp doesn't trap all the free air molecules. A way around that is to turn on the warp only when it's approached by something that passes the required tests to identify it as garbage.

Strange things happen aboard the *Redshift*. Although this base of hypotheses is large enough that I've had to pick convenient assumptions when offered a choice, I have made every effort to play fair with the established rules.

To those of you who think it must have been time-consuming to work out all the equations to describe activities that take place in this ship; you're right. But pity the person who ever considers turning *Redshift Rendezvous* into a film.

John E. Stith
Colorado Springs, Colorado
June 1987

FIGURE ONE

CONFIGURATION OF THE *REDSHIFT*

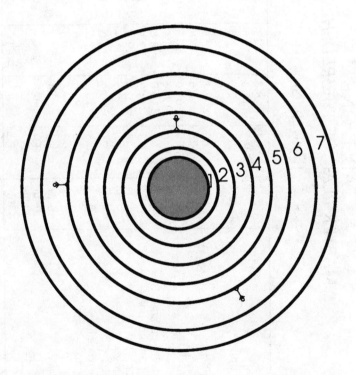

Scale: 1 centimeter = 6 meters

TABLE ONE
MASTER PLAN OF THE REDSHIFT

	(Downstairs)					(Upstairs)		
Level:	1	2	3	4	5	6	7	Outside
Radius, floor (m)	5	7	9.8	13	16	19	23.5	27
Radius, ceiling (m)	6.8	9.5	12.3	15.5	18.5	23	26	Inf
Height of ceiling (m)	1.8	2.5	2.5	2.5	2.5	4.0	2.5	Inf
Gravity, floor (g)	4.62	2.36	1.20	.68	.45	.32	.21	.16
Gravity 1.5m up (g)	2.74	1.60	.91	.55	.38	.28	.18	.14
Gravity, ceiling (g)	2.50	1.28	.76	.48	.34	.22	.17	.00
Circumference (m)	31.4	44.0	61.6	81.7	100.5	119.4	147.6	169.6
Floor Area (m²)	314	616	1207	2124	3217	4536	6940	9161
Orbital velocity, 1.5m up, (m/s)	13.2	11.5	10.0	8.8	8.1	7.4	6.7	6.3
Escape velocity, 1.5m up, (m/s)	18.7	16.3	14.2	12.5	11.4	10.5	9.5	8.9
Rate of time, floor	.31	.38	.46	.53	.59	.63	.67	.70
Rate of time, ceiling	.37	.46	.52	.58	.62	.67	.70	1.00
Rate of time/level 4	.57	.71	.87	1.00	1.10	1.17	1.26	1.32
Red shift %, floor to ceiling	-18.4	-16.3	-10.9	-7.5	-5.6	-6.5	-3.1	-29.6
Elevators leading up	4	6	6	6	6	6	0	
Stairwells leading up	0	8	8	16	16	16	0	
Appearance	bowl	bowl	flat	sphere	sphere	sphere	sphere	sphere
Uses	high-value cargo	cargo	cargo	guest galley bridge	guest recreation	bulky cargo	cargo	

TABLE TWO
RELATIVE SPEEDS AND DISTANCES IN HYPERSPACE LAYERS

Hyperspace Layer	Speed of Light (m/s)	SOL Improvement Factor	Dimension Equivalents Compared to Layer Zero	Use for this Layer
0	3×10^8	1	1.00	Normal Space
1	5.36×10^7	2	.08938	
2	9.59×10^6	4	.007989	
3	1.71×10^6	8	7.141×10^{-4}	
4	3.06×10^5	16	6.383×10^{-5}	
5	5.48×10^4	32	5.705×10^{-6}	
6	9790	64	5.100×10^{-7}	
7	1750	128	4.558×10^{-8}	
8	313	256	4.074×10^{-9}	
9	55.9	512	3.64×10^{-10}	Ship Travel
10	10.0	1024	3.26×10^{-11}	
11	1.79	2048	2.91×10^{-12}	
12	.32	4096	2.60×10^{-13}	
13	.060	8192	2.32×10^{-14}	
14	1.0×10^{-2}	16384	2.08×10^{-15}	
15	1.8×10^{-3}	32768	1.86×10^{-16}	High-speed comm net

By going one layer higher, the speed of light drops to .1787 (about 1/5.6) of current, and relative distances drop to .08938 (about 1/11.2) of current, so speed-of-light travel is twice as effective.

TABLE THREE
FUNDAMENTAL ASSUMPTIONS, EQUATIONS, AND CONSTANTS

c = velocity of light on the *Redshift* = 10 meters per second

Pseudo-Mass at center of ship = 1.7×10^{13} Kg

Gravitational Constant (G) = 6.67×10^{-11} nt−m²/kg²

Gravity (in gees) = (G × Mass / Radius²) / 9.81 (Newtonian)

Circumference = 2 × Pi × Radius

Area = 4 × Pi × Radius²

Orbital Velocity = (G × Mass / Radius)·⁵ (Newtonian)

Escape Velocity = (2 × G × Mass / Radius)·⁵ (Newtonian)

Rate of time = 1 / (1 + (G × Mass / c² × Radius))

Red shift % change = rate of time difference: floor to ceiling

Notes:

Dimensions are in meters. Masses are in kilograms.

Most of the above equations are easily available in many physics texts. The rate-of-time equation is derived from one in *Gravitation and Spacetime* by Hans C. Ohanian:

$$dt_2/dt_1 = 1 + Gm/r_1c^2 - Gm/r_2c^2$$

by assuming r_2 is infinite—meaning a point infinitely far from the gravitational field, at which time progresses unslowed by gravitational fields.